## "Mom, Tommy and Mr. Forrest are going fishing. They invited me along. Is that okay?"

Molly couldn't miss the glow on her daughter's face. She hadn't ever been fishing before—and Liza was an adventurer at heart. She loved nothing better than trying something new.

"What about homework?"

"Just math. I can do it after dinner." Liza pressed her hands together imploringly. "Mom, please?"

How could anyone resist that smile? And yet, Molly felt herself hesitating—her mind scanning for excuses. The thought of her daughter spending all afternoon with Jackson made her nervous. Suppose he started asking Liza questions? Molly hadn't prepared Liza— though she'd been perfectly willing to lie herself, her conscience had balked at the idea of rehearsing her daughter in perjury. Liza knew only that her father had died before he'd been able to marry her mother. Molly had promised to tell her all about him when she was a little older. But that information might be enough....

Jackson was no fool.

# THE REAL FATHER
## Kathleen O'Brien

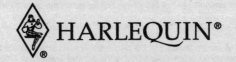

HARLEQUIN®

TORONTO • NEW YORK • LONDON
AMSTERDAM • PARIS • SYDNEY • HAMBURG
STOCKHOLM • ATHENS • TOKYO • MILAN • MADRID
PRAGUE • WARSAW • BUDAPEST • AUCKLAND

To Laura Shin,
who always makes my work so much better.
And who always makes it so much fun.

ISBN 0-373-70927-7

THE REAL FATHER

Visit us at www.eHarlequin.com

**Printed in U.S.A.**

Dear Reader,

When I was a little girl of three or four, the family lore goes, I climbed comfortably onto my father's lap and snuggled there for several minutes. But then, chattering happily, I chanced to look up. Openmouthed, I looked again. It wasn't my father at all. It was my uncle, my father's identical twin.

Even today, everyone laughs at the memory of my panicked, poleaxed little face. With one violent shove, I wriggled down and fled—not because I didn't love my uncle, who was a gentle, darling man, but because I had been so thoroughly deceived.

Later I learned that I was just one of many such victims, both innocent and deliberate. Confusion followed wherever they went: "I saw you at dinner the other night," a wounded friend would complain. "Why didn't you say hello?" The tales of their early years were legendary—including nights when, midevening, the young men would trade dates, their lady friends never aware of the switch.

And the most amazing case of all… One day, when they were little boys, my uncle Matt ran down the hall and slammed into a full-length mirror. His mother, comforting him, was moved to ask, "But Matt, dear, why on earth did you do that?" To which my uncle replied, "I thought it was Mike, and he ought to get out of the way."

I felt less foolish when I heard that one. After all, if even *they* couldn't tell the difference, how could I?

Perhaps, since I'd been brought up on such wild—and possibly a tiny bit embellished—stories, it was inevitable that someday I would want to explore the plot and character possibilities of twinship.

Jackson and Beau Forrest, the twins at the heart of *The Real Father,* are purely fictional creations. However, the trials they endure are not, thank goodness, based on any real events in the lives of my father and his brother.

But in building Jackson's personality—in understanding his guilt, his grief and the intensity of his loss—I did draw on what I had witnessed at home: the love that was more than love, the connection so profound, it approached the mystical, the communication that ran along lines buried much deeper than words.

My father and uncle had the luxury of growing old together. Jackson and Beau did not. As I tried to comprehend what such a loss would mean to an identical twin, as I asked myself how such an emptiness could ever be filled, I realized that it would take more than the perfect heroine.

It would take at least two.

And that's how I found Molly and Liza Lorring. A landscape architect and her daughter—or the Most Royal Queen and Beauteous Princess of the Planet Cuspian…depending on who you ask. Between them, they're quite equal to the task of slaying any dragons that might be plaguing a hero.

I hope you enjoy their story.

Warmly,

*Kathleen O'Brien*

# PROLOGUE

HE COULDN'T DECIDE whether to pass out or punch something.

Jackson Forrest hung on to the dresser with the heels of both hands, using its mahogany bulk to keep him standing erect until he made up his mind. He didn't look into the mirror. The first glimpse of his reflection had shown him two bleary-eyed silhouettes weaving sickeningly in and out of each other, and he'd lowered his head quickly. Right now he couldn't bear the sight of himself once, much less twice.

Instead he stared at the ring, which lay on the dresser like an accusation, winking aggressively in the lamplight. The Forrest ring. Eighteen-karat gold forged into a pattern of interlocking leaves—the metal so soft and precious, the design so intricate that it was hard to imagine the thing surviving even one owner. Yet it had been worn by every first-born Forrest male since the Civil War.

His brother's ring.

"Damn you." He spoke aloud. His voice was husky and slurred. "What a snake you are, Forrest...."

His voice trailed off. Who was he talking to?

Beau? Or himself? He wished he hadn't had so much to drink—it limited his vocabulary. But maybe there wasn't a word in the entire English language that could sum up the disgust he felt for the both of them tonight.

Clenching his teeth against the stale memory of Michelob, he raised his head. "Jeez," he muttered to the haunted man that stared back at him. "You are one pitiful son of a bitch."

The ring winked its golden eye again, and a new wave of nausea rolled over him.

*How could he stand it? How could he live with what he'd done?* With a slurred curse he swept his hand across the dresser top, sending everything spinning to the floor. Coins, cuff links, keys—they all fell in a discordant metallic jangle along with the ring.

As the noise echoed hollowly through the large, high-ceilinged room, the door opened. Somehow Jackson managed to look up without losing his balance. It was Beau. At the sight of his brother, one lucid fact finally pierced Jackson's mental fog. He didn't want to punch *something*. He wanted to punch *somebody*.

He wanted to punch Beau.

And he wanted Beau to hit him back. He wanted a fierce, primitive battering that would draw blood or tears or both. He wanted to hurt and be hurt. To punish and be punished. As if that alone could cleanse him now.

But Beau wasn't interested in Jackson's fury. He wasn't even aware of it. He didn't notice the mess on the floor. He was, as usual, entirely focused on his own emotional state.

Which clearly wasn't any happier than Jackson's. Beau slammed the door shut behind him, cursing with a vivid vocabulary that put Jackson's earlier drunken mumbling to shame. His blond hair was tousled, hanging down over his forehead as if he'd pulled his fingers through it a hundred times. Under the tangled fringe, his green eyes were hard and angry, and the golden tan of his face had darkened to the unmistakable deep bronze of rage.

He looked nothing like the sunny angel he was known far and wide to be. Nothing like the coddled darling, the sweetheart of awestruck little girls in pinafores, sex-crazed cheerleaders in pom-poms, lonely old ladies in blue hair—and everything in between.

He looked almost ugly. And he looked mean. For a piercing instant of self-serving spite, Jackson wished that Molly could see Beau now, like this, with his true nature stamped on every feature.

But he mustn't think about Molly. He needed to clear his head. He needed to find out what had made Beaumont Forrest, his *beloved* twin brother, the elder by fifteen minutes and the favorite by a country mile, so furious that he forgot to be charming.

What if he had found out—?

But no. Jackson rubbed his eyes, trying to adjust his vision, which was still offering him double images. Beau couldn't have found out anything, not this soon. That was just Jackson's guilty conscience working overtime. Might as well get used to it. He had the sick feeling that he was going to be living with a guilty conscience for the rest of his life.

Beau shoved Jackson aside and began yanking open the dresser drawers.

"Where the hell are my keys?" Beau tossed clothes roughly as he dug through stacks of neatly folded T-shirts and jeans, turning pockets inside out. "I know I put them in this goddamn room somewhere."

"God, Beau. Chill." Denied the support of the dresser, Jackson sat on the edge of Beau's four-poster bed, hunching over, hands dangling between his knees. "What's got you in such a lather?" He tried to keep the bitterness out of his voice, but he couldn't quite do it. "Something go wrong? Did your bimbo du jour fail to show up for the fun?"

Beau didn't even turn around. "Shut up, Jack," he growled, slamming one drawer and wrenching open the next. "I'm not in the mood for any of your crap right now."

Jackson's inner radar began to pulse. Being an identical twin meant that you heard things no one else could hear, felt things no one else could sense. Something was wrong. Really wrong. This wasn't just another of Beau's sulks. This was trouble.

"What's the matter, Beau?" He stood, ignoring the dizzying nausea as best he could. "Is it Molly?"

"To hell with Molly." Beau shoved the drawer shut violently and kicked at the dresser in frustration. He spun around and turned his savage gaze on his brother. "Damn you, Jackson. If you've got the keys to my car, you'd better cough them up pronto."

He was losing control. Jackson could feel the blood pounding in Beau's throat, at his temples, behind his eyes—just as if it were happening to him. He took two steps forward, reaching for the edge of the dresser. "They're on the floor—"

With an ugly oath, Beau lunged toward the fallen keys.

"Where are you going?" Jackson's nerves were tingling with a nameless dread. He suddenly wished he had hidden the keys. "Tell me what's going on."

"I'm getting out of here, that's what. If that tramp thinks she's going to ruin my life, she's got another think coming."

Jackson tried to shake the Michelob from his brain. "Who? Molly?"

Beau's face was frightening. "Molly? Hell, Jack. Get real. Who gives a damn about that frigid little bitch?" He moved toward the door.

Jackson followed on legs that seemed to be made from something numb and wobbling. "Beau, wait. Why don't you let me drive?"

Beau didn't even bother to answer. And Jackson knew it was a ridiculous suggestion. Beau might be deranged with fury, but Jackson was so drunk he probably couldn't get the car out of the front drive without climbing an oak tree. Still, every instinct was screaming for him to stop his brother. He lurched down the stairs, keeping Beau's retreating back just barely in sight.

When he reached the low-slung red sports car that sat waiting in the moonlit drive, Beau had already ground the engine to snarling life. There was no time to waste. Jackson vaulted over the convertible's closed door and dropped onto the black leather seat. For a long, tense moment, he met his twin's furious gaze with an unyielding stare. Beau could breathe fire if he wanted to. Jackson wasn't getting out.

Finally Beau looked away. He jammed the car into reverse, gears screaming, and backed out of the drive at a mad, blind tear. At the front gate, he swung the wheel, sending the car into a sliding spin that somehow ended up facing the road.

After that there was only hissing wind, blue moonlight and the silent madness of breakneck speed. Neither of them spoke a word as the little car tore through the empty streets of downtown Demery. Stop signs, stoplights, sharp curves—nothing slowed Beau's fury. Jackson watched quaint storefronts and stately homes streak by like bleeding paint on an Impressionist canvas. He wondered how much fuel was in the tank, hoping that Beau would run out of gas before he ran out of luck.

They nicked a curb, jolting every bone in Jackson's body. If Jackson had hoped that the potent cocktail of sheer danger and mute fear would drain the rage from his brother's heart, he'd been deluding himself. Beau seemed to grow more inflamed with every wild mile. The streets grew narrower, less carefully cultivated. They weren't far now from Annie Cheatwood's house. The dread in Jackson's body began to take a clear and terrible shape.

"Beau," he called over roar of the engine. "Beau, knock it off. You're going to kill us both."

But Beau didn't hear him. Or wouldn't hear him.

Eyes narrowed against the wind, he steered the car grimly, his foot never lifting from the accelerator. Jackson watched him, strangely hypnotized, and he thought he saw Beau's lips form a word.

"Bitch," he seemed to say. And then over and over, "Bitch, bitch, bitch."

Jackson turned his gaze back to the road just a fraction of a second too late. With a cold horror he saw the statue flying toward them, like something out of a bad dream, a fifteen-foot marble monster suddenly coming alive and hurtling toward the little car.

"Beau!" Jackson grabbed the wheel and shoved it desperately to the left, though he knew it was hopeless. Nothing could stop the insane advance of the statue, the figure of a Civil War general that stood in dignified sentry in the center of Milton Square, a sweet, civilized plot of land at the edge of town.

Beau was clawing at the wheel, too, finally aware of their danger. But even the combined strength of their young, athletic bodies could not wrench the car free of the relentless, magnetic pull of the statue.

Metal exploded against marble. Bone crushed against chrome. Steel ripped through leather and flesh.

And for Beau and Jackson Forrest, twenty-two years old, the world went black and ended.

# CHAPTER ONE

"WHAT A DELIGHTFUL little girl your daughter is, Ms. Lorring."

Janice Kilgore, vice principal at Radway School, was beaming. Even her dense network of freckles seemed to glow. "She's so easy with the other children. She fits in beautifully here, don't you think?"

Molly nodded, not wanting to spoil Miss Kilgore's pleasure by pointing out that Liza usually fit in comfortably wherever she went. The other woman naturally preferred to believe it was some magic chemistry provided by her exclusive private school. It would help to justify the exorbitant tuition she was going to have to discuss with Molly later on.

Besides, Miss Kilgore's enthusiasm was undoubtedly influenced by the fact that Liza came recommended by Miss Lavinia Forrest of Everspring Plantation. In Demery, South Carolina, population fifteen thousand, the Forrests reigned supreme. Forrest children, including Miss Lavinia, had attended Radway for three generations.

Still, Liza's bright, uninhibited smile was quite a recommendation all its own.

Molly looked across Radway's large, well-equipped playground now, drawing comfort from the sight of her daughter. Liza's smile had brought sunshine into some of the darkest days of Molly's life.

Liza hadn't noticed her mother and Miss Kilgore standing at the fringe of the playground. She was busy hoisting a smaller child onto a swing. Both little girls giggled as Liza lowered the safety bar, gave the child a push and then stood back, her wispy blond hair flying in the February wind, her cheeks as red as her winter coat.

The coat was getting too short, Molly noticed absently. Liza's legs seemed to stretch by inches every day. It was impossible to keep her in clothes that fit. Her lurching growth spurts seemed to promise that she would be dramatically tall and slim.

Just like her father.

"What a cutie," Miss Kilgore said, sighing. "You must be very proud of her."

Molly didn't answer right away, struggling to subdue the absurd tightness that had overtaken her vocal cords at the sight of Liza's long, coltish legs.

The answer was easy, if only she'd been able to control her voice enough to speak it. Yes, Molly was proud. These past nine years—first struggling as a frightened teenage mother to bring up her newborn daughter alone, then going to school at night, and finally piecing together a career and a business as a landscape architect—had been almost unimaginably difficult.

Some nights she'd been so lonely she'd talked to the walls. Some days she'd been so tired she wanted to cry. But she hadn't wept. She had endured it, all of it. She had fought the odds, and she had won.

And Liza made it all worthwhile. Her little girl was smart, sweet, amazingly courageous. She was everything Molly had hoped she'd be. Everything Molly herself had not been—not at nine, not at nineteen, not ever. Not even now, at almost twenty-nine. For Molly, the daughter of a resentful, alcoholic father, being brave was still very much a decision, not an instinct.

So how could Molly help being proud? She had taken her one small talent, a gift for growing things, and she had turned it into a career so successful that she and her daughter wanted for nothing.

Well, nothing but a new coat. She blew Liza a kiss and made a mental note to buy her the most beautiful red coat in all of South Carolina.

"She's a fantastic kid," Molly said finally, turning back to Miss Kilgore. To heck with false modesty. She let her joy in her daughter break through in a wide smile. "I consider myself very, very lucky."

"You are. Believe me, they're not all like that." Miss Kilgore seemed to have been born with a smile on her face, and she directed her dimpled grin toward Molly. "Would you like to see the rest of the school? The music rooms? The science lab? The swimming pool?" She held out her hands, palms up in refreshing candor. "How can I impress you, Ms. Lorring? I have to admit, I'd love to see Liza at Radway."

"Call me Molly. And I'm already impressed."

"Fantastic. I'm Jan. Tommy Cheatwood! Stop that! Put Peggy down this instant!"

Molly was momentarily bewildered, until she realized that Janice Kilgore's practiced gaze had been scanning the playground even as she wooed and flattered her new candidate. An impish, gap-toothed boy in the corner was holding on to a small, squealing girl's ankles, guiding her around like a human wheelbarrow.

For one intense moment his blond hair and green eyes, his irreverent grin, his animal pleasure in his mischief, reminded her forcibly of the Forrest twins. Well, Jackson Forrest, perhaps. Beau had never looked quite that cocky and defiant.

At the sound of his teacher's voice, Tommy looked over, grimaced, and let go, plopping Peggy into the sand without ceremony. His face sobered, and the fleeting impression disappeared. Molly breathed again.

Jan rolled her eyes and turned back to Molly. "So you're impressed. Good. Now before one of my beloved monsters does something to turn you off, shall we just move right along to the ceremonial signing of the contract?"

Molly shook her head. "It's a little early for that," she said, smiling.

Jan sighed, her cheerful face coming as close to somber as her snub nose and freckles would allow. "Already heard about the tuition, have you? I know it's a heart stopper, but we're not offering just snob appeal here, Molly. We can give Liza the education she deserves. Even tossing aside the sales pitch, we really are the best.''

"I believe you." And she did. Molly had been born here in Demery. She'd grown up here. There weren't many social, political, economic or even academic nuances that she didn't grasp. Jan wasn't exaggerating: If you lived in Demery, Radway School was the best.

But that was the catch. *If* you lived in Demery. At the moment, Molly and Liza lived in Atlanta. Even if she accepted the Everspring restoration job, she would be here only a couple of months.

"It's not the tuition," Molly explained. "My plans are really still up in the air. I haven't even committed yet to taking the job."

Janice looked confused. "But when Miss Forrest called, she said…she seemed to think it was all settled."

"I know." Molly could well imagine how Lavinia Forrest would have made it sound. Lavinia wanted Molly to do the landscape renovations at Everspring Plantation, and Lavinia was so accustomed to getting what she wanted that she probably considered the whole thing a done deal.

And truthfully, the contract was so lucrative, the benefits so generous, that only a fool would have wasted a single second before leaping up to sign on the dotted line.

Maybe that's what she was, Molly thought. A fool. But she wouldn't be rushed into this decision. Once, ten years ago, she had allowed herself to be pressured into doing something foolish, something she knew in her heart was wrong. The consequences had been staggering, life altering.

The consequence had been motherhood.

On the day she had learned she was pregnant, while she sat on that cold, metal examination table with her tears barely dried on her cheeks, she had made a promise to herself. She had vowed that no one would ever again force her to act against her own judgment.

Beginning in that frightened moment, with grim, blind determination she had taken control of her life and Liza's. She wasn't about to turn over the reins now.

Lavinia would have to wait. There was something Molly had to do before she could commit to this project. Something she had to know about herself— and about exactly how far she had come in the past ten years.

Had she come far enough that it was now safe to come full circle? To come home?

"I'm meeting Lavinia in a few minutes," Molly explained, wishing in spite of herself that she could take that disappointment from Janice Kilgore's face. "I think she said you wouldn't mind letting Liza stay with your class, just for an hour or so?"

Jan's grin broke through. "You know I'd love it. Look at her with the little ones. Why, it's as good as having another teacher's aide." She chuckled. "A great deal better than our last one, who liked to sneak off and smoke cigars in the closet."

Molly picked her way across the winter-brown field of laughing, twirling, seesawing children to kiss Liza goodbye. As she breathed in the fresh, soapy scent of her daughter, enveloping her in a long bear hug, she assured the little girl that she'd be back very soon. As usual, Liza nodded with untroubled acceptance, quite content to be left in her new surroundings.

As Molly headed toward her waiting rental car, she resisted the urge to look over her shoulder. Liza was fine. Her confidence was a gift, and Molly didn't want to undermine it by communicating insecurity. It was just that Molly's own childhood had been quite different. She had dreaded new places and strange people, sensing that the world was unpredictable. She had always felt just one slippery step from some nameless disaster.

Living with a family like hers could do that to a person.

Molly knew that Liza sometimes longed for a daddy—and the knowledge often filled her with a sense of failure. But then she reminded herself of the truth she'd learned so long ago, listening to the sound of her father's drunken rages: No father was a thousand times better than a bad one.

TWENTY MINUTES LATER, Molly stood in a churchyard, tightly gripping a velvety cluster of deeppurple pansies. The cemetery was only five miles east of Radway School by car. Emotionally it might as well have been in another world.

Where Radway had rung with the laughter of a hundred children and teemed with young, vigorous life, this place was almost preternaturally quiet.

Black-armed oaks, drooping willows and barely budding dogwood crowded together, blocking all sound from the street. The winter sunshine fought its way through the tangled branches, but at a price. It lay like a broken thing on the grass, a fractured mosaic of white-gold light amid the olive-green shadows.

Molly hadn't visited Woodlawn Cemetery in almost ten years, but she had no trouble finding the Forrest plot. It lay deep in the center of the seven acres of gray marble headstones and mildewed angels, deep enough to signify that the Forrest family had been in Demery since its founding.

Ten generations of Forrests lay beneath these silent trees. The carvings spoke of brave Confederate soldiers, some only sixteen years old when they were delivered here straight from battle. Headstones told of young mothers who died bearing Forrest infants, who then were brought here, too, lost to influenza or typhoid fever. More-modern graves were less tragic, reflecting long lives and easy passing. The natural ebb and flow of life.

Until she came to one of the newest graves, where someone had recently placed a bouquet of sweet peas. Until she read the headstone. Placed here less than ten years ago, its letters still formed fresh, sharp angles in the sparkling granite.

Beaumont Cameron Forrest. Cherished son, beloved brother.

Twenty-two years old the day he died.

Just twenty-two. For a disoriented moment Molly

couldn't make sense of it. Her handsome Beau, her older, more sophisticated hero...just twenty-two?

She had idolized him ever since she was eight years old, when he had chivalrously paused in his majestic twelve-year-old pursuits to rescue her doll from the creek. And yet Molly now was older than Beau would ever be. His twin brother, Jackson, was older now, too—almost thirty-two. No longer the identical twin.

Molly fought back an unfair flash of resentment that Jackson should have lived, aged, prospered, while Beau...

But this was what death did. It warped perspectives, inverted relationships, rendered obsolete concepts of older, younger, bigger, smaller. It froze you in time, forced others to go on without you.

She squeezed the flowers so tightly she could smell the sharp scent of broken stems. Her legs felt suddenly soft, as if the weight of her body would sink through them, driving her to the ground. She wondered irrationally if the earth would still be damp from all the tears she had cried in this spot ten years ago.

"I thought you might be here." The dry, husky voice came from a mere three yards behind her, and Molly turned with graceless shock. She had believed she was alone here. She had certainly *felt* alone.

Lavinia Forrest, Beau's aunt, stood there, watching. She looked exactly as she had looked ten years ago—the way she'd looked, in fact, for as long as Molly could remember. Tall, lanky, square-jawed. Dressed as always in slacks and jacket of no-

nonsense navy blue, her straight white hair bobbed for maximum efficiency. She eyed Molly with her familiar candid scrutiny.

"You're not crying," Lavinia said matter-of-factly. "That's good. No use crying over him, not after all these years."

Molly smiled, strangely reassured by the older woman's crusty manner. Though the whole world might tilt and sway, though strong, glorious young men might die too soon, some things, apparently, never changed.

"I was just about to head over to the church to meet you," Molly said. "Am I late?"

Lavinia shook her head. "No. I finished early. I decided to let the other volunteers arrange the flowers for once. They could use the practice. Never saw so many women with five thumbs on each hand." She dismissed the volunteer guild with one wave of her own long-fingered, capable, quintessentially *Forrest* hand. "But what is this sudden formality, little Miss Molly? No hug for an old friend?"

Molly murmured a wordless apology as she held out her arms and let herself be enfolded in Lavinia Forrest's comforting embrace. Lavinia was unusually tall—it was a Forrest trait—so even though Molly herself was almost five-eight, she felt childlike beside the older woman.

It felt like coming home. Lavinia's scent was so familiar—a mixture of clean soap and the natural earthy perfumes of a woman who loved to work with flowers. Through the years, Molly had enjoyed more hugs from Lavinia Forrest than she had from her own mother.

This hug was long and warm, and Molly sensed that it was Lavinia's way of saying that she understood, even shared, Molly's grief at the sight of Beau's grave. Though Lavinia had loved her twin nephews equally, Beau had always been her favorite. Of course, Beau, with his sunny disposition and his charming manner, had been everyone's favorite. Jackson had never gone out of his way to charm anyone.

The whole community had mourned Beau's death, but Lavinia's loss had been devastating. She had no husband, no children of her own, and she had lavished her stockpile of affection on the darling nephew who teased and flirted with her as no one else had ever done. Now that Beau was gone, Lavinia had only her flowers to spoil.

Molly knew that Lavinia would never speak openly of her heartache. It wasn't in her vocabulary. But that was all right. This hug was eloquent, and it was enough.

Finally Lavinia broke away, clearing her throat roughly. "Well, then, that's that. You've seen his grave. It stings a little, but you survived it. Now what do you say let's get out of this gloomy place?"

Molly hesitated. Then, with a deep, steadying breath, she bent down and placed her bouquet of pansies neatly alongside the sweet peas that already lay at the base of the headstone. Her fingers were gratifyingly steady as she smoothed the ribbons that bound the blossoms together.

Straightening quickly, Molly brushed her hands together and met Lavinia's uncompromising Forrest-green gaze squarely.

With a smile she took Lavinia's arm and nudged her toward the path that would lead them back into the sunlight.

"You're right, Aunt Lavinia. We'd better hurry and get that landscaping contract signed. It will be spring before you know it, and I've got about a million flowers to plant."

JACKSON FORREST LEANED against an oak at the edge of the soccer field, watching as Tommy Cheat-wood loped his way down the grass, way ahead of all the other boys, using those long, skinny legs to kick the stuffing out of the little black-and-white ball.

Tommy's blond hair was standing up in wet spikes of perspiration, and his face was a flushed study in complete concentration. Sixty pounds of talent and intensity. As he reached the other side, he gave the ball one last, whopping thrust, sending it into the net, sailing neatly past the awkwardly flopping goalie.

*Damn, the kid was good.* Jackson whistled his admiration above the cheers of the watching parents. Hearing the familiar notes, Tommy looked back at him, grinning through the sweat, and the two males exchanged a thumbs-up.

But already Coach Riser was striding toward the boy, his clipboard tucked tightly under his arm. His glowering face didn't seem to promise a congratulatory pat on the back. Tommy stood ramrod straight, awaiting his fate.

"What the heck was that, Cheatwood?"

Ross Riser's voice was rough, the muscles in his neck rigid. Tommy stared at his coach, mute with misery.

Jackson found himself tensing, ready to jump between coach and player. *What do you think it was? It was the go-ahead goal, you moron.* But he didn't say it. He knew better than to interfere, though every instinct was telling him to get in there and shove Ross Riser out of little Tommy's face.

He tightened his jaw. Good grief. Had he turned into the typical overbearing, overprotective parent? Riser was just a volunteer coach, and he was doing the best he could. Jackson took a deep breath and waited. Tommy was a tough kid. He could handle it.

Coach Riser squatted in front of the boy, and, though he lowered his voice diplomatically, everyone could tell that Tommy was getting a verbal lashing. Jackson reminded himself of the hundreds of times his own track coach had lectured him with that same exasperated look on his face. But Jackson had been in high school, for God's sake, not in fourth grade. And he'd been a…well, he'd been what was politely known as "a discipline problem." Tommy wasn't.

Besides, it was only a game. Ross Riser needed to lighten the hell up.

Annie Cheatwood, Tommy's mother, had just arrived at the soccer field, peeling off her orange Low

Country Hardware Store apron and tossing it into the back of her beat-up green sedan. Glad of the distraction, Jackson watched her pick her way through the crowd of mothers in tennis togs and diamond earrings, fathers in khaki slacks and golf shirts. Most of them spoke courteously to her as she passed, but the reserve in their faces told a different story.

Jackson knew that, if she hadn't been a special friend of his, none of them would have offered her so much as a nod. A hardware store clerk who had the nerve to possess a large bustline and a small waist, and didn't bother to hide either one, was ordinarily invisible to this crowd.

As Annie reached his side, Jackson found himself chuckling out loud at the idea of his being anyone's social sponsor. He was the ultimate black sheep. These same people wouldn't have spoken to him, either, if he hadn't inherited his daddy's plantation.

Annie looked puzzled, studying him as she folded a piece of Juicy Fruit into her mouth. "What's so funny?"

He held out his hand, asking for a stick of gum. He didn't chew gum, didn't even like it, but he knew that the diamond moms and khaki dads thought chewing gum was vulgar, and the idea suddenly appealed to him.

"Life. People. Soccer. Chewing gum." He shrugged. "Actually, just about everything seems pretty funny right now."

She handed the gum over with a sideways smile.

"Oh," she said. "You're in one of *those* moods. Great."

As if he'd been pulled by a magnet, Coach Riser came striding over. His scowl had been replaced by a goofy grin, which Jackson realized was every bit as irritating. Riser had begun dating Annie recently, and he was clearly infatuated.

"Hi, there, you two," the coach said, directing that lovesick smile toward Annie, but sending a perfunctory smile toward Jackson as if the two of them were good friends. Jackson knew better. Ross Riser didn't quite know what to make of Jackson's friendship with Annie, but he definitely didn't like it. And the whole issue of Tommy confused and alarmed him, though he wasn't close enough yet to Annie to ask her to explain it.

"Hi, Ross," Jackson broke in before Annie could speak. "Tell me, coach, what's your problem with Tommy? Didn't you *want* him to score? Don't you *want* us to win?"

Riser's pale skin flushed, and his brown eyes tightened. He eyed Jackson narrowly, as if he feared a subtle threat lurked beneath the innocent words. As if Jackson might be referring to Riser's one shameful secret, which darkened the air between them like a shadow every time they met.

But Jackson kept his expression bland, and Riser relaxed, obviously deciding that, this time at least, no deeper implications had been intended. "Not like that, I didn't," he said. "I've told Tommy not to go galloping down the field all alone. He's a team player, and he needs to wait for his team."

"Even if they're half an hour behind him?"

Riser's voice hardened. "That's right, Forrest. Even then. You have a problem with that?"

Annie groaned and swatted lightly at Jackson's arm. "Knock it off, you two. If I'd wanted to get caught in a macho slime-fest, I would have stayed at the hardware store."

Jackson grinned. "Sorry," he said, recognizing the truth of her comment. He wasn't going to get into a wrestling match with Ross Riser over how to handle Tommy. Or over Annie, either, for that matter. Frankly, he didn't have to.

"Whatever you say, Ross," he offered with an easy shrug. "You're the coach."

Annie patted his cheek. "Good boy," she said. Then she turned to Ross, whose handsome face had already begun to darken again. "Are we still on for Friday?"

Ross nodded, glancing covertly at Jackson. "You bet we are. I'll be there at six." And then, with an awkward lurch of boyish defiance, he leaned over and pecked Annie on the lips before turning and hurrying back toward the field.

Annie and Jackson watched the game in a pregnant silence for a couple of minutes. Finally Annie spoke.

"I know you don't think I should be seeing him."

Jackson kept his eyes on Tommy, who was reining himself in and staying with the pack. What a shame. "That's right," he said. "I don't."

Annie made a small popping sound with her chewing gum, something she never did unless she was angry. "But, doggone it, Jackson, you haven't got any right to tell me who I can and can't see."

Jackson nodded. "That's right," he agreed equably. "I don't."

Annie growled, obviously losing patience with him. "Listen here, Jackson Forrest. You'd better come on out and tell me what your problem is with Ross, or you'd just better hold your tongue and stay out of it."

He swiveled, slanting her a laughing glance. "Think back, Annie, darling. Did I say a word against Ross? I think this topic was your idea, not mine."

She narrowed her eyes, considering. He could tell when she realized he was right—her hazel eyes began to flash. Annie hated being wrong.

"Yeah, well, you didn't have to say anything, did you? You know I can read your mind. You don't like Ross, Jack. I want to know why."

The chilly February wind had blown pieces of her hair up against her flushed cheeks. Jackson reached out and gently tucked the fine, light-brown strands back behind her ears. "Maybe I don't think he's good enough for you and Tommy. Maybe I think you deserve better."

She looked unconvinced. "Yeah? Why, do you see the King of Siam standing in line to date me?"

"Annie—"

"I'm serious, Jack. I'm not exactly the catch of the century, you know, a single working mom." She cast a wry gaze over the crowd of upscale parents.

"Can you imagine any of these guys inviting me to the country club for dinner?"

"Annie—"

She shook her head, rejecting his assurances of her worth. She'd always hated soft soap and platitudes. "Besides, Jack, I'm just dating him a little, that's all. It's not as if I'm going to marry the guy. You don't have to worry that he's going to try to step in and be Tommy's dad or anything."

Jackson managed not to flinch, although she had hit a bull's-eye with that one. Canny Annie. She always could cut right through to the truth of things. He turned toward the soccer field, as much to avoid letting her read his expression as to follow the progress of the game.

Tommy was working his way downfield, threatening to score once again. Jackson's gut twisted a little, watching those bony, knob-kneed legs churn with every ounce of energy in the boy's body. The kid had so much heart, so much spunk. He needed a dad. He deserved one.

"I'm sorry, Annie," Jackson said. "You're right. It's none of my business."

A moment's silence. And then, slowly, her hand slid up and rested against his forearm. When she spoke her voice was softer, less agitated. "Besides you've got other things to worry about right now. Isn't your old girlfriend supposed to show up at Everspring this afternoon? You know, that pretty, prissy girl from high school?"

Jackson frowned. "Beau's old girlfriend," he said

curtly. Annie knew all this. What was she playing at? "Not mine. Beau's."

Annie tucked her hand cozily into the crook of Jackson's arm. "Right. Whatever," she said. "If you say so."

## CHAPTER TWO

IT WAS A TYPICAL late-winter morning at Everspring Plantation—dull, lifeless, the doldrums season for gardeners. Too late for the red blush of berries, too early for the yellow splash of bulbs. Brown grass slept, still exhausted, under gray skies.

But Molly, standing on the mossy brick steps of the old plantation kitchens staring down toward the banks of the slow-moving river, didn't see winter. Everywhere she looked, she saw flowers. She saw spring days banked high with azaleas, sprinkled with candy-colored tulips, crocus and lilies. She saw green summer acres bordered with pink phlox, white candytuft, blue columbine and crimson dianthus. She saw fall afternoons lit by chrysanthemums as fiery gold as candles.

And if she closed her eyes very tightly, she could see Beau, too, walking across those flower-filled lawns, coming toward her with the summer wind ruffling his silky blond hair, the sun lighting the intense green of his eyes. And a smile on his lips.

"Mom! Come quick!" Liza's eager voice broke into Molly's yearning daydream. "It's a maze, just like in the puzzle books!"

Opening her eyes, Molly shook away the images,

forbidding tears to even think about forming. How absurd of her to give in to maudlin sentimentality the very first moment she set foot on Everspring earth. This was why she had left Demery in the first place, why she hadn't come back in ten long years. She knew that here at Everspring, where Beau had lived, where she and Beau had loved, the memories would be as overpowering as quicksand.

But she could resist it—and she would. She refused to live in the past, no matter how beautiful its gardens might have been. She was lucky. She had a life, a career, a future....

She had a *child.*

And she intended to give that child her full attention.

"Mom!" Liza stood at the opening to the thick, six-foot high maze, her fists planted on her boyish hips with exaggerated impatience. "Come look! It's *so* cool!"

Molly smiled. "It's boxwood," she said. "Little-leaf box, actually. It's from Japan." She always used playtime to teach Liza about plants. And at least half the time, Liza listened.

This wasn't one of those times. Ignoring the botany lesson, Liza grinned as her mother drew closer. Her eyes sparkled with mischief. Suddenly, she reached out and tapped Molly's arm.

"You're it!" she cried triumphantly, and then she started lithely into the maze, disappearing immediately behind its leafy walls.

Molly hesitated only a second before taking off after her. Liza's legs might be younger, but Molly had the advantage of familiarity. She knew every twist and turn, every blind end, and every secret pass-through. At eleven, she had cleverly eluded Jackson, who was always chasing her through the maze with a tree frog, a lizard or a garter snake in his hand.

And at sixteen, she had allowed Beau, sexy, laughing Beau, to catch her.

She heard Liza just ahead, giggling. The sound was infectious. She laughed, too, giving herself over to the pleasant adrenaline rush of the chase, the cool, invigorating feel of wind across her cheeks.

"You can run, dearie," Molly called out in her best movie-villain voice as she rounded the second left turn, scuffing the boxwood with her shoulder in her haste, "but you can never hide!"

An answering squeal told her Liza was just around the next turn. She turned up the speed, and she was already stretching out her hand for the capture when she heard a sudden thump, and a small, high shriek of fear.

"Liza!" She took the corner with her heart knocking at her throat. *Liza*...

She froze in her tracks, which, she realized with numb horror, was actually quite fortunate, because if she had kept running she would have collided with the man who stood there, holding a shocked Liza in his arms. Just as Liza had obviously collided with him.

She looked at Liza first, caring only if her daughter was safe. Then she looked at the man.

A small, breathless voice in her mind whispered the name on a sudden leap of joy.

*Beau.*

Her dreams had seen him just like this. The vivid-green eyes, the dark, proud arch of eyebrow. The squared chin, the shining thickness of waving blond hair. The long, capable fingers. She felt a sudden, familiar lurch of pure physical desire.

But finally, probably in no more than the space of a heartbeat, common sense clamped down on the wishful madness.

Of course it wasn't Beau. Beau was dead. It would never be Beau again.

It was Jackson.

Her gaze clearing, she began to see the details. Like Beau, Jackson had always been devastatingly handsome. It was his birthright. Forrest males were always glamorous far beyond normal men.

And today he was, if anything, even more attractive than he had been at twenty-two. His athletic body was still lean and rangy—a runner's body. While Beau had been the football hero, Jackson had been the high school track star. Quite natural, the gossips had suggested. He got plenty of practice running from sheriff's deputies and outraged fathers.

He smiled now, watching her study him. The grin was as deeply dimpled and rakish as ever, but it was subtly different. It was as if the years had erased just a little of the defiance that had once been his hallmark.

"Hi, Molly," he said, using that voice that was so like Beau's—and yet so different. He bent down to Liza. "Are you okay? That was some crash. You must have been going about a hundred miles an hour."

Liza grinned up at him. Molly winced at the sight of that familiar, dimpled grin. "Yes. I'm a fast runner," she said proudly. "I hope I didn't hurt you."

He massaged his ribs dramatically. "I think I'll live." He straightened and met Molly's gaze over the little girl's head. "It's been a long time, Molly. How are you?"

Her throat felt strangely dry. It seemed to take away her powers of speech to look at him like this. It was like looking at a ghost. A ghost who made her tingle, remembering things that hadn't ever happened—at least not with him.

"Liza," she said, touching her daughter's hair softly. "Would you go out to the car, please, and get my purse?"

Liza looked confused. "What do you need your purse fo—"

"I'd really appreciate it," Molly interjected, her voice still soft.

Liza got the message. She looked from Jackson to her mother once, curiously, but without anxiety. She smiled. "Okay."

Molly watched her disappear back through the maze, and then, clearing her throat, she turned to Jackson.

"I was so sorry," she said. "So terribly sorry about Beau." She knew that wasn't the best way to begin, but she couldn't think of anything else. She hadn't expected to find Jackson at Everspring. Lavinia had hinted that, as Jackson's main address these days was New York—where he'd moved as soon as he'd been released from the hospital—he probably wouldn't be in town during her own stay here. She wondered now whether Lavinia had deliberately misstated the case.

Whatever the reason, she had no speeches ready. Still, why was this so hard? It was just Jackson, the boy she'd played with since she was a child, the boy whose shoulders she had soaked in tears whenever Beau's careless ways had broken her heart.

"I can't appreciate the magnitude of your loss, of course, but I—" She took a deep breath, hating the stilted expressions that seemed to spout unbidden from her lips. "I loved him, too, Jackson. I loved him desperately."

He nodded. "I know you did." His eyes took on some of the old sardonic quality. "And blindly, too, if I remember correctly. But hey—" he cocked that disarming smile at her, and suddenly the mockery was gone again "—didn't everyone?"

The sound of Liza's favorite nursery rhyme jingle broke into Molly's response, the little girl's high, clear notes making their way like birdsong through the boxwood wall.

Jackson looked toward the sound, then slowly turned his gaze back to Molly. "I don't have to ask if she's your daughter, do I?" He smiled. "She's exactly like you at that age."

Molly took a deep breath. She knew the similarity was dramatic. Molly had been lanky, too, always outgrowing her clothes just like Liza. And both of them had identical wispy blond hair, wide-set blue eyes, and fair cheeks that pinked at the slightest breeze.

"Do you think so?" As Molly tried to think of what else to say, Liza's song changed to a show tune, her young voice swaggering with a pretty good approximation of early Madonna. Molly couldn't help smiling, meeting Jackson's raised eyebrow. What an amazing kid she had. Where did she learn these things?

"As you can hear, though, the similarities are all on the surface," Molly said over the noise. "Liza's nobody's clone. I never could carry a tune. And she's got tons more gumption than I ever dreamed of."

Jackson tilted his head and let his gaze settle on Molly's face. "Maybe," he said, answering her smile with one of his own. "But, you know, M, I sometimes thought you might have underestimated yourself in that department."

"Are you kidding?" Molly shook her head incredulously. It felt surprisingly nice to hear Jackson's old nickname for her. "I was a mess. I was afraid of my own shadow."

Jackson shrugged. "I think you're still selling yourself a little short. After all, your daughter must have inherited all that confidence and charisma from somewhere."

She stared at him, realizing, suddenly, just like that, the moment of truth had come. This was where she should say, quite casually, "No, actually, she inherited that from her father." Jackson obviously was expecting that, waiting for it, as if he had planned it.

Perhaps he had. Perhaps, without realizing it, she had been running through a conversational maze, and now she had hit the dead end, the unanswerable question that rose up between them as insurmountable as a thick, thorny hedge.

The big question. The sixty-four-thousand-dollar question, the one no one ever quite spoke out loud.

The question Jackson had nonetheless been leading her deftly toward since the first moment he set eyes on Liza.

If these lucky genes had not come from Molly, then where?

Who was Liza's father?

ORDINARILY LIZA WOULD have been in no hurry to get back to the grown-ups, who talked about the most boring things on earth. Meeting *new* grownups was the worst, because they always wanted to ask her the same dumb questions, like what subject do you like best at school, or how did you get so tall?

But this new grown-up was different. She'd been looking for someone to be King Willowsong for nearly a year now. She'd almost given up. But it was as if the maze had led her to him, as if she had banged into him for a reason. When she had looked up into his awesome green eyes, and seen his hair shining all silvery in the sun, her first thought had been that maybe, finally, she had found a King for Planet Cuspian.

But it would take more than silvery hair and green eyes if he was *really* going to be King. The true test was much harder. If he was truly the King, he had to be able to recognize that her mother was the Queen.

So she had to hurry. She'd noticed a funny look in his eyes when he had said hello to her mother. It might have been the right look, the look a king should give a queen. But her mother had sent her away before she could be sure.

She was almost at the entrance to the maze when she heard people coming up the walk behind her.

"Hello?"

For a minute Liza wished she could just pretend she hadn't heard the lady calling out. But that wasn't nice. The Princess of Cuspian didn't do things like that. At least not very often.

She turned and saw a woman about her mother's age, but sexier, like someone on TV, and not quite as soft, with her tight shiny black belt and tight blue pants. Still, somehow Liza knew that the lady wasn't a Mudbluff. She might smell like too much hair spray, and her lipstick might be the color of a really bad bruise, but she wasn't a Mudbluff.

Her mom thought it was weird, but Liza always tagged everyone right away using the different species from her imaginary planet. Everyone was either a Willowsong or a Mudbluff. A good guy or a bad guy.

It wasn't that she didn't understand the difference between made-up and real. It was just that tags made life simpler. Mostly, she had discovered, people were Willowsongs, which was kind of a relief, kind of comforting, when you thought about it.

Most of the Mudbluffs she'd seen were in the movies. Well, there was Mrs. Geiger who taught piano and hurt your fingers trying to make them reach the keys—she was a Mudbluff. And once Liza had watched a woman at the grocery store squeezing her kid's arm until he cried. Definitely a Mudbluff.

But mostly Liza's world was made up of Willowsongs.

As Liza slowed down to see what the lady wanted, she noticed that a little boy slouched along behind the woman, scuffing his sneakers across the brick walk. Liza looked closely at his blond hair. She knew him. She had seen him at the Radway School when she'd gone to visit a couple of weeks ago.

Tommy, maybe? Yes, she was pretty sure he was Tommy.

Tommy was hard to forget. He'd spent the whole day in trouble with the teacher. At first, Liza had thought Tommy was a Mudbluff for certain. But then she had looked into his eyes, cool eyes the color of rye grass, and she hadn't been so sure. Those were the tricky ones, the people who did Mudbluffy things, but their eyes were sad, or tired, or scared, and you suddenly could tell they had reasons, big reasons, for the bad things they did.

"Hi," the woman said as she drew closer. "I'm Annie Cheatwood." Her blue eyes swept Liza's face, smiling and frowning at the same time. "I guess you're Molly's little girl, aren't you? Good grief, look at you! Is this déjà vu or what?''

Liza nodded. She knew what the lady meant—her grandmother said that all the time. And she'd seen pictures of her mom as a little girl, so she knew they looked alike. Especially the ones where her mom was smiling. There weren't very many of those, as if her mother had always been hiding a missing tooth or something.

''Yes,'' she said, curious to think that her mother had ever known this lady, who, now that she was up close, smelled of hair spray, Juicy Fruit gum, and, most surprisingly, wood chips.

It was actually kind of a nice smell. Nothing like her mom, but still. Definitely not a Mudbluff. ''I'm Liza,'' she added politely.

''Well, it's great to meet you, Liza,'' Mrs. Cheatwood said, sounding as if she meant it. ''It's really kind of a kick. This is my son Tommy. I guess you two are probably about the same age.''

Liza looked over at Tommy, who had his hands behind his head, stretching his head back to stare at the sky, thought there wasn't anything happening up there, not even an airplane. There didn't seem to be any point in saying ''hi.''

''Actually, we're looking for Jackson,'' Mrs. Cheatwood said. ''Jackson Forrest. He lives here, but nobody answered the door up at the house. Is he around?''

''Maybe,'' Liza said. ''My mom just met a man in the maze, but she didn't say his name.''

''Hot damn, he cornered her in the maze, did

he?'' Mrs. Cheatwood shook her head, as if she couldn't believe how funny that was. Then she wrinkled her nose. "Sorry, didn't mean to say 'damn.' That's what comes from selling lug nuts to guys in dirty shirts all day. Anyhow, was it a tall, gorgeous guy? Blond? Green eyes to die for?''

Tommy groaned. "For crying out loud, Mom.''

Liza flicked a look at him. He'd begun tearing the leaves from a low-hanging oak branch, and he still didn't acknowledge her presence.

"I guess so,'' she said to Mrs. Cheatwood. "He had green eyes. I think they're still in there.''

"Great. I hate to bust up a party, but I need to see Jackson ASAP. He's going to help me get this little devil of mine under control.''

*"Damn it,''* Tommy muttered with feeling. He swatted violently at the denuded branch. *"Goddamn it.''*

"And maybe he'll wash that filthy mouth out with soap while he's at it,'' Mrs. Cheatwood said. She stalked toward the maze, assuming without even looking back that her son would follow her.

Which, after a long, tense second in which his hard green gaze locked defiantly with Liza's, he did.

Liza hung back a moment, but her curiosity overcame her hesitation, and she decided to tag along.

Green eyes, she mused as she followed the woman's pointy heel marks that dug a string of small circles in the earth, like a connect-the-dots game. That's what King Willowsong *should* have.

*Green eyes to die for.*

As NOISES CARRIED toward them through the maze, and the irregular pattern of thudding footsteps grew loud enough to announce the imminent arrival of at least three people, Molly breathed a sigh of relief. She didn't even ask herself who it might be. She just closed her eyes and thought that she'd never been so glad to hear anything in her life.

*Hurry,* she implored mentally. Someone, anyone, to break up this awkward moment.

She still hadn't answered Jackson's unspoken question.

But she wasn't sure why she hadn't. She had a lie ready. A good lie. Carefully thought out, embroidered with so many little homespun details that sometimes she half believed them herself. A lie good enough to fool the entire population of Demery, South Carolina, if necessary.

But this wonderful lie, which she'd practiced a thousand times, training it to issue confidently from her lips, had simply refused to be spoken. It had lodged like a chicken bone in her throat, and, while Jackson stood there watching her in growing bemusement, she had been able to manage only a few stupid syllables of stumbling evasion.

"Molly. You can tell me. Who—"

But he didn't have time to finish. The approaching hubbub separated into individual voices. One adult—a female, clearly irked by something. One disgusted little boy objecting sulkily to everything the woman said. And then Liza's voice, breaking in politely, instructing the others to take the next left.

"Thank goodness!" A voluptuous brunette

emerged from the opening like a diva making her grand entrance.

She pressed the heel of her hand dramatically to her forehead. "I swear, Jackson, if you don't make this little rascal see reason, I'll—" She ducked her head to Jackson's collarbone and went limp against him. "I don't know what. Toss him into the volcano? Grind him into hamburger meat and have him for dinner?"

Jackson grinned, but over the woman's bent head he tossed a quick wink to the little boy, who had come sulking in behind her. "Why don't you just sell him to the Gypsies? Make a few bucks while you're at it."

The woman moaned. "They won't take him."

Jackson put his hands on the woman's shoulders and eased her erect again. "Then I guess we're stuck with him. We'll have to see what we can do to straighten him out."

He rotated her slightly. "Annie, say hi to Molly." He tilted his head. "You remember Annie Cheatwood, don't you, Molly? She was ahead of you in school—she graduated the same year Beau and I did."

Reaching out with his right hand, he touched the little boy's shining blond head. Molly noticed that the child, though still noticeably surly, did not pull away. "And this is her son Tommy, who, though his mother seems to have forgotten it, is a pretty cool kid."

Molly recognized him immediately. It was the little boy from Radway School. The mischievous blond child who'd been wheeling another student around by the ankles. The one who had reminded her of—

Suddenly Molly's brain began to blink and spin, like a computer being violently overloaded. So much was going on in the scene before her—so many complicated nuances, so many unspoken implications. She hardly knew where to begin processing it all.

Out of the chaos, one bewildering question pushed to the fore, blinking in a neon urgency.

Could Jackson be this little boy's father?

Bluntly stated like that, it seemed absurd. *Annie's son,* he had said, not "mine." And somehow, to Molly, it was inconceivable. Could Jackson have a child he refused to acknowledge? A pregnant lover he had refused to marry?

Surely not. But still... Look at the boy. The lanky limbs. The silver-blond hair. Those Forrest green eyes. That straight, high-bridged nose with slightly flared nostrils...

It could be true. That moment on the playground hadn't been an illusion. In a few years this handsome little boy would definitely possess the arrogant Forrest profile.

"Hi, Molly." Annie was smiling at her warmly. "Good to see you. It's been years. You grew up nice, kid." Annie poked Jackson in the ribs. "Didn't she grow up nice, Jack?"

Somehow tearing her gaze from the mysterious child, Molly smiled back. Of course she remembered Annie Cheatwood. Beautiful, sexy, brassy Annie, who had entertained a steady stream of the school's most popular boys in her ancient yellow sedan. *The Yellow Peril,* the boys had called it. Molly had been officially horrified but privately awed. She'd never known a girl whose car was infamous enough to earn a nickname of its own.

Annie had lived just down the street from Molly, in that modest neighborhood just on the wrong side of the tracks. Molly's mother had always looked down on Annie's family, who didn't care if crabgrass took over their little square of lawn, who let the paint peel on their walls and slats droop in their shutters. "Thank God we're not as tacky as the Cheatwoods," her mother had always said, sniffing with the desperate superiority of the chronically insecure.

Molly hadn't been friends with Annie, exactly. In high school, four years made a huge difference, and besides, Molly was too diffident, too prissy and far too uptight to interest the dynamic older girl.

But Molly had always admired her and had secretly wished to be more like her. Annie wasn't ashamed of being poor, and she obviously didn't agonize over what the neighbors thought. Even as a teenager Annie had believed herself the equal of anyone, somehow aware that human value wasn't measured by whether a man had spindly crabgrass or lush boxwood hedges in his front yard.

It was an enviable level of wisdom that Molly herself hadn't found until much later in life.

"Thanks, Annie," she said. "You're looking wonderful yourself." Molly intensified her smile, hoping that Annie might sense a little of that long-standing respect.

Maybe, Molly thought suddenly, it had been Annie who had refused to acknowledge the father of her child—not the other way around. That would be like her. She'd no doubt consider little Tommy just as "legitimate" as a Cheatwood as he could ever have been as a Forrest.

"Sorry to bust in on you guys, but I need Jack's help with Tommy." Annie cast a daggered glance toward her son, who simply looked away, feigning boredom. In that pose of deliberately casual defiance, he looked more Forrest than ever.

"This one's in big trouble. *Huge*." Annie turned back to Jackson. "He broke Junior Caldwell's nose, and now he won't go over there and say he's sorry."

Tommy raised his pointed chin. "I'm *not* sorry. You want me to lie?"

Annie narrowed her eyes dangerously. "You bet I want you to lie, buster. It's called good manners. It's called do it or your sorry behind is grounded for the rest of your sorry life."

Tommy's chin didn't waver, though his voice did, just a little. "I won't apologize. He deserved it. Junior Caldwell is a big, fat, stinking parasite."

Jackson made a sound like a muffled laugh, and Annie jabbed her elbow in his ribs. "Straight off this week's science vocabulary list," she said, and Molly could hear strangled mirth in her voice, too. "Talk to him, Jack. The Caldwells are raising Cain. They're trying to get Tommy kicked out of Radway."

"I don't care," Tommy said firmly. "Radway stinks. It's just a bunch of snobs and mamma's boys."

"Some things never change," Jackson observed cryptically. He slid his arm around Annie's shoulders. "Okay, cool down. Tommy and I will talk."

Annie let out a groan of relief. "You're an angel of mercy, my friend. And maybe, while you're at it—" she pointed toward her head with two fingers and made a scissoring motion "—this, too?"

Jackson glanced toward Tommy, as if assessing the need. Tommy, who Molly realized was plenty smart enough to know what his mother was talking about, simply stared off into space. Only the unnatural stillness of his body indicated any interest in the outcome.

"Sorry, Annie. Can't help you there." Grinning, Jackson chucked two fingers under Annie's chin. "You got to learn to pick your battles, sweetie."

Strangely mesmerized, Molly watched the two of them, still unable to come to grips with what she saw. Jackson and Annie were so comfortable together, so clearly partners in the awesome task of rearing this bright, handsome, willful little boy. Their communication was relaxed, largely nonverbal, and yet amazingly complete.

Molly had to pinch off a trickle of envy. It would have been nice to have someone like that, someone to bring your troubles to, someone who would help you sort out the mountains from the molehills. Molly had always been alone with her worries, sometimes struggling from bedtime until dawn to find the simple perspective Jackson had been able to offer Annie in a matter of minutes.

She felt a small hand creep up toward hers, and she looked down with a smile to find Liza standing close, her expression wistful. Molly's heart ached, recognizing that wordless longing. Never mind that the threesome in front of them weren't really a family, the couple not man and wife, the boy's background murky.

In every way that mattered, they *felt* like a family.

Molly and Liza were like children pressing their faces against the candy store window. She didn't know what to say to take that look from her daughter's eyes.

"I love you, honey," she said, for want of anything more inspired.

"I know," Liza answered softly, but she didn't take her eyes from Jackson even long enough to blink.

## CHAPTER THREE

TOMMY SAT NEXT TO Jackson on a big iron bench that overlooked the river. Though they'd been sitting there at least five minutes, Tommy hadn't said a word. He knew why he'd been brought here. Jackson was going to give him a lecture about how you shouldn't fight with people at school.

Well, he could just lecture away. Tommy didn't care. Grown-ups didn't know about Junior Caldwell, about what a creep he was. He deserved to have his nose broken.

Besides, Jackson didn't have any business giving Tommy a lecture. He wasn't his dad. He wasn't his uncle, or his brother, or even the principal. He wasn't anybody. He was just a guy who hung around with his mom. Lots of guys did that.

And they all wanted to impress her by trying to play daddy. Lots of big, fake smiles and head patting. And all that ''How's my little man?'' crap. Oh, yeah, everybody wanted to be Tommy's dad.

Everybody, that is, except his real dad. Wherever *he* was.

*Who*ever he was.

If he ever met his real dad, Tommy decided, he'd break *his* nose, too.

Tommy impatiently kicked at the small rocks that decorated the little picnic area where they sat. It was getting hot out here. Jackson had pretended he needed Tommy's help moving a bunch of boxes around for that old Miss Forrest. It had been hard work, and it made Tommy mad because he knew it was just an excuse to get him out here and bawl him out.

He stole a look at the man sitting next to him on the bench. So where was the lecture?

Almost as if he had forgotten Tommy was even there, Jackson leaned down and picked up one of the flat white pebbles at their feet. He eyed it carefully, tested its shape and weight, and then tossed it with a perfect flick of his wrist toward the river. It skipped three, four, *five* whole times before it finally sank.

"Awesome," Tommy said in spite of his determination not to speak first. He picked up a stone himself and tossed it. Two measly bounces, and it sank with a hollow plop.

Jackson sorted through the stones, picked up two and handed them to Tommy. "Flat is better," he said matter-of-factly. "And use more wrist."

By the third stone, Tommy had made it up to four skips, and he was feeling a little less grumpy. Maybe he'd been wrong about the lecture.

"So," Jackson said as he demonstrated the wrist motion one more time. "This Junior Caldwell kid. He's pretty big?"

Tommy made a rude noise and tossed his pebble. Four skips. He was finally getting the hang of it.

"Heck, no. He looks like a girl. He cried when I hit him. He cried so hard snot was dripping out of his nose."

Jackson paused midtoss and arched one eyebrow blandly at Tommy. "You hit a kid who looks like a girl?"

Tommy flushed, feeling suddenly uncomfortable. "Yeah, well, he's a major creep. He was really asking for it."

"Yeah?" Jackson shook a couple of pebbles in his palm thoughtfully. They made a noise like Monopoly dice. "Well, I guess you had to, then."

"I guess I did." It was so darn hot—how could a winter afternoon be so hot? His mother shouldn't have made him wear this jacket. His face felt red.

Tommy heaved four pebbles, fast and hard, into the river, which was sparkling now under the high, yellow afternoon sun. They all sank immediately. "Darn right I had to."

Jackson handed him another stone. "Take your time," he advised. "Don't try to bully it. You can't intimidate a rock." He demonstrated the sideways wrist flick one more time. "It's subtle. But remember you're always smarter than the rock, if you'll just take the time to finesse it."

Tommy took a deep breath, twitched his wrist a couple of times in practice, and then let the pebble glide easily through his fingers. Five skips! As much as Jackson's best.

*Finesse.* He liked that word. And he liked the way it worked.

Too bad you couldn't finesse a jerk like Junior Caldwell.

"You know what he said?" Tommy cast a quick glance toward Jackson, then looked away. "You know what that moron said?"

Jackson seemed entirely focused on finding the perfect pebble. "No. What?"

Timothy frowned, fighting back the sudden stupid feeling that he might cry. He hated even remembering what Junior had said.

"Somebody at lunch said they saw Coach Riser buying nails in the hardware store where my mom works. So Junior said that was because he's nailing my mom. And everybody laughed." He gritted his teeth and drew in a big breath, which hurt, as if his lungs were too tight. He made a fist around his pebble. "You know what that means, Jackson? Nailing somebody?"

"Yeah, I know." Jackson's face looked hard. "Mostly it means your friend Junior Caldwell is a stupid little punk."

"He's not my friend," Tommy said roughly. "I hate him. He's a spoiled sissy. I spent the night with him one time, and you know what? He's got twenty-five video games. He's got his own TV in his room. He sleeps with a stuffed puppy named Bitsy, and he doesn't even try to hide it."

"Bitsy?" Jackson's slow chuckle was appreciative. "Man. That's really embarrassing."

"And it gets even worse," Tommy said, remembering that night at the Caldwell mansion with a sharp, uncomfortable clarity. The whole thing had made him feel rotten somehow, even though it hadn't been so bad, really. Mr. Caldwell had been kind of nice, even if he did spoil Junior something awful. He played ball with the boys, and he had even watched them play video games for a while. He had particularly admired Tommy's skill at the Vampire Blaster game.

"Get this. Junior can't get to sleep unless his dad comes in and reads a bunch of football stats to him like a bedtime story. It's just plain pathetic."

Jackson's eyes were thoughtful, and Tommy wondered for a moment whether he had sounded jealous. He wasn't jealous, not one bit. Junior Caldwell was a nerd. It was just that Mr. Caldwell's voice had been really nice, and it felt kind of safe to have a strong man there, reading numbers and names in that comforting voice—especially after that weird vampire video game.

But still, it was sissy stuff. No guy should need a bedtime story to get to sleep.

When Jackson finally spoke, his voice was normal. He didn't sound as if he felt sorry for Tommy at all, thank goodness. Tommy couldn't stand for people to feel sorry for him.

"Absolutely pathetic," he agreed. "The kid is a zero. So what do you say, Tommy? You think you could give your mom a break and maybe tell this zero kid you're sorry?"

Surprisingly, Tommy suddenly felt as if he maybe could. Though he wasn't sure why, it had helped to talk about it. The worst of his anger was gone, like when you twist the top off a cola and all the fizz shoots out.

"Oh, okay," he muttered, skimming his last pebble expertly across the silver sparkles of the river. "If it'll make everyone chill about it."

They stood side by side, counting the skips together. Four, five, *six!* They high-fived each other, grinning.

As they walked back toward the plantation house, Tommy decided that, in a way, Jackson might make a pretty good father after all. Tommy knew he'd been lectured just now, sort of, but he really didn't mind.

"But remember," Tommy said firmly, pausing as they reached the carriage house, where his mother was waiting, "sorry or not, if Junior Caldwell doesn't shut up about my mom, I'll finesse his ugly nose all over again."

"Wow. You sure do travel light," Annie said as she deposited the last of Molly's suitcases onto the polished honey-pine floor of the Everspring carriage house. "I couldn't even get all my makeup in these puny little bags, much less my clothes." Straddling the arm of the sofa, she leaned back and gave Molly an appraising once-over. "But I guess the good-girl look doesn't call for all that much makeup, does it?"

Molly laughed. It was impossible to take offense at Annie's candor, especially after she'd offered to help unload the car and lug the suitcases upstairs to the small guest quarters.

"Not really. And the gardener look doesn't call

for that many clothes, either. I've got six pairs of jeans, all with torn, dirt-black knees, and a couple of mud-colored T-shirts.'' She surveyed the luggage ruefully. ''Most of these are full of Liza's toys and video games.''

Annie leveraged her legs over the sofa's arm, no mean feat considering there wasn't a spare millimeter of fabric in her electric-blue pants, and slid down the padded upholstery to a comfortably reclined position, kicking her shoes off as she went.

''No kidding? Tommy plays video games, too. All the time.'' She grimaced, wriggling to get the pillows just right. ''When he's not out breaking other kids' noses, that is.''

Molly couldn't help noticing how instinctively Annie made herself at home here. Was that just Annie's style—or had she spent time in this little secluded suite of rooms before?

Molly had been here before herself—years ago, with Beau. They had wrangled on that very sofa, Beau pressing and Molly retreating, until finally they had ended the dance the same way they so often ended it, with Molly crying as a coldly disgusted Beau drove her home.

As she thought back on it all now, Molly realized how sadly clichéd it had been. The more sophisticated boy growing bored with his too timid younger girlfriend, making demands and issuing threats. The girl weakening, fearful of losing the love of her life...

But at the time it hadn't seemed like a cliché. It had been confusing and terribly painful. Molly had begged for understanding, for patience. But she had been so afraid. If one night he made good his threat, if he left her, if he found another girl... How could she live without Beau?

Ironic, wasn't it? She had ended up having to live without him anyhow.

She wondered what it had been like for Annie and Jackson—if her suspicions were correct and the other couple had sneaked up here, too. Very different, she suspected. She imagined sexy whispers and muffled laughter, beer bottles knocking together as boots and underclothes rained across the floor.

Not that it was any of her business.

"Mom!" Liza appeared suddenly in the doorway, clutching a copy of *The Wizard of Oz* and a lovely doll dressed in a pink satin princess gown. "These were in the little bedroom. There's a teddy bear, too. Do you think it's all right if I play with them?"

Molly smiled at her daughter's eager face. "Of course," she said. "I'll bet Aunt Lavinia left them for you. You'll meet her tomorrow—you'll like her a lot."

Liza nodded, obviously hardly hearing anything beyond the "yes." She turned back toward the bedroom, already murmuring to her new pretend playmate, stroking the doll's long, silky blond curls and straightening her tiny rhinestone tiara.

"Aunt Lavinia, huh?" Annie sounded amused. "That's mighty cozy. I guess that means the Forrests considered you practically one of the family?"

One of the family. Molly tried not to think about how desperately she had once longed for that to be true. Those hopes had died ten years ago, as if they had been riding in that little car with Beau. She felt a tingle of discomfort burn along her cheekbones as she remembered how Beau's mother had shunned her at the funeral. How the older woman had turned her away from Jackson's hospital room. He was rarely conscious, Mrs. Forrest had said frigidly. Molly's condolences would be conveyed. There was no need to come again....

"Well, I wouldn't go that far." She worked at keeping her face neutral. No need to dredge all that up now—though she could see an avid curiosity shining in Annie's eyes. "Lavinia was always kind to everyone. I started calling her that when we were all very little, and I guess it just stuck."

"Yeah, Lavinia's a peach," Annie agreed. She rested her cheek on her knuckles and sighed. "That other one, though. The mother. She sure was a puffed-up peacock, wasn't she? Thought the Forrests were too good to breathe the same air as the rest of us plebes."

Molly smiled. Giselle Forrest *had* looked something like a peacock, actually, with her jewel-toned designer clothes and her stylishly spiked and highlighted hair.

"She was pretty aloof, wasn't she? But I think maybe she was just difficult to know."

"Difficult?" Annie laughed. "Honey, I know the mannequin down at Bloomingdale's better than I knew that woman. Like her better, too."

Molly didn't argue. She had felt that way once. She remembered being amazed, that day at the hospital, that Giselle could look so perfectly groomed, complete with flashing diamonds, sleek nylons and perfectly applied lip liner. Molly herself had been a mess, tearstained and disheveled. For weeks she had found it a struggle even to run a comb through her own hair.

She had hated Giselle that day, both for turning her away and for looking so completely unaffected by Beau's death.

It wasn't until years later—when she heard that Giselle Forrest had died of liver disease—that Molly had finally understood how personal, how unique, grief really is. That compulsive poise had been Giselle's protection. Her exquisitely cut diamond brooch had been nothing but armor placed over a heart as mangled as Molly's own.

Annie shifted to a sitting position, stretching like a cat. "Yes, ma'am, I've always said it beats me how a cold-blooded witch like that could have a decent son like Jack."

"Or Beau," Molly added, feeling strangely as if Annie had slighted him.

"Yeah, sure." Annie shrugged. "Whatever. Heck, it's a mystery how she had any children at *all*, if you know what I mean. Deserves its own segment on 'Tales of the Unexplained,' don't you think?"

Liza appeared in the doorway once again. "Excuse me," she said politely, "Mom, where are my suitcases? I want to play with all my dolls together."

Molly picked two pieces from the pile of luggage and passed them to her daughter, who eagerly hoisted them both and trotted back toward her own room. Molly envied the little girl her easy ability to adapt wherever she went. A few spangled scarves for costumes, a few hand-drawn pictures for backdrops, a few smiling princess dolls for companionship, and that little bedroom was well on its way to becoming the Planet Cuspian.

Annie was expertly eyeing the diminished stack of luggage, which, now that Liza's bright-pink pieces were gone, did look a little skimpy, Molly had to admit.

"Even allowing for the minimalist approach to wardrobing," Annie said dryly, "I'd have to guess you haven't exactly come home intending to put down roots." She laughed. "No pun intended."

"Nope. Just the landscaping kind," Molly said with a smile, sliding the largest of the suitcases, which held her seed catalogues, garden brochures and drafting supplies, toward the window. She'd probably work over there—the light was perfect, the view of terraced lawns marching down to the river inspirational. "We'll only be staying a couple of months, just until the renovations are done. Liza and I consider Atlanta home now."

Molly felt Annie's gaze on her as she unzipped the bag and began stacking supplies on the large desk. "Got your own landscaping business in Atlanta, I hear," Annie said. "Doing pretty well there?"

Her voice was almost too bland. Molly looked up, wondering what the other woman was getting at. "I can't complain," she answered evenly.

"Yeah, I can see you're not the complaining type." Annie sighed. "Still, it would be a heck of a lot easier with a second paycheck in the house, wouldn't it? What about it, Molly? Ever think you ought to go down to the husband store and pick yourself out a new one?"

Molly bent over the table, arranging her colored pencils in their holder. She let her hair fall across her face. "I haven't thought about it," she said, wishing her voice didn't sound so tight. "We really do just fine."

"Oh, now. Don't go all huffy on me." Annie grinned as she inspected a pink-hued fingernail. She nibbled carefully at a ragged edge. "I'm not trying to pry your tax statement out of you. I'm a single mom myself. I know all about it. Frankly, I'm just wondering why you've come back here at all."

Molly took a deep breath, forcing herself to relax. She leaned against the edge of the desk, pencils in hand, and looked at Annie.

"Sorry. It's simple, really. I've been doing mostly business landscaping for the past few years. I'd rather be doing houses, but the domestic market in Atlanta is pretty hard to break into. The same companies have been designing those old estates for generations." She rubbed the soft pencils against her palm, leaving rainbow-colored smudges on her skin. "But Everspring could change all that. Scarlett O'Hara herself would be impressed with my résumé after this."

Annie was nodding. "Makes sense." She narrowed her eyes. "So you really came just for the job?"

"Of course," Molly said. "What else would I have come for?"

"Well, I wondered..." Annie seemed unsure how to proceed, and the hesitance sounded unnatural, as if she rarely bothered to plan or polish her utterances. "Oh, hell, I'll just say it. I wondered if maybe you had come because of Jackson."

Finally, Molly understood. Of course—how could she have been so dense? Annie was interested in Jackson, and she didn't want any competition.

Molly almost laughed at the thought. If only Annie knew how wrong she was! If only she knew how difficult it was for Molly to even look at Jackson, who wore Beau's face, inhabited Beau's body, so casually—as if he didn't suspect what it did to her. Jackson, who without meaning to awoke a thousand dreams in Molly's breast, who with one smile, a ghost's smile, stirred emotions that should have slept forever.

She shook her head emphatically. "No, Annie," she assured the other woman. "I didn't come because of Jackson. I came *in spite of* him."

JACKSON TRIED to concentrate on the cards in his hand. He tried to ignore the small square of light that glowed, like backlit amber, in his peripheral vision. The light from one of the carriage house bedrooms. He especially tried not to see the slim silhouette that occasionally moved across the golden curtains.

But he hated canasta. He was terrible at canasta. What had possessed him to tell Lavinia he would play canasta with her tonight?

And for that matter, when had his spicy maiden aunt taken up this monotonous game herself? And why? Hadn't she always lumped canasta in with bridge as the "pastimes of the half-dead or the half-witted?" Yes, last time he was in town, he distinctly remembered Lavinia and her cronies staying up half the night drinking mint juleps and playing cutthroat poker.

"So," he said, laying down all his fours and stifling a yawn. "What's with the canasta, Vinnie? And where's the brandy? Did a traveling missionary come through town cleaning things up or what?"

She didn't bother to look up from her cards. "I've been reading Great-great-aunt Maybelle's diaries, and apparently this was her favorite game. I thought I'd better find out what the attraction was."

Oh. That cleared things up. Lavinia was the family historian, and she took her research very seriously. She could tell you what the Forrest family had served President Zachary Taylor for dinner back in 1850. And she was likely to try out the recipe herself, just to see how it had tasted.

It made for some interesting dinners, especially since Lavinia was the world's most terrible cook.

"So what *is* the attraction?" Jackson's gaze flicked toward the carriage house, but he forced it back to the cards. Which were the good threes—the red or the black? God, he hated this game.

"Don't you try that sarcastic tone on me, young

man," Lavinia said tartly. "And just because you haven't got the guts to climb those stairs and talk to her, don't take your frustration out on me, either."

Jackson glared at his aunt over the pile of cards between them. "What baloney," he said. "Just because I'm bored stiff with this moronic game—"

"It's not just that," she said, snapping her cards shut irritably. "It's because for the past two hours you've been twitching around this house like a fly in a glue pot. It's because you showered before dinner. And it's because you can't keep your eyes off that window."

Jackson drummed his fingers on the table. "I showered before dinner," he said grimly, "because I'd been moving your filthy boxes all afternoon and—"

"Oh, stuff and nonsense," Lavinia said with a hint of laughter buried beneath the peppery tone. She plopped her cards on the table and began to gather up the deck. "Get out of here, Jackson. If you're not going to go up there, at least go somewhere. You're driving me crazy, and I've got some reading to do."

He surrendered his cards with a chuckle. Lavinia had always been able to see through him. "Actually," he admitted, "I was thinking I might see if they needed something to eat. They can't have had time to stock the refrigerator yet."

Lavinia huffed and continued stacking the cards in her mother-of-pearl lacquered box. "They had the same dinner we had," she said. "I sent food up on a tray hours ago."

Jackson declined to comment. Somehow he couldn't see Lavinia's culinary experiment du jour, spinach-and-chickpea casserole, appealing to a nine-year-old little girl. It had taken a good deal of character for this close to thirty-two-year-old man to swallow down his own portion.

"Still, maybe I'd better check. See if they need anything at all."

Lavinia smiled at him archly. "Of course. How thoughtful. Maybe you'd better do that, dear."

Jackson kissed her cheek on the way out. "You are an adorable old termagant, did you know that, Auntie?"

"Thank you," she said sweetly. "I do my best."

HALF AN HOUR LATER, a large, warm, aromatic box of mushroom pizza balanced on his forearm, Jackson climbed the stairs to the carriage house. The night had turned cold and clear. Stars glinted against the black sky, as sharp as bits of broken glass.

He paused at the door, uncomfortably aware that he was rushing things. She was probably still unpacking—she was undoubtedly tired. He should have given her time to settle in. He should have waited until tomorrow.

But how could he? He had waited so long already.

Still, he wished he could shake this ridiculous sense of guilt. Why should he feel guilty? She wasn't Beau's girl anymore. Beau was gone. He'd been gone for ten years—long enough, surely, for his claim on Molly to fall forfeit. Surely the invisible walls behind which Beau had cloistered her had long since crumbled to dust.

Damn it, no more guilt. He exhaled hard, his breath materializing, silver and ghostly, in front of him. He raised his hand and knocked twice. Low, in case Liza was sleeping. But definite. Unashamed.

He heard her light footsteps as she came toward the door, and he ordered his heart to beat in even time.

No more guilt. He was betraying no one. He had every right to be here, to offer pizza, to offer help, to offer friendship.

To offer, in fact, whatever the hell he wanted.

# CHAPTER FOUR

"OH, YOU WONDERFUL, wonderful man." As soon as she opened the door, Molly tilted her head back, closed her eyes and inhaled a long, deep, sensual breath of the pizza-scented night air. Her hair streamed unbound over her shoulders and twinkled in the light, as if she'd stood in a shower of glitter. "I could just kiss you."

Jackson gripped the pizza box a little more tightly, hoping he wouldn't end up with tomato sauce all over his shoes. But the sight of her was enough to make his fingers numb.

How could she have become even more beautiful? Ten years ago he would have said it wasn't possible. But if Molly at eighteen had been a fairy princess, the woman before him was the Gypsy queen. Her coltish, utterly virginal body had softened in all the right places, and each curve seemed to be issuing wordless invitations to his hands.

The pizza box buckled at one corner.

"Well, by all means," he said, somehow managing to keep his voice from squeaking like a kid's. "Feel free."

She laughed, a low trickle of warmth that slid across his skin like sunshine. "It's actually real!"

She put one hand on the box and breathed deeply again, as if she couldn't get enough of the scent. "I thought I smelled pizza, but then I thought, no, I must be dreaming. Like the man in the desert who thinks he sees water."

Jackson chuckled. "I gather you and I have approximately the same opinion of spinach-and-chick-pea casserole."

"Please don't tell Lavinia." She stepped back, opening the door wider to let him enter. "I managed two bites, then I gave the rest to Liza. Believe it or not, she absolutely loved the stuff."

"Good God, what's wrong with her?" Jackson grimaced. "I slipped mine under the table. Stewball and I have a pact. I won't tell Vinnie he sleeps on the Chippendale sofa if he'll clean my plate for me."

Molly was already opening the box and peeling apart the gooey slices hungrily. She handed one to Jackson. "Poor Stewball," she said as she bit into the hot cheese. She moaned with delight. "Mmm. Mushroom. You remembered I love mushroom."

Jackson busied himself piling melting strands of cheese on top of the crust. Of course he remembered. Molly would probably never believe how little he had forgotten. He remembered how, back when they were kids, she used to sign her name with a smiley-face inside the *O*. He remembered the opening lines of the sonnet she'd written for senior English. He remembered how her mascara used to smudge around her lower lashes when sad movies or stray dogs—or Beau—made her cry.

And about a million other things. It was a wonder he had ever been able to learn how to build buildings, considering all the Molly trivia that still cluttered his feeble mind.

And yet, tantalizingly, he sensed that there were a million new things to learn about her, too. That womanly quality in her body, for instance. The faint shadows in her face, where pain had left its mark. The deep, satisfied glow in her eyes when she looked at Liza.

The Gypsy queen knew things the fairy princess hadn't dreamed of.

"And thick crust. Jackson Forrest," she mumbled, her mouth stuffed with cheese, "I positively love and adore you."

He grinned. "I'll bet you say that to all the pizza delivery boys." He grabbed another slice for each of them, tore off a couple of paper towels from the rack, and made for the sofa. She followed without hesitation, as if she were magnetized to the pizza.

She plopped down beside him, curling her bare legs up under her. She swallowed the last bit of crust, reached for her second slice and dug in greedily.

He stared at her, marveling. Though she wore only a long, grass-stained T-shirt, which had obviously been washed so many times it settled around the curves of her body like a second skin, she was completely uninhibited.

She must not even realize how damned sexy it was to watch her slide that wedge of pizza between her teeth. Or perhaps she just never imagined that good old Jackson would be thinking about such things.

"What?" She blinked at him over the pizza, hesitating midbite. She looked self-consciously down at her hands. "Oh, I'm a mess, aren't I?"

He looked, too, suddenly, noticing that she had stray smudges from multicolored markers all over her fingers. And, now that they were in a better light, he could see that the gold glittering of her hair was just exactly that—glitter. The sparkling flecks dusted her forearms and the backs of her hands, too.

"What on earth have you been doing?" He rubbed his forefinger along her wrist. "You look as if you stood too close to a preschool explosion."

She drew herself up with as much hauteur as she could manage in that position, with that silly dab of oil from the cheese shining on her chin. "For your information, I have been in another galaxy," she said loftily. "I come to you straight from the Planet Cuspian, where I just happen to reign as Queen."

He looked toward the kitchenette. He knew Lavinia had generously stocked a minibar before Molly's arrival. "You don't say. And exactly how many mint juleps does it take to blast you to that particular galaxy?"

She smiled as she popped the last bit of the second piece of pizza into her mouth and wiped her hands on the paper towel.

"None," she said. "I've been decorating Liza's room. Cuspian is her imaginary planet." She pulled her hand ruefully through her hair, trying to pick out the glitter. "Unfortunately, it's a very messy planet."

Jackson couldn't stop himself from leaning over and smoothing his fingers across her cheek, brushing away one stray fleck of gold. "Well, if you're the Queen," he said, "why don't you do something about that?"

Her skin was warm and soft, and he felt the gentle rounding of her cheek as her smile deepened. He ought to take his hand away, but he couldn't. Luckily, she didn't seem to find anything at all unsettling about having Jackson's fingers on her skin. They'd been there before, wiping away mud or mosquitos, mayonnaise or makeup or tears.

"It's a purely ceremonial title," she explained. "You see, on the Planet Cuspian, all the real power belongs to the Princess."

"And that would be…"

She grinned. "Exactly. Princess Liza, who even now sleeps under the golden moons of Cuspian, which we transported all the way from Atlanta in a hefty bag." She shook her fingers playfully, releasing a tiny sparkling rainfall of gold. "The Princess is hopelessly fond of glitter."

Jackson closed his throat hard, blocking the words he wanted to say. He wanted to ask her to show him—wanted it so much it was a physical thing, like thirst. He wanted to see the golden moons; he wanted to memorize the innocent face that slumbered beneath them. He wanted to know everything there was to know about Molly and her little girl, the child who obviously owned every square inch of her mother's heart.

But he had to wait. Somehow, he had to be patient.

As a rule, patience didn't come naturally to him. That had always been the one advantage to being the "bad" brother. Everyone expected Jackson to be outrageous, to say and do whatever he wanted, no matter who didn't like it. He could think of a hundred people—most of them women—who would laugh out loud at the idea of Jackson troubling himself to resist temptation.

But maybe those hundred skeptics didn't know him quite as well as they thought they did. They had no idea that resisting Molly was not a new experience for Jackson. It was a way of life.

"And speaking of the Planet Cuspian—as long as you're here, is there any chance I could rope you into helping me with the decorations in Liza's room? I'm in desperate need of someone tall and strong and brave to hang the third moon." She grinned. "I can't promise you won't go home glittering like the Sugar Plum Fairy, but who knows? You might decide it's a good look for you."

He cocked one eyebrow and thanked fate for seeing fit to reward him so quickly for his five seconds of patience. "We tall, strong, brave guys aren't afraid of a little glitter. Especially when the Queen tells us she believes we can hang the moon." He glanced toward the bedroom hallway. "But didn't you say Liza was sleeping?"

"That's okay. She sleeps like a stone. And I did

promise her that everything would be in place when she wakes up tomorrow.''

He stood and held out his hand. ''Then I'm yours, my Queen,'' he said. ''Take me to your leader.''

When Molly eased open Liza's door, Jackson stared, hardly able to believe the magic she had performed in that tiny, ordinary bedroom. A dozen large posters—drawings of castles and dragons and shooting stars, of tall green towers and fantastic red roses and sloping blue mountains—had turned the plain white walls into an elaborate stage set. Most, he guessed, had been created by Molly. He recognized her special eye for color and composition. But some of them had been enhanced by a younger, less sophisticated artist who was spectacularly liberal with glitter.

Two huge golden globes hung in one corner of the room, swaying slightly in the breeze from the half-open window, catching the lamplight and tossing it out across the room in a luminous shimmer. Multicolored, gold-spangled scarves had been tied to the headboard of the little twin bed, drawn up to a point and attached to the wall to create a royal canopy.

Under that canopy, honey-brushed by the light from the Cuspian moons, lay the princess. He looked for one long minute at the peaceful profile, the yellow hair splayed against the frilly pink pillowcase, the absurdly incongruous Atlanta Falcons nightshirt. But then his throat did something painful, and he couldn't look anymore.

He turned to Molly. "Does the moon go over there, with the others?"

He had instinctively whispered, but when Molly answered she spoke at a nearly normal level. "Yep. It's the biggest moon—so big it pulled the hook right out of the ceiling." She walked to the corner, casually brushing the silky bangs from Liza's forehead as she passed, and picked up a huge gold ball from the floor. She grinned sideways. "See? Cuspian's dominant moon. It needs to be screwed into a beam, but this good old wood is really hard. It's difficult to get enough leverage while I'm standing on the chair."

He almost laughed. The foam globe was as big as a beach ball and had been rather clumsily decorated with everything from the gold aisle at the craft store: gold spray paint, gold sequins, gold velvet ribbons, gold braided trim, rhinestones and, of course, glitter. But he could imagine Liza's earnest little face as she went over her work, gluing the glamour onto her wonderful fantasy moon, and the urge to laugh faded. This was an amazing child.

But what had he expected from Molly's daughter? He remembered Molly herself at that age, bent over a frostbitten lilac, focused, intense, determined, as if this were the last flower on the planet, as if she could somehow will life back into the blackened petals.

"Okay, let's see if we can make it stay. Where's the hook?" He took the large white-iron hanger from Molly's hand, climbed on the chair and pressed the screw end of the metal into the beam. Nothing. Molly was right—the wood had hardened over the past hundred years, and it was almost like trying to break through metal.

But if she believed he could hang the moon, then he'd hang the thing or die trying. He pushed harder, refusing to let the strain show on his face—God, was that adolescent show-off still lurking in his psyche? "Look, M! No hands!"—and finally the oak surrendered, and the point pierced through.

After that, it was easy. She handed up the slender fishing line that almost invisibly extended from the ball, and he slipped it over the curve of the hook. A thousand twinkling gold moonbeams shot across the walls, across the sleeping little girl, across Molly's happy smile, turned up toward him like a gift.

"Voilà," he said softly. "Let there be moonlight."

She put out her hand, sweetly—though irrationally—offering to help him down, as if her fragile form could possibly hold his weight. But he took it, because it would have been rude not to. Because it would have been impossible not to. It had always been impossible for him not to take whatever she offered.

The chair rocked as he descended, and she inhaled, startled, putting her hands on his shoulders while he got both feet back on the floor.

"Careful," she said, running her fingers along his sleeve, checking to be sure he was stable.

He couldn't have been less so. Though the ground was solid beneath his feet, his brain was reeling, trying to find center. But she was too close. Her hand was on his arm, her warmth seeping into him. Her eyes were so liquid-blue in the lamplight that, looking into them, he stopped breathing. He felt his interior shift, as if his whole body had been constructed over a dangerous, unseen fault line.

He didn't speak, and neither did she, but something passed between them anyway. Slowly, over long, elastic seconds, her lips parted, and her eyes widened. Her fingers tightened on his sleeve, and her breath hitched, tight and shallow.

"Molly," he whispered. He touched her cheek. "God, Molly—"

At the sound of his voice, she blinked. She frowned. And then she pulled away.

"Molly—"

"I'm— Oh, God, I'm sorry." She ran her hands through her hair, then wiped them across her face, as if trying to wake herself up from a confusing sleep. "Oh, Jackson, I am so sorry."

She faced him, her eyes pinched with distress. "I didn't mean to—" She took a deep breath. "I think it's just that… Being here, you know? After all this time. And you—" She shook her head helplessly. "You understand, don't you? It's just that, for a minute there, you looked so much like Beau."

"I MUST HAVE BEEN CRAZY," Molly muttered under her breath as she tried to make her way to the one remaining empty park bench. "Mad, roaring crazy. If you hadn't looked at me like that, with your eyes all big and pitiful, you'd still be at home with your head in a flowerpot."

Stewball, the thirteen-year-old springer spaniel who had always belonged to the Forrest family, didn't hear her, of course. He was slightly deaf, and he was not interested anyway. He didn't know he was aging, didn't know he was half-blind, didn't know he was driving her crazy. He knew only that he was out in the world for the first time in weeks, and he wanted to lunge and bark and chase everything that moved. Demery Park at noontime gave him plenty of scope.

"You're a crafty soul, I'll give you that," she added, wondering if Stewball was big enough to actually pull her arm out of its socket. "Doing that sleepy old helpless hound impersonation so that I'd feel sorry for you."

Stewball darted between her legs to growl at a trash receptacle. At home he looked so harmless. Jackson had been in New York for days—an emergency with one of his building projects, she'd heard from Lavinia—and Stewball had spent the entire time mooning pathetically on Everspring's shady front porch, watching the drive with his long, sad face propped against a huge clay pot of pansies.

In a fit of pity, Molly had invited him to come along to the park, where she was to meet Lavinia at noon. And now she was stuck with the demon dog he had become the minute he bounded out of the car. Maybe, she thought, hoping against hope, when Lavinia got here she could make him behave.

Or maybe not.

Molly tried to unbraid the leash Stewball had diabolically wound across her legs. But he kept circling, and she only seemed to grow more tangled.

"Need some help with that mutt?"

Stewball knew it was Jackson before Molly, absorbed in extricating herself, could focus on the words. With a loud, welcoming bark, he suddenly raced forward, nearly toppling Molly in his haste to tackle Jackson, who was approaching with Lavinia. Molly had no choice but to follow, her fingers tangled in the leather lead and her feet clumsily weaving their way several inches behind her outstretched torso.

Drat the mangy mutt. She had been dreading seeing Jackson again after the way she had embarrassed herself the other night. She had almost kissed him, for heaven's sake. Jackson, who had been her most loyal friend since her pigtail days—but who had never once looked at her *that* way. And why would he? Everybody knew that Jackson liked his women exotic and sassy and hot. Jackson wouldn't ever have wasted his kisses on a common domesticated house-female like Molly.

What a miserable moment it had been! She had tried to explain. His resemblance to Beau had momentarily confused her. It had been a little like being caught in a dream. It had been—oh, it had been crazy. There weren't any words to explain it, not really.

He'd been nice about it, but she had sensed his discomfort. He had invented an excuse to leave the carriage house almost immediately. And before the sun came up the next morning, he was on his way to New York, like a starling winging mindlessly away from the sound of gunfire.

So she would have liked to show a little dignity, at least right at first. And now here she was throwing herself at him all over again. With a little help from this damned dog.

"Stewball, down! Down!" Lavinia was laughing and backing away at the same time. Stewball was ignoring her, intent on getting his mouth close enough to Jackson's face to properly welcome him home.

Jackson ruffled the dog's hair playfully, somehow managing to keep clear of that soggy, enthusiastic tongue. He reached for the lead, which Molly surrendered gratefully, and within a few seconds he had shortened Stewball's range so drastically that, after a few abortive lunges that went nowhere, the animal had no choice but to sit at Jackson's feet and pant his adoration quietly.

"Hi, M." Jackson smiled at Molly, who hoped she didn't look too mussed. "You okay?"

She nodded. "But happy to see reinforcements." She frowned down at Stewball. "Didn't he once qualify as a good dog?"

Jackson chuckled. "God, no! Don't you remember the Fourth of July picnic the first year we had him? He scarfed down two dozen deviled eggs and a blueberry pie before anyone could stop him."

Yes, of course she remembered. "And on the way home he threw up all over your car," she said, grinning at the memory of Jackson's face when he'd seen the mess. "It was so awful. I thought you were going to strangle him."

But Jackson hadn't strangled him. Funny—she could suddenly remember the whole thing. Jackson had taken one look at the pitiful puppy, whose head was swaying with dizzy misery, and his anger had evaporated. He had reached over and stroked Stewball's ears, murmuring gently soothing sounds.

Actually, it had been Beau, sitting in the back seat with Molly, who had lost his temper. Beau whose face had reddened with fury at the sight of the soiled upholstery. A shiver passed over her as she remembered his tone as he informed Jackson that *he* was not going to clean up that mess.

Strange. So incredibly strange that she had forgotten all that.

"And then there was the night Beau went skinny-dipping down at the river," Lavinia said, shaking her head in helpless amusement. "Stewball ran away with his jeans and the poor boy spent an hour trying to find them before he finally came creeping home in his underwear."

Molly looked at Jackson, confused. "I thought that was you," she said. "Beau told me—he told me that happened to you."

Lavinia and Jackson exchanged a swift look. "Maybe it happened to both of us," he said easily. "Stewball's list of sins is so long no one can keep it straight."

Molly didn't believe him, but she wasn't sure what to say. Perhaps she was the one who remembered wrong. And did it really matter? It had happened more than ten years ago.

But it felt strangely unsettling. Her memories were all she had left of Beau. She didn't like to think they were unreliable.

"So." Lavinia put one hand on Molly's cheek, the other on Jackson's shoulder. "I'll bet you two are wondering why I called this meeting."

Molly smiled, nodding. She was curious. She had assumed Lavinia asked her here for purely social reasons. She hadn't realized Jackson had been invited, too.

"I've got a plan. A wonderful plan. But I need your help, both of you." Lavinia began walking toward the eastern edge of the park. After a few yards she turned and frowned at them. "Are you coming, or do I need to put you on a leash, too?"

As soon as Lavinia was confident that she had them in tow, she picked up her pace, striding along in her chunky white running shoes as if she were trying to beat a time clock. Molly hoped they weren't going far. Her espadrilles weren't made for marathons. Jackson seemed fine, but Stewball obviously hated to abandon his dream of sniffing every tree trunk they passed.

Lavinia talked as she walked, but she didn't bother to turn around, so most of her words were lost on the wind. Once Molly frowned quizzically toward Jackson, but he just shrugged his shoulders and smiled, obviously equally mystified.

As suddenly as she had begun, Lavinia stopped. She turned around, beaming at Molly. "So here it is. What do you say? Can you get it done by April, do you think?''

Molly looked around. Nothing presented itself as the obvious explanation. In fact, they had reached the extreme eastern boundary of the park, where the brick paths and iron benches gave way to a rather large, empty plot of undeveloped land.

She returned her gaze to Lavinia. ''Get what done?''

''The landscaping, of course!'' Lavinia looked impatient. ''Good heavens, haven't you two been listening to a word I said? I'm donating this land to the city so that they can expand the park. We're going to build a pavilion here. It will be the Beaumont Forrest Pavilion, and I want you to design the landscaping.''

''Oh.'' Molly was stunned, but pleased. How lovely to honor Beau's memory this way, with something permanent that the whole city could share. And how gratifying it would be for Molly herself to have a part in creating it. ''I think it's a wonderful idea.''

''Good.'' Lavinia nodded her satisfaction to Molly, then turned to Jackson. ''But remember I said I needed help from both of you.''

''Yes?'' Jackson's face was impassive. ''What do you want from me?''

''If Molly can get things ready in time, we'll officially open the new park at the bicentennial celebration in April. I know that will be a push, because she's got to get the house ready for the spring tour that same week. But I'll get her plenty of workers—it should be manageable.''

''Lavinia.'' Jackson held her gaze steadily. ''What do you want from me?''

''Well, Jackson, you know that no one knew Beau better than you did,'' she said. ''No one loved him more. I want you to give the dedication speech.''

Of course. How perfect. Molly smiled and touched Jackson's arm, delighted. It would be difficult for him—quite emotional, of course. But it would be so right.

''Well?'' Lavinia raised her eyebrows. ''Will you do it, Jackson?''

''No,'' Jackson answered flatly. ''I won't.''

MOLLY ARRIVED HOME FIRST. She couldn't help being glad that she hadn't needed to ride with Lavinia. The air in that car had probably been glacial. Jackson had been steadfast, categorically refusing to give the speech, and refusing with equal implacability to explain why. Lavinia had finally given up, her bewildered frustration stamped on each of her features.

As Molly got out of her rental car, struggling to make Stewball believe that their outing was truly over, she saw that a strange man was standing at the edge of the drive. He didn't look like a salesman. He had his hands in his pockets, and he was staring down at the brick path as if it were the gateway to another world, and he wasn't sure he should risk setting foot on it.

Well, she could certainly sympathize. She had always thought Everspring was like another world, coming from her cramped, bitter household into this peaceful expanse of grace and luxury.

As she watched him, she realized that the man looked familiar. Did she know him? She smiled warily, unable to shed her big-city caution just yet, even though she was well aware that in Demery no one ever met a "stranger."

Stewball finally decided to cooperate. As he climbed reluctantly down out of the car, she snatched hold of the leash before he could escape again.

At the noise, the man looked up, giving her a clearer view of his pleasant, even features. And then it came to her. Coach Riser. Good heavens, it was Beau's old football coach.

"Hi, Molly," he said, reaching down to pat Stewball, who, back on home turf, was once again masquerading as an obedient dog. "I think I would have recognized you even if I hadn't known you were back in town. You haven't changed a bit since high school."

She smiled, knowing it for a lie but appreciating the sentiment anyway. She wasn't surprised that Coach Riser remembered her, even though she hadn't been any kind of athlete in high school. She hadn't even been a cheerleader. But she had been the biggest distraction for Coach Riser's prize quarterback, and therefore she had definitely made an impression.

Coach Riser worried about everything Beau Forrest did—whether he ate enough greens and got enough sleep, whether he was slacking off in history, and whether he quarreled with his girlfriend. A tiff with Molly had been known to affect Beau's passing game, and Ross Riser, a young coaching phenom who had a record of thirty-eight wins, two losses and one tie at Radway, wouldn't stand for that.

"Coach," she said with pleasure. "It's wonderful to see you. I heard you were still at Radway. Are you still winning every game you play?"

To her surprise, he looked uncomfortable. "Not really," he said. "We do all right, but it's not like before. Not like with Beau."

Of course not, she thought. Beau had been one of a kind. She made her smile firmer so that it wouldn't turn tearful. She was absolutely not going to start blubbering every time she ran into another old memory.

"Yes." She tightened her fist around Stewball's leash. "Beau was wonderful, wasn't he?"

Ross Riser's jaw hardened. Molly wondered if he, too, might be fighting back tears. He stared into the middistance, as if he didn't want to catch her eyes. "Beau was—" He broke off, chewing on his lower lip and squinting at something she couldn't see. "Oh, hell, he was a Forrest. What else can I say?"

That didn't sound right. His voice was strangely rough, and he thrust his hands in his pockets harshly. She could see that his fingers had curled, making fists under the fabric. He looked angry, and the sight surprised her. Why on earth would speaking of Beau make Coach Riser angry?

But perhaps he was just angry at his own display

of emotion. He probably prided himself on being tough, a man's man. A coach was supposed to control his players, cheer them on or chew them out as necessary. Not cry over them.

Still, the moment felt awkward. She looked around the front yard, wondering what to talk about next. It was a beautiful afternoon, cool and blue-skied with a hint of spring sweetening the breeze. The bulbs would be pushing up any day now. The crape myrtle bushes over by the fountain were overdue for pruning. But she couldn't imagine saying any of that to the suddenly tense man in front of her. She wished she had listened better while Beau had bragged about his football exploits. Or at all.

"Well, speak of the devil."

"What?" Molly looked at the coach, confused. Speak of the devil? She frowned, instinctively disliking his tone. "Who?"

She heard voices just a split second before she saw Jackson and Lavinia rounding the corner. Molly had parked in the back drive, nearest to the carriage house, but the family always used the front entrance.

"Hello, Riser," Jackson said without any particular inflection. "What's up?"

Molly's inner antenna quivered slightly. So she hadn't been imagining the cloaked hostility she'd thought she glimpsed in Ross Riser's face when he saw Jackson approaching. The same thinly veiled antagonism lay beneath Jackson's clipped words just now.

She looked from one man to the other curiously. Both were tall, athletic, extremely good-looking—

and tense as bowstrings. Ross Riser was almost ten years older than Jackson, a gap that back in high school had given him an air of unassailable authority. But now the balance of power had shifted, and they were just two grown men who obviously didn't like each other very much.

She wondered why.

"Jackson," Ross responded tersely. "I've been looking for you." His tone was oddly accusatory, and Molly's curiosity deepened. Why should Ross Riser take that attitude with Jackson?

Jackson obviously found it inappropriate, too. "Did you look in New York? Because that's where I've been for the past three days." He smiled without warmth. "I hope I haven't violated my parole."

"Oh." Ross's fair skin flushed, and he lowered his eyebrows in a self-conscious scowl. "Well, I need to talk to you." He shrugged one shoulder and slipped his fists into his pockets again, obviously working for a more conciliatory tone. "If you have a minute."

"Go ahead, Jackson," Lavinia said. "We'll meet you back at the house."

Stewball didn't like it, but Molly kept him tightly leashed as Ross and Jackson walked away, so the disappointed dog had to content himself with a few plaintive whines.

"What on earth," Molly said quietly, as soon as the men were out of earshot, "was that all about?"

Lavinia looked thoughtful. "I'm not sure. Things haven't been right between those two for years." She sighed. "I've always wondered…" She patted

Stewball absently and gazed after her nephew. "Ross and Beau were very close. I've always wondered whether Ross blamed Jackson for Beau's death."

"Blamed Jackson?" Molly was incredulous. "Why?"

Lavinia slipped her arm through Molly's. "A lot of people did, you know. Right away a rumor began spreading around town that Beau hadn't really been driving, that Jackson had been responsible."

Jackson? Molly felt herself filling up with resentment. How unfair—and how cruel. Jackson had been a rebel. He had been cocky, irreverent and stubborn. But he had never been a liar. And, while a lesser man might have envied his smooth-talking, prom-king brother, Jackson had always been intensely supportive of Beau—even protective.

"You see, the police couldn't actually tell who'd been behind the wheel," Lavinia said her deep voice sad but resigned, as if she'd been over this a million times. "We had only Jackson's word for it."

"Well, that should be enough," Molly said hotly. She had adored Beau, but even she knew that his halo had been kept in place more than once by virtue of having a loyal identical twin. She remembered one day particularly, when Beau had been in bed with a hangover, unable to face Saturday football practice. Jackson had suited up and played all morning as Beau. Not even Coach Riser had noticed the difference.

"Yes, well, you know how gossips are." Lavinia buttoned her cardigan against a sudden, distinctly wintry breeze and, letting out the leash, let Stewball prance ahead of them down the brick path. "Anyhow, it may be Annie Cheatwood, for all I know. She's dating Ross and is the type who has always got men at each other's throats like dogs."

Annie. Of course. If Ross was dating Annie, he might have some questions about Tommy—and Tommy's parentage. And if he cared about Annie, he wouldn't be very fond of any man he suspected of leaving her holding the diaper bag alone.

Molly turned without thinking. The men were just barely visible, standing in the front driveway near a large blue Ford truck. Even at this distance it was obvious that Ross was furious. Jackson looked bored.

"You mean that Ross and Annie are…" She hesitated, wondering suddenly how much Lavinia knew—or suspected—herself. "I mean, that Jackson and Annie are—"

"Oh, who cares?" Lavinia snorted softly. "It's just some stupid testosterone skirmish or another. Besides, it's the world's worst waste of time to try to figure out what men are thinking anyhow, right?"

"Right," Molly agreed halfheartedly. But, she realized as she turned reluctantly back to follow Lavinia into the house, this was one time she would certainly have liked to know.

# CHAPTER FIVE

ROSS DIDN'T SPEAK until he and Jackson were almost at the driveway. Better to get as far away from the women as possible. This might turn ugly, and he'd rather not have an audience.

Jackson had parked his shiny green 1958 Thunderbird right next to Ross's bunged-up truck. Of course. The way Ross's luck had been going lately, where else? The two cars looked like a textbook illustration of the difference between "collectible" and "old."

But screw that. He didn't care if Jackson drove a platinum Rolls-Royce with diamond-studded hubcaps. This wasn't about money. This was about character. This was about honesty. And fair play.

And Annie. It was definitely about Annie.

"So what's on your mind, Riser?" By the time they reached the truck, Jackson already had his keys out, signaling that he didn't intend to waste a lot of time here. Well, that suited Ross fine. He was sick of trying to pull an end run around Jackson Forrest. He was ready to go right up the middle.

"I want to talk to you about Annie," he said. Jackson didn't look surprised. And why should he be? What else could it have been about? The New

York architect and the small-town football coach didn't exactly have a whole lot else in common. Except Beau. And Jackson knew Ross would rather cut out his own tongue than bring up Beau.

"Okay." Jackson leaned against the hood of Ross's truck and let his keys dangle loosely at his side. "Talk."

"It's pretty simple." Ross filled his chest with air and set his shoulders. "I want to know what your intentions are."

Damn. That line had sounded much better in his head.

Jackson's eyebrows went up lazily. "You know, Riser, I've heard people complain that you were too old for Annie. This is the first time I've wondered if they might be right." He chuckled. "Are you auditioning for the part of her father?"

Ross felt himself flushing. Jackson had always had the effect on him, even when he was a teenager. Something in that bored green gaze could always find your weak spots, like a heat-seeking missile. But damn it, how had Jackson guessed that Ross was feeling particularly shopworn today?

Like there weren't a million signs. He probably had noticed that Ross was favoring his bad knee. The Ace bandage around his elbow was in plain sight. And, even without those clues, Jackson was smart enough to deduce that any forty-year-old workhorse with a pin in his knee would feel pretty decrepit standing next to a thirty-year-old Thoroughbred.

"I'm only ten years older than Annie is, damn

it.'' His voice sounded slightly hoarse. ''Who says I'm too old for her?''

''Oh, you know.'' Jackson shrugged carelessly. ''People.''

''Really.'' Ross stepped a foot or two closer. ''Would you be interested in knowing what people say about *you*, Forrest?''

''Not even remotely.'' Jackson's smile tightened, and he straightened to go eye to eye with Ross. ''Listen, Riser, I haven't got time to stand here trading insults. And frankly I don't recognize your right to grill me about Annie, so, unless you've got another subject you'd like to try, I'm out of here.''

For a minute, Ross thought he was going to have to smash that arrogant Forrest nose so flat Jackson would breathe through his mouth for a year. But somehow he managed to keep his fists where they belonged. Ross's mother, a science teacher who had been widowed young, had drilled into her three brawny sons that fighting was always a last resort, except for the most pea-brained species.

He took a deep breath and tried to use his human-size brain, trusting that he still actually had one under this testosterone fog. He had gone about this all wrong. Whether he liked Jackson Forrest or not, the man stood in his way like a two-ton nose guard. Antagonizing him wasn't going to do anything but make matters worse.

He moved aside, abandoning the up-in-the-middle strategy. He sucked in another chestful of oxygen, and, rubbing hard against a smudge on the truck hood with the pad of his thumb, tried to regroup.

He had meant to have a simple, sane, man-to-man talk with Jackson. He'd failed miserably. One snarky comment from the younger man and he'd let himself get overheated.

No, damn it, that wasn't true. He had to be honest with himself. He wasn't overheated. He was just plain jealous.

Jealous of that fast, sexy car. Jealous of that perfect air of insouciance, an attitude you were born with or lived without. Jealous of those Hollywood-green eyes that looked as if they'd been stolen from a jeweler's shelf. Jealous of that runner's body, which still looked more twenty-something than thirty. Ross's own ex-football muscles threatened every day to turn to flab unless he worked himself to death, which led to that mummy look of Ace bandages and the subtle stink of liniment.

Hell, yes, he was jealous. And even less dignified, he was afraid.

He was afraid that he might lose Annie to this man. This rich, smug, disgustingly lucky son of a bitch, Jackson Forrest.

Annie was less impressed by cash and cachet than any other woman he'd ever known. But she was human.

And he was afraid that, when Forrest got bored—*which he would*—Annie would get hurt. Tommy, too.

So he had to get his envy back under wraps and appeal to Jackson's better nature. Jackson might like Annie—who didn't like Annie? He might even want her—after all, Jackson was human, too.

But he didn't love her. Ross did.

"Annie's starting to make noises about maybe cooling things between us for a while," he said, working that smudge as if he were getting paid to polish the car. "She says she needs space, time to think. But I know what that means. It means you've said something."

"Something like what?"

"I don't know. Maybe you don't even have to say anything. Maybe you can just give her that look. But somehow you've been turning her against me."

"Ross—"

"Don't deny it, Forrest. I've seen you do it. I just don't know whether you're doing it because you want her—or because you hate me."

A long pause beat against the air between them. Ross didn't dare look up, for fear he'd lose his control again. He was coming pretty damn close to whining here, and he didn't like the sound of begging on his lips. But for Annie he could do this. For Annie he could do almost anything.

"You're wrong." When Jackson finally spoke, his voice was low and controlled. Ross thought he heard a note of sympathy somewhere deep in the short, simple syllables. "I don't hate you, Riser."

Ross looked up and forced his burning gaze to meet the other man's calm eyes. "Okay, you despise me, then. Choose any word you like. The bottom line is, you don't think I'm good enough for her. You don't think I'm good enough for Tommy."

"It doesn't have anything to do with 'good enough,'" Jackson said carefully. "I don't think you're good *for* him. There's a difference—although I guess from where you sit it appears to come to the same thing."

Not good for him? Jackson Forrest could dare to stand there and say that Ross Riser was not good for Tommy? He might have laughed if he hadn't been so furious.

"I'd marry his mother, if she'd have me. I'd be a full-time father to that kid, Forrest, if you'd just get the hell out of the way. I guess that's a damn sight better for them than anything you're offering."

Jackson's mouth hardened. "No, Ross, you won't do that," he said with a deceptively soft voice—like the sound a Doberman makes in the back of his throat to warn you to freeze in your tracks. "Don't even think about it."

Suddenly it was just too much. Ross banged the flat of his hand against the hood of the truck. The metal bowed under the force then bounced back into shape.

"This is still all about Beau, isn't it?" He wiped his hand across his face, pulling his mouth so hard it hurt. "God, Forrest, that was fourteen years ago! It was one game, one lousy high school football game. It was wrong. It was a terrible, terrible mistake."

"But it was your mistake, Riser. And you used my brother to fix it for you."

Ross let loose a short bark of harsh laughter. "What, your saintly brother? Have you been telling yourself that I corrupted him? Well, I'm sorry to disillusion you, but Beau was delighted to do it,

Jackson. He thought it was funny. God, how he laughed in the locker room! I wish you could have seen him laugh.''

"Ross,'' Jackson said, still softly. "Shut up.''

"No.'' Ross couldn't stop himself. "Goddamn it, I've earned a reprieve. It's been fourteen *years*. Aren't you ever going to let me off the hook?''

Jackson palmed his keys, and something in the way his knuckles whitened around them proved that his temper was just as close to slipping its reins as Ross's.

Jackson shouldered past him roughly, without apology, as if he didn't trust himself to stand so close. With the truck between them, he turned.

"No,'' he said. "I'm not. Not where Tommy is concerned.''

He stared at Ross over the rusted flatbed, his green eyes as hard and dangerous as a snake's. "Listen carefully, Riser. I don't give a damn whether you gamble or not. Lose your truck at the poker table and walk to work. Bet your kidneys at the dog track and pee through a machine for the rest of your life, for all I care. But know this—if you let your problems come within a hundred miles of that little boy, I'm going to bring you down.''

MOLLY KNELT in the empty garden bed, sifting the soil through her fingers, searching for stray roots. She had been working this bed for nearly two hours, and finally she was almost finished. She had long ago flung her sweater across an overhanging branch, working too hard to notice the chill. She had abandoned her gardening gloves so that she could feel the resistance of weeds as she pulled them. Her cheeks felt gritty where she had wiped away sweat with blackened fingers, and her knees were numb where the cold, damp dirt had penetrated her jeans.

She rocked back onto her heels, satisfied. This was the sort of job she generally left to hired hands these days—in fact, there were three day workers even now doing similar clearing at other spots on the Everspring grounds and two whole crews at the park grounds. But she had needed to do some big-time thinking this afternoon. And, as she had learned years ago, she thought better with dirty hands.

As usual, the earth had not disappointed her. While she had knelt here, rhythmically sifting and pulling, she had come up with a new, fully formed vision for the Everspring landscaping.

The proposal she had submitted to Lavinia when she bid for the project had been done from memory. The reality of Everspring, after ten years of storms and disease, bad pruning and uncontrolled growth, was somewhat different. The stately, spreading oak out back, for instance, the centerpiece of the family sitting garden, had been taken down yesterday, the victim of a lighting strike that had left the core dead, vulnerable to disease.

With the oak gone, she had seen instantly that she was going to need new plans.

Which thankfully had come to her. She could hardly wait to start sketching, taking her ideas, which right now existed only in her mind, as fragile as bubbles of air, and giving them a substance, a color, a tangible reality.

Dirt and imagination. What more could a person ask from a job? She lifted a handful of the rich black soil to her nose and inhaled its loamy scent with a sensual appreciation. She let her gaze roam across the bed of bulbs, which were just now beginning to sprout tender green shoots above the dirt.

Her heart beat a pleasantly rapid rhythm high in her chest, as it always did when she was exhilarated.

She loved this work. She loved this plantation.

"Hi, Mom." She looked up to see Liza standing at the edge of the flower bed, her book bag in her hand. Molly lifted her wrist, guiltily checking her watch—though of course it was caked in soil and unreadable.

Was school out already? She'd been so engrossed she hadn't heard the bus arrive. "Oh, sweetheart, I'm sorry. I meant to meet you at the stop."

Liza smiled. "That's okay. Tommy Cheatwood walked with me. He came to Everspring because he and Mr. Forrest are going fishing. They invited me to go with them. Is that okay?"

Molly couldn't miss the glow on Liza's face. She hadn't ever been fishing before—and Liza was an adventurer at heart. She loved nothing better than trying something new. From origami to paintball, from ant farming to line dancing, Liza's instincts were always clamoring "yes!"

"What about homework?"

"Just math. Page 242, the evens. I can do it after

dinner.'' Liza pressed her hands together imploringly. ''Mom, please?''

How could anyone resist that smile? And yet, Molly felt herself hesitating—her mind scanning for excuses. The idea of Liza spending all afternoon with Jackson made her nervous. Suppose he started asking Liza questions? Molly hadn't prepared Liza—though she had been perfectly willing to lie herself, her conscience had balked at the idea of rehearsing her daughter in perjury. Liza knew only that her father had died before he had been able to marry her mother. Molly had promised to tell her all about him when she was a little older. But that might be enough. Jackson was no fool.

''Honey, I don't know. Mr. Forrest might have felt awkward. I mean, if you were standing there, they might have invited you because they thought it would be rude not to—''

''You know me better than that, M.'' Liza and Molly looked up to see Jackson coming around the corner from the main house. He wore faded jeans and a sweatshirt, carried a trio of fishing poles, and looked immensely amused. ''I'm not at all allergic to being rude, if the occasion calls for it. We invited her because we thought it would be fun.'' He winked at Liza, who grinned back happily. ''What do you say, Molly? We won't let her fall in.''

Liza didn't beg any further, but her longing was almost like a humming in the air. Her eyes were locked on Molly's face, trying to read her chances.

''Okay,'' Molly said, and the syllables were barely out of her mouth before Liza squealed with delight and rushed over to give her a grateful hug. "Let me clean up, and I'll get you a snack before you go."

"No need," Jackson said. "Lavinia's already making sandwiches for the two of them. Peanut butter and—" He paused, giving Molly a deadpan expression. "I suggested jelly, but Vinnie seemed to be leaning toward cucumber."

Molly wrinkled her nose instinctively, but Liza looked fascinated. "Cool," she said. "I've never had that before."

"Better hurry to the kitchen, then, before Tommy eats them all." He raised one quick wry smile toward Molly. "I'll wait for you here."

When Liza was out of earshot, Molly chuckled. "Coward," she said.

"I don't notice you running in for a bite yourself," he countered. "Not that Lavinia would let you in her kitchen looking like that." He dragged a nugget of pine bark from her hair and flicked it back into the mulch. "I thought you were the brains of your landscape company, not the brawn."

She smiled sheepishly, knowing she must look a wreck. She probably had a mud mustache—she remembered carelessly wiping her upper lip with grimy fingers. "But this is the part I like," she said plaintively. "Don't you think it's perverse that the more successful you are, the less time you spend actually doing the work you love?"

"Extremely," he agreed, rolling her small plastic gardening cart closer so that he could make a seat out of it. "Being an architect is no different. I seem to have become a professional luncher. I'm in charge of sweet-talking the clients over white wine while my staff gets to design the buildings. I might as well have become a snake oil salesman."

Molly laughed. "Since when have you been willing to sweet-talk anyone? Aren't you the guy who once told me that all silver tongues were forked?"

"Did I say that?" He grimaced. "God, teenagers can be obnoxious, can't they? I must have been caught in a particularly vicious bout of Beau-envy that day."

She didn't really believe that, though the twins had been as different in their social manners as any two people could possibly be. Beau could charm the blue out of the sky if he put his mind to it, while Jackson was usually blunt to the point of discomfort.

Long ago Molly might have believed it was envy—that Jackson had developed his trademark vinegary candor merely because his brother had cornered the market on honey. By their teenage years, though, she had begun to realize that it was something else—a reaction, perhaps. Or an antidote, the way you might add lemon to an oversweetened tea.

"Well, Beau could flatter a girl until her head spun," she admitted, remembering how she had longed for, *lived* for Beau's pretty compliments and thrilling declarations of undying love—even when she had often feared that he might be fibbing. Not lying, exactly. Just exaggerating. Just a little.

She reached out and touched Jackson's arm, hoping he wouldn't mind her black crescent-moon fingernails. "But it was awfully reassuring to know that, if I really needed to hear the truth, I could always come to you.''

He didn't look at her. He seemed to be mesmerized by her fingers, staring down at them as if he didn't want to meet her eyes until he had decided how to respond. Could he think she was flirting with him? Discomfort wriggled in her stomach, and she eased her hand away as smoothly as possible.

She wasn't flirting. She wouldn't dream of flirting with Jackson. But even as she reassured herself, she admitted that something was different between them today. Some new, slightly edgy tone had crept into their easy intimacy, and their casual good-buddy relationship suddenly felt just a little more complicated.

This was her fault. If only she hadn't been so foolish the other night, letting his resemblance to Beau knock her into an emotional tailspin.... But the truth was it had felt strangely exciting to be with him. He was such a dynamic, gorgeous man. A real man, whose arms were real, warm, masculine. And ten years of nothing but memories...

Now she was the one looking down, incapable of straightforward candor. She had left tiny beads of soil on his arm. ''Oops. Sorry,'' she said, whisking them away efficiently with her fingertips. ''I'd better finish up here, I guess. I'm a menace to any clean person who gets near me.''

''Need any help?'' He looked around appraisingly. ''Wow. Things sure look different without that oak tree.''

She nodded as she stood up and, still holding the

muddy spade she'd been working with, brushed the dirt from her knees with her free hand. It had been painful to observe the workers dismantling the two-hundred-year-old tree, their cruel machines buzzing through the limbs section by section. When they had begun to drive their jagged, whirling blades deep into the stump, grinding the roots to sawdust, she had turned away, unable to watch.

"The garden looks positively lost without it, doesn't it?" She scanned the perimeter, thinking out loud. "Whenever you have something that dominant, you tend to make it the focal point. Then everything else you plant has to be chosen to work with it. Eventually, the garden becomes dependent on it."

"Dependent?" He looked toward the gaping hole where the tree had been. "That sounds a little extreme."

"But true," she insisted, absently rubbing the loose dirt from the edges of her spade. "See how the azaleas and oleander were grouped to balance the sides of the tree? And the dogwood over there—they were chosen because their texture and dimension provided the perfect foil. Even the brick paths were laid using the tree as the central axis."

She sighed. "Without that tree as the focal point, the garden falls apart."

She stopped, glancing over to see if he was bored. He probably couldn't understand why she felt so passionate about this. He couldn't know how intensely she identified with the problem. She had done very much the same thing with her own life, once upon a time. She had let Beau become her focal point. She had, without quite realizing it, built everything around him, made even the tiniest decisions with him in mind.

And when he had died, her life had disintegrated into a hodgepodge of meaningless trivia.

But Jackson didn't look bored. He was scanning the garden, his gaze sober and evaluating. "Actually, it's the same when you're designing a house. You start with a central element, then let the rest of the house group around it. It's just easier, I suppose, because we're not working with animate objects. An arch or a column or a chimney can't die on you. So it's a little safer to let yourself depend on it."

How strange that he should put it like that. She wondered for a moment whether he had read her mind. He was watching her with something that might be pity in his gaze.

"Exactly," she said brightly, hoping to cover her discomfort. She moved toward the empty spot where the tree had once stood. "That's why I've decided to put something inanimate in its place. A gazebo, I think." She held out her hand and urged him to follow her. "Come see—the view of the river is wonderful from there, actually. I know the perfect design—I saw it in a catalogue only a couple of months ago."

"A gazebo?" He joined her on the bumpy earth, lightly touching her elbow for balance as they walked carefully over the crazy minefield of mounds and depressions left by the extricated roots. "You're not willing to try another tree?"

She shook her head—and she also tried to shake the sense that he wasn't just talking about the garden. "No, it would be impossible. And it's not just because I'm afraid of losing it. Trees like that take years and years to grow. If I tried to stick some new one in the ground there, the proportions would be all wrong."

"Sure," he said agreeably. "Makes sense." Stretching his neck as if he'd begun to grow stiff, he stood next to her, looking down toward the river with such a casual air that she suddenly realized she had probably imagined the whole subtext. He'd just been indulging her, showing interest in her work to be polite. Nothing deeper than that.

"You're sweet to listen to all my rambling," she said, smiling up at him. "I know I get carried away. It drives Liza crazy." She laughed softly. "Beau used to call me The Garden Bore."

To her surprise, Jackson turned roughly, a pulse beating in his tightened jaw. "Molly," he said, speaking slowly. "I am not Beau."

She looked at him, at the dark slash of brow over blazing green eyes. He looked so hard. So suddenly tense. "I know," she said hesitantly.

"I don't think you do," he said. "Not really. Not always."

"Yes, I do." She moved closer, and once again she touched his arm. "I'm sorry, Jackson. I really do know."

He exhaled harshly, and gradually the tension in his muscles seemed to relax slightly under her fingertips.

"Okay. Then prove it, M. Stop comparing me to him." Jackson put his hands on her upper arms and brought her in closer. Her face was only inches from his. From this intimate perspective he looked less like Beau than ever. Tiny laugh lines radiated out from his shockingly green eyes—lines that had never touched Beau's twenty-two-year-old skin. Jackson's mouth was harder than Beau's, too, and was framed by a light-brown dusting of stubble that Beau would never have tolerated. And the heat. Jackson seemed to generate an appalling amount of heat.

"I don't," she said, surprised at how shaky it made her feel to stand this close to him. "I mean I won't…"

"And for God's sake don't judge me by Beau's standards. I haven't got the time or the inclination to pretty up everything I do with a coat of social whitewash. If I don't drown you in flattery, it's because I respect you too much. If I listen when you talk, it's because I am interested, because I want to know how you think."

She knew it was true. It felt almost disloyal, but Molly knew deep inside that her friendship with Jackson had always been more honest, more reliable, somehow, than her love affair with Beau.

But she couldn't say that. In a way, it would be just another comparison, and she had promised… "Okay," she said simply. "I understand."

He nodded, but he didn't let go of her. They stood in silence a moment, wrapped in an intense intimacy created by the green, dappled sunlight and the cool, whispering wind. Their eyes held, unblinking and searching. Finally his thumbs moved almost imperceptibly across her upper arms, rubbing the soft flannel of her shirt against her skin.

When he spoke, his voice had dropped to a warm, slightly amused intimacy. "And if I kissed you…"

She felt her heart stall, startled into momentary paralysis. She gripped the molded handle of her spade so hard it hurt her palm.

"If I kissed you," he said again, "it would be because you have grown into a damned sexy woman. It would be because I get the feeling your mouth would taste as red and warm as summer roses."

This couldn't be happening. She searched his face to see if he might be making fun of her. But though his eyes held a spark of laughing fire, it wasn't unkind. And the heat was pulsing out from his body to hers.

"I think maybe you are flattering me, now," she said unsteadily, trying for the same casual tone he had taken. "At the moment I suspect my lips taste more like winter dirt."

He reached his right hand up and traced her lower lip with his knuckle, smiling into her eyes. "Shall we find out?"

Something electric snaked through her veins. She could hardly believe what she was doing, but she felt her whole body pressing toward him, the way the tulips at her feet were even now thrusting through the cold earth, seeking the spring.

"Molly?"

She took a deep breath. Before she could allow herself to change her mind, she put her hands on Jackson's chest, ignoring the darkened, muddy tip of the spade as it grazed his sweatshirt. As softly as she could, she touched her lips to his.

Hot skin and cold air. Scratchy beard and velvet lips. Musky male and sweet soap. The unmistakable power of Jackson.

Not Beau. Jackson.

He made a small sound at the back of his throat. Her head swam, trying to feel everything. Trying to understand anything.

But then the air was filled with the footsteps and laughter of approaching children. Jackson's hands dropped. She backed away, as scalded and self-conscious as if she'd been a teenager again, caught necking in Beau's little sports car.

She looked at him, bewildered.

"Darn it, Jackson, it's gonna get dark pretty soon." Tommy stomped around the corner, his voice aggressive and aggrieved. "My mom will bust my behind if I'm not home by six."

"I'm ready," Jackson said calmly, ignoring the brand of mud she had left on his chest. "Your pole's over there by the hedges."

Liza, who arrived right behind Tommy, looked curiously from her mother to Jackson, then back to her mother. "Don't you want to come with us, Mom?"

"I'd better not," Molly said. Thank heavens, her voice was calm, too. Unlike her insides. "I need to finish up here. By the time I've had my shower and made dinner, you'll be back.''

The children began to debate who should get which fishing pole. And just before he joined them, Jackson turned back to Molly with a wicked grin.

"You were right about the dirt, M," he said, staring boldly at her lips. He raised his warm, laughing green gaze to her eyes. "But I was right about the roses."

# CHAPTER SIX

THE ALTERNATIVE Classroom didn't have its heat on, and it felt cold, colder than the Planet Cuspian in the dead of night, in the dead of winter. Liza thought maybe that was deliberate. Probably the teachers wanted you to sit in here getting colder and scareder, thinking about the bad things you'd done until you were so sorry you could almost cry.

Well, she was cold all right, but she wasn't scared. Not very scared, anyhow. She didn't get in trouble very often. When her mom got here, Liza would explain everything, and it would be okay. Her mom would understand.

Probably.

She looked over at Tommy Cheatwood, the only other person in the room. Tommy definitely wasn't scared. They had been told not to get up out of their desks for Any Reason Whatsoever, but Tommy had been up and down a dozen times. He was shooting a rubber band at the alphabet border that had been hung along the top of the blackboard, aiming for one letter at a time. He was already up to *J*. He was a very good shot.

Now he was perched on the flat part of his desk, his feet on the chair, facing the back of the room, where *J* through *P* were displayed. He held up his finger and loaded the rubber band around the tip. Squinting narrowly, he pulled hard and let it fly. The elastic made a snapping sound as it thwacked the paper border, right in the center of the *J*.

Tommy cackled triumphantly and climbed down to retrieve his ammunition.

"Aren't you afraid they'll catch you?" Liza knew he didn't want to talk to her. She knew because for the past twenty minutes he'd been pretending she wasn't even in the room. She'd been pretending the same thing, actually. She'd been drawing King Willowsong's coronation on a torn piece of paper she'd found in the desk. But she didn't have any crayons for color, and she was getting bored. Tommy's rubber band game seemed like more fun.

He gave her a look that said she was pathetic. "Oh, yeah, terrified." His voice was sarcastic, in that ultracool way the other boys always tried to imitate. "What would they do?" He took aim at the *K* and shot. Another bull's-eye. "Call my mom?"

She saw his point. They already had called his mom.

"Is your mom going to be mad?" Now that she had made him talk, she didn't want to go back to silence. If she just sat here and worried about it, she might end up thinking she was scared after all.

"You bet she will." Tommy grinned suddenly. He had a great grin. It made you want to smile back, for no reason at all.

"Hopping mad," he elaborated gleefully. He picked up his rubber band, then came back. Sitting wrong-ways on the desk, he looked at her. "Yours won't be, though."

Although that was exactly what Liza had been thinking, it annoyed her for him to sound so sure. "Oh, really?" She lifted her chin. "How do you know that?"

Tommy idly snapped his rubber band against the blue denim that covered his knee. "She's not the type. Your mother is the kind that gets—" he lowered his voice, making a tragic face "—disappointed."

Liza bit her lower lip, knowing that somehow it would be wrong to laugh. But the way he said that—it sounded just like her mom.

"And besides, grown-ups get more upset when boys fight," he said thoughtfully, as if the subject interested him. "They think it's a Bad Sign." His voice capitalized the phrase, as if it came straight out of a parenting handbook. "When girls fight, they just think it's cute and brave."

Liza wasn't sure that was true. But she'd never hit anyone before, so she didn't know for sure. "What will your mom do to you?"

Tommy sighed, either at the prospect of his mother's temper or at Liza's constant questions. "She'll yell a lot. My mom is a big yeller. And she'll ground me for life. But that's okay—she'll forget about it by next week. The part I really hate is that all her boyfriends will start telling her how I need a man in the house." He looked disgusted. "A male role model. Can you believe that? Like my having a dad would somehow make me get along with that jerk Junior Caldwell.''

Liza nodded in complete sympathy. ''No one can get along with Junior,'' she said. Junior Caldwell was the reason she had been sent to the Alternative Classroom. She had seen him sneaking up on Tommy at recess with a big gob of dog-do in his hands, getting ready to throw it all over him. She knew Tommy and Junior fought a lot, but this didn't seem fair, hitting him from behind. So she had shoved Junior out of the way, calling a warning to Tommy. Tommy had swung around, thrusting his fist out instinctively. Junior had fallen and started bawling his eyes out.

And before she even had a chance to explain, she and Tommy were sent to the AC in disgrace, their parents summoned. Junior got a tissue and a Coke in the clinic.

''Junior acts so tough,'' she added, feeling wronged all over again. ''But he's really just a big baby.''

''You got that right.''

Tommy looked almost friendly, and she began to hope that maybe he had forgiven her for interfering. ''Next time, stay out of it,'' he had said—quite rudely, she thought, considering. ''I darn sure don't need any girl to protect me.''

''Well, I guess you do,'' she had countered angrily. ''You'd look pretty stupid right now with dog-do in your hair.'' That was when he had stopped talking to her.

''What are you drawing over there?'' Tommy

squinted toward the paper she had on her desk. She instinctively covered it with her forearms, not sure she wanted to tell him about it. He could be pretty nice sometimes, like the other day when Jackson took them fishing and Tommy taught her how to bait her hook. But she didn't know what he'd think of her planet. And she didn't feel like being laughed at right now.

"Just a picture," she hedged, fiddling with her cuff so that it covered more. "I like to draw."

"Let me see." Tommy actually got down off the desk and wandered over to her chair, twisting the rubber band around his fingers in a complicated, rhythmic pattern, as if he just couldn't ever be completely still. Boys were weird like that.

Reluctantly she moved her arm aside and let him look. He stared a long time without saying anything, and she peeked down, suddenly nervous. Darn. She had liked the picture a minute ago. Now it looked really stupid. King Willowsong's crown was way too tall for his head. And his cape, which was supposed to be regal ermine, looked like a big freckled blob that had landed on his back.

"Who is that guy?" Tommy was staring at Liza now. He was frowning, as if he were trying to figure out a really hard math question. "Is that supposed to be Jackson?"

She felt herself flushing. "Kind of," she said uncomfortably. Would Tommy think the whole thing was just completely dumb? Would he tell all the other boys?

"Man," Tommy said, rubbing the pencil marks

with his thumb, as if he thought it might be a trick. "You're pretty good. It really looks like Jackson, I think. And is the queen supposed to be your mom?"

She wondered how he knew that. She hadn't drawn the queen very well. It must be the ponytail, which looked just like the one her mother wore when she was working on the landscaping. "I guess so," she admitted. She waited to hear what Tommy's reaction would be.

He looked at her, his eyebrows still drawn together, but not as if he were mad. Just as if he were thinking hard. "Does this have anything to do with Jackson kissing your mom the other day?"

"No," she said hotly, pulling the picture off the desk and folding it up into tiny pieces, making a paper triangle the way she did with her notes to friends. "Of course not."

"You're not thinking he and your mom might get together, are you? You're not thinking he might move in and be your dad, are you?"

Liza stood, forgetting that she wasn't supposed to. "Of course not," she said again. "That's dumb."

"'Cause he won't. My mom kissed Coach Riser, but that darn sure doesn't mean he's going to move in with us." Tommy began snapping the rubber band again, this time against his own palm. He was still looking at her in that funny way. "Do you ever wish you had a dad?"

Liza squeezed her hand around the triangle of paper. She felt the edges curl in under the pressure. "No," she said. "Not at all."

Tommy nodded, his frown easing.

Suddenly there was noise in the hall. Voices and footsteps coming their way. Tommy slid into his chair, set his jaw hard and then squared his shoulders.

"Me, either," he said firmly, giving her one last glance. "Especially not that dumb old Coach Riser."

AS SHE DROVE OFF from Radway, Molly watched Liza out of the corner of her eye, marveling at her daughter's quiet dignity. At Liza's age, Molly would have been an absolute wreck if such a calamity had happened to her. Sent home from school in disgrace—for fighting, of all things! She remembered once having to tell her father that she had failed a Latin test. She hadn't dared to cry—her father hated what he called her "Goddamn waterworks." But her fingers had felt numb when she handed over the paper, and her throat had worked in dry, desperate spasms as she tried to swallow or speak.

Liza, on the other hand, was contrite but hardly crushed. She had agreed that shoving was inappropriate and listened cooperatively as Molly discussed other options that might have been more effective.

And now here she was, a mere fifteen minutes after Molly had picked her up, sitting in the passenger seat, humming quietly to herself as she worked on a spelling ditto.

She seemed to sense her mother's glance. She looked up with a smile. "Are we almost there? I can't wait to see your old house. It sounds so cool."

"It does?" Molly wondered what she had ever

said about her childhood home that would make Liza believe that the boxy little structure deserved such a description. "Cool?"

"Totally," Liza confirmed enthusiastically. "Remember how you said the baby oak tree had grown so big its roots started tearing up the patio? Doesn't that sound cool and magical? Like Jack and the Beanstalk or something."

Molly smiled, and she was suddenly glad that Liza would be with her when she saw the house again. In the nightmarish months after Beau's death, when she had discovered that she was pregnant, she and her mother had fled from this house as if it had been on fire. And they had never looked back. Her mother had finally divorced Molly's abusive father, and had busied herself in a new marriage. Molly had immersed herself in motherhood.

After the divorce, Molly's father had left the house, too—changing cities every few months until he finally died a few years later in another state. Even then, neither Molly nor her mother could face returning. They had hired someone to clean the rooms out, listed the property with an agent who was hardly enthusiastic, and then they'd let the house stand vacant, paying the annual taxes by impersonal air mail.

So it had stunned Molly this morning when the real estate agent called, telling her there was finally an offer. She had agreed to meet the woman at the house at three o'clock, though the prospect made her stomach feel tight and queasy. Yes, it was good that

Liza would be with her. The world always looked better viewed through Liza's eyes.

And hadn't there been something magical about that oak, after all? The buckled concrete had horrified Molly's mother, but Molly herself had been thrilled to see the sapling become a mighty tree, with limbs strong enough and high enough to lift her above the house, away from her father's anger and her mother's weeping.

But when she and Liza arrived at the cul de sac, the reality was even more depressing than she had remembered. The neighborhood had improved—obviously it had caught on among young professionals, and most of the houses had been given face-lifts and clever new landscaping.

This minisuburban renewal had not touched Molly's house. Now instead of being the most compulsively self-respecting address on the block, it was the most conspicuously neglected. The paint was dingy, stained with rust from the well water of badly aimed sprinklers. The lawn was more dirt than grass, except where weeds had filled in the gaps. The knee-high wall around the tiny front courtyard was missing several bricks, and the gate had lost a slat, giving the house a slightly loony, gap-toothed smile.

In fact, it was a miracle anyone had made an offer on it. Molly felt a sudden fear that the agent wouldn't show up—that the call had been a hoax. This house was a disgrace, and she warmed with shame. Had she really believed that by turning her back on the past she could obliterate it? She had merely left it to rot on the ground, like discarded flowers.

Even Liza's determination to be cheerful seemed to falter in the face of this sad little house. She stared with her mouth open slightly, her pencil frozen an inch above her last spelling word.

"I know," Molly said ruefully. "It's pretty terrible. The kind of house where Mudbluffs would live, right?"

Liza frowned thoughtfully. "No," she said. "Not like that at all. I think it's a Willowsong house deep inside. It's just kind of—" Her gaze was wide, taking in the curtainless windows, the empty, rotting wooden planters, the mildewed sidewalk. "Kind of like a house that's been put under a spell. Like Sleeping Beauty's castle when the thorns grew all over it. You could make it pretty again, Mom, you know you could. It needs roses, I think." She smiled at her mother. "Willowsongs love roses."

Molly laughed, shaking her head helplessly. Anything less like a castle, cursed or otherwise, would be hard to imagine. But still—somehow Liza's silly optimism was infectious. The oppressive sense of decay and failure lifted, and the house was once again merely a house. Nothing wrong here that a coat of paint and a good landscape architect couldn't cure. And maybe even a few roses...

She tweaked her daughter's long, silky ponytail. "Only you, sweetheart. Only you."

Liza grinned. "Well, you know I'm right," she said, hurriedly stuffing her spelling ditto into her backpack. "Big red roses. And some ruffly white curtains. Come on. Let's go see."

AN HOUR LATER, the agent had come and gone, leaving behind an offer so low that, in spite of her eagerness to be rid of this house, Molly had not been able to say yes right away. She'd sleep on it, she had promised the woman. She'd call tomorrow with an answer.

She stood at the kitchen window, watching as Liza climbed the long, low arms of the huge oak, her red coat flashing in and out of winter-bare branches. Had the buyers even noticed how lovely the tree had grown? Yes, it needed trimming—the lowest limbs almost brushed the earth. But a tree like this didn't grow over night. In summer, it would provide cool green shade over the whole yard. Surely the tree alone made the house worth more than this paltry offer. If she spruced things up a bit—curtains, paint, and yes, even roses...

"Hi, Ms. Lorring. We thought that was your car out there. Is Liza with you?"

Molly turned, surprised to see Tommy Cheatwood standing behind her at the kitchen door. She had assumed that Annie would probably have Tommy chained to his bunk bed by now, forcing him to write "I will never hit anyone again" in perfect cursive about a thousand times.

"Hi, Tommy," she said, stifling the shock she got every time she realized how much he looked like Jackson. "Are you with your mother?" Molly hoped so. Annie had grown up around here, too.

She'd be able to tell Molly what the houses in this neighborhood were really worth these days.

"Nope. She's still at work." Tommy's restless gaze found the kitchen window, which framed a picture of a little girl swinging upside down, her blue jeans curled over the oak's lowest branch, her red coat flapping over her face. "Is that Liza?"

"Yes. But Tommy," Molly called as the little boy turned and scooted back down the kitchen stairs, "how did you get he—"

"He's with me." Jackson appeared in the doorway, his lanky form so like a larger version of Tommy's that Molly momentarily caught her breath. "I picked him up at school, and we're waiting for his mom to get home from work. The condemned boy's last wish was to find Liza and climb a couple of trees. I didn't have the heart to say no."

"*You* picked him up? The school calls *you* when Tommy gets in trouble?"

The minute the words were out of her mouth she regretted them. It wasn't any of her business, and she knew it. Jackson didn't owe her explanations about Tommy—any more than she owed him explanations about Liza. Far less, in fact.

And, of course, he didn't offer any. He merely cocked his head at a quizzical angle and smiled as he moved into the kitchen. "Actually, they called Annie, but she couldn't get away from work, so she called me."

"Oh, of course." Relieved that the awkward moment had passed safely, Molly sought a smooth way to shift the subject. "You know, from what Liza told me, I honestly don't think the fight was their fault. Will Tommy be in much trouble at home?''

Jackson shrugged. ''Annie makes a lot of noise, but in the end she's pretty much a pushover for the little devil. Can't stay mad at him more than thirty minutes at a stretch. In a couple of years, he's going to figure that out, and then she'll really have her hands full.''

A father's discipline might help, Molly thought. Poor Annie. Molly knew all too well how exhausting single parenting could be, even with a daughter as easy as Liza. She could hardly imagine trying to cope with a moody, willful boy like Tommy. Not without backup.

But she didn't speak the words out loud. It was, she reminded herself sternly, none of her business.

Jackson didn't seem to notice her tension. Hoisting himself to a seat on the bare countertop, he studied the empty kitchen. ''I'd almost forgotten this place. It's been a long time.''

''For me, too.'' She scanned the room, too, trying to see if through his eyes. Perhaps, without all the unhappy memories, it looked perfectly normal, just another collection of the same cheap appliances found in middle-class kitchens all over America. Jackson wouldn't know how many tense, angry meals had been eaten here. He wouldn't hear the echoes of her father's broken beer bottles, her mother's muffled weeping, her own desperately pounding heart.

Suddenly she realized he had stopped looking at

the kitchen. Now he was looking at her, with the same air of curious speculation.

"A long time. But maybe," he ventured, "not quite long enough?"

She met his gaze, flushing slightly. "Am I that transparent?"

"Sort of," he said evenly. "I know you pretty well, M. Want to talk about it?"

No, she didn't want to talk about it. That had always been her mother's cardinal rule: never tell anyone what happened at home. It was a sad, ugly little secret that the three of them conspired to hide from the rest of the world.

Molly touched the chipped Formica on the front of one of the cabinet drawers. She remembered the day that piece had broken off. Her father had been furious at her mother, as if it had been her fault, though even a child could see that the material was shoddy and crumbling with age.

"My father drank," Molly said suddenly, shocking herself. She hadn't ever discussed this with anyone, not even with Beau. Why now? Why Jackson? "He drank a lot. It didn't make for a very happy childhood. Frankly, if I had never seen this house again, it would have been fine with me."

She forced herself to look over at Jackson, expecting to see her inner shock mirrored on his features. But he didn't look horrified. He met her words with a calm acceptance, merely waiting for her to go on.

And instantly she saw why it was Jackson she had finally chosen as her confidant. Though she had

adored Beau—beautiful, universally adored Beau—
he had somehow been too lucky, too self-assured.
Too perfect. She had always felt it was a miracle
that he had picked ordinary Molly Lorring to be his
girlfriend. She had struggled daily to live up to the
honor.

But rough-and-tumble Jackson, who had spent
half of high school in the dean's office, who had
thumbed his nose repeatedly at the world's expectations, had always understood that people were
flawed. Molly remembered now that Jackson had
been the defender of the underdog, the champion of
damaged things.

She was suddenly glad she had told him. Even
after all these years, the memories were oppressive—and sharing them lightened the load.

"You don't seem surprised," she said. "Did you
already know?"

His smile was wry, tucking itself into one corner
of his cheek. "Know what? That the 'sweet bird of
youth' is pure myth? That being a kid is hard as
hell? Yeah, I already knew that."

She laughed quietly. "No, I mean about my father. Did you know he was an alcoholic? Did everyone know? My mother tried so hard to keep it a
secret."

He eyed her thoughtfully. "No, I didn't, not for
sure. But I knew something was wrong. I knew you
were afraid of upsetting him. In fact, I knew you
were irrationally afraid of upsetting anyone—that it
was easy for people to take advantage of you." His
gaze softened. "And I knew you were unhappy."

A foolish lump formed in her throat, and she looked away, toward the wall, where she could almost see herself at fifteen, bending over next to her mother, helping to clear up wet bottle shards in complete, despairing silence.

But that was long ago. And right here on the countertop was her one-way ticket out of the past forever. The contract for the sale of this house.

"Yes," she admitted. "There were some pretty grim days." She blinked the image away and looked back at him, smiling. "But there were good days, too. I can remember watching you and Beau drive up in that little red sports car, your blond hair shining in the sun. I was sure you were my white knights, riding up to rescue me and carry me off to Castle Everspring."

Jackson raised one eyebrow. "Castle Everspring... Is that, by any chance, located on the Planet Cuspian?"

She knew that voice, that lurking mischief. He was teasing her again, just like in the old days. She wished she had something to chuck at him, something harmless like a dish towel, but the kitchen was completely empty. She settled for wrinkling her nose nastily in his direction.

"Are you implying that Liza has inherited my delusional tendencies? Are you suggesting that our reality wires might be just a little loose?"

"No," he said, dropping deftly down from the countertop and coming to stand next to her at the window. "That's not what I'm suggesting, and you know it." He put his hands lightly on her shoulders.

"I'm saying you've done well, M. Just look how well you've done."

They both gazed out at the backyard, where Liza and Tommy were doing battle with a half-dead holly bush. Each child flourished one hand high in the air—something they had learned from *Zorro* reruns, no doubt—and with the other thrust a branch-sword toward their thorny enemy. What they lacked in style they made up in energy, and their faces were ruddy with laughter.

"I'm saying that she's inherited your ability to create beauty and happiness wherever she goes," he said, "using whatever tools come to hand. And if Everspring helped, I'm glad."

"It did," she said softly. "More than you'll ever know. And you helped, too. You and Beau."

He tightened his hands on her shoulders, just a little. Just enough to make her shiver under the skin. "It was our pleasure, ma'am."

She didn't turn around. She hardly knew what to make of these new feelings—these stirrings of awareness whenever she was around him. They were complicated—composed partly of confused, half-remembered yearnings for Beau, and partly of strange shimmers of delight in Jackson himself. His laughing eyes, so like Beau. His hard-edged lips, so definitely Jackson. His teasing, lightly offered wisdom, not like either of the boys she had once known, but some new, more mature person she was only now coming to understand.

Suddenly she wanted to kiss him again, as she

had done in the garden. To explore once more the powerful differences between his lips and Beau's.

But already his hands were moving away. He reached down toward the contract that lay faceup on the table, the paltry offer typed in with embarrassing clarity.

"Good God." He tilted the page up to double-check the figure, as if he couldn't believe it. "You're not going to accept this, are you?"

She felt herself stiffening, and she took a deep breath. "I might," she said. "I haven't decided yet."

"Well, don't." He let the contract fall. "It's ridiculous."

"I'm not sure it is. The house is a wreck. It wouldn't be realistic to expect anyone to offer full value unless I fixed it up."

"Well, why don't you?" He scanned the room. "A new roof, an updated facade, maybe tile on the floors in here and in the baths. And you could restore the yard yourself. Heck, M, you know the value of that kind of thing. For every thousand you put into the house, you'd get back three."

She took a deep breath. "I haven't got the time, Jackson. With the Everspring renovation and now the park landscaping, too—"

"Sure you do." He seemed impatient, the competent architect analyzing the problem. "You'd hire out the work in the house. I could put together the facade plans for you in a couple of days, and I know people you could use. And this yard is tiny—you know it would be easy."

"I don't want to," she said, aware that she sounded stubborn, irrational, but unable or unwilling to change her tone.

He paused, and she could feel the speculation in the silence. "Okay," he said slowly. "Why not?"

She picked up the contract and rolled it safely into a tube that she gripped with both hands. "I would have to spend time here. Not much, maybe, but more than I want to spend. I just want to sell this wretched house and move on. Can't you understand that?"

Without answering, he turned her around slowly. When she faced him, she saw that his eyes were a dark, shadowed green. They betrayed no irritation with her mulishness. They betrayed nothing at all.

"I know you must be able to understand," she insisted. "You have a past, too, Jackson. A past you'd rather forget."

"Of course I understand," he said finally. "I spent five years avoiding this city and everything it stood for."

"Well? Then you do know—"

"I know that running from the past is easy, M." He touched her cheek gently and smiled a shadow smile. "But the problem is you have to keep on running. And eventually it catches you anyway."

# CHAPTER SEVEN

TOMMY KNEW he didn't have much time left. Pretty soon Jackson was going to come and get him. Pretty soon he was going to have to face his mom, which would really stink because she was going to be popping, steaming mad. She'd be yelling for hours about how she was going to bust his behind.

But that was okay. He could take it. Just as long as she didn't end up in her room, crying that weird way she cried sometimes, like she was trying to swallow it, like she'd choke before she'd let anyone hear her. Tommy figured it was because she almost never cried. She probably didn't really know how to do it right.

Oh, heck, he wasn't going to worry about that now. Right now he was having fun. For a girl, Liza was pretty cool. She wasn't afraid to get dirty. And she hadn't shrieked when they found a dead lizard in the backyard a few minutes ago. She had picked it up, with her bare hands. Even though she buried it, which was a pretty sissy thing to do, she didn't get all mushy about it. She just dug a hole and got it over with.

"Let's go check out the house, okay?" Liza rose

from the mound of dirt, wiping her palms on her jeans. "I want to see my mom's old room."

Tommy looked at her from where he stood on the lowest branch of the oak tree. "I don't like being inside. Besides, it's boring—there's no stuff in there. I don't believe anybody ever lived there."

Liza frowned. "Yes, they did. My mom told me all about it."

Tommy held his arms out and stepped along the branch like a tightrope walker. It felt cool. It probably looked cool, too. He bounced a little to show he wasn't even scared. "Oh, yeah? How do you know it's true? She could have been making it up."

Liza's frown deepened. "You mean lying? My mom never lies."

Tommy laughed out loud. "Yeah, right. Moms lie all the time, dummy."

"Not mine."

"Want to bet? I'll bet she tells you your cough medicine won't taste nasty."

Liza crossed her arms, but she didn't say anything, so Tommy knew he was right. He grinned triumphantly. "And she probably tells you about how you won't grow big and strong if you don't eat your vegetables."

"Well, that's true. You won't."

"Ha! Jackson told me he never ate vegetables. And look at him."

Liza looked annoyed. "Those aren't really lies. They are just—" she stopped for a minute, squinting in concentration "—just little white fibs. Everybody tells those."

Tommy rolled his eyes. "God, you're such a girl."

He surveyed the tip of the branch, decided it was too skinny to hold him, and then plopped down, straddling the limb with his legs. He wanted to pretend it was a motorcycle, so he grabbed a couple of smaller branches, gripped them like handlebars, and made loud engine-revving noises.

"I'll bet I know what else she's lied about, too," he said. "I'll bet she's lied about your dad."

Liza looked really mad for a minute, and Tommy almost wished he hadn't said anything. He liked being friends with Liza. She felt comfortable, kind of like having a sister. Tommy sometimes wished he had more family. Not that he wanted all the hassle, but it was just that other people had lots of family— sisters, brothers, grandparents, cousins…fathers. So when you had only a mom, you felt kind of outnumbered—like trying to play soccer without a whole team.

"You don't know anything about my dad," Liza said frostily. "My dad died before I was born."

Tommy gunned his imaginary engine. "Well, that's what your mom told you anyhow."

Liza marched over and shook the tree limb. Shook it really hard. Though he hated to be a sissy, Tommy had to hold on to keep from getting dumped on the ground.

"It's true!" Liza held on to the tip of the limb, threatening to shake it again. "Why wouldn't it be true? You don't know anything about it!"

"Moms always lie about dads who aren't around.

My mom lies about it, too. She just says my dad can't live with us. Whatever that means."

Liza's hand stilled on the branch. She looked at him seriously. "What do you think it means?"

He shrugged. "Who knows? It probably means she had sex without getting married, and then the guy wouldn't marry her." Perversely, though he had meant to shock her, he didn't like the horrified look he saw on Liza's face. He would bet his best—his only—video game that no one had ever said the word *sex* to her before. She really needed to get a clue.

He put on his best tough, bored expression. "But who cares, anyhow? I figure it was probably just Jackson. Or maybe even that jerk Coach Riser."

Liza's mouth dropped open into a dumb-looking O. "Really?" She swallowed. "Really? You really think Jackson might be your father?"

He shrugged again, though suddenly there was a weird lump in his throat. The way she said "father"... She made it sound like a word you'd use in your bedtime prayers. He wished like fire he hadn't ever brought it up. He'd thought it would make him feel better, smarter and tougher and cooler than Liza, who didn't know anything about anything. But he felt rotten. Really rotten.

"Maybe. Or like I said, maybe Coach Riser." He tried not to say Coach's name any differently. He wouldn't want Liza to think he was hoping it might be Coach, deep inside. "Who knows? Who cares? Obviously whoever it is doesn't want to admit it, right?"

"Oh, Tommy." Liza's eyes were shining with tears. He wanted to laugh at her for being such a sissy, but he couldn't quite get it out. He began to be afraid that his eyes might start shining, too.

"Anyhow, let's talk about something else. This is a dumb conversation." He narrowed his eyes at her. "And you'd better not ever tell anyone what I said."

"I won't," Liza promised softly. She stared at the ground a long time, and when she looked up, her face was really sweet, but with a wet line on each cheek. "I know. I'll tell you a secret, too, okay? Something I don't want other people to know, so we'll be even. But you have to promise you won't laugh about it."

"About what?"

She flushed, but she lifted her chin bravely. "About the imaginary planet I've invented."

"Sounds dumb."

"It's not. It's a cool story. It's exciting. Right now King Willowsong—"

"Is that the guy in your picture? The guy who looked like Jackson?"

She ignored him. "King Willowsong is lost in the ice cave, and the Planet Cuspian is about to be taken over by Mudbluffs who have set up a death ray on the first golden moon."

In spite of himself, Tommy was interested. "What are Mudbluffs? Are they monsters? You can't have a very exciting story if there aren't any monsters."

She tilted her head and gave him a look. "If

you're going to keep interrupting, I'm not going to tell you."

He considered telling her to take her dirty look and get lost, but he really wanted to know about the Mudbluffs. So he faked a yawn and settled back against the tree trunk. "Oh, okay, fine. Tell me about your dumb old planet."

MOLLY LOOKED DOWN at the science fair entry on the table in front of her, a rather clever experiment involving tender green cress seedlings and damp cotton. It demonstrated the effects of drought on root depth. For a fourth grader, the student had done a beautiful job. If it had been any other school, Molly might have suspected that the work was not the student's own. But at Radway, overachieving was a way of life.

She moved on to the next project, an ambitious attempt to invent ways to save the aquifer, complete with full-color computer-generated charts and graphs. The name on the expensive tri-fold display was Junior Caldwell, so she gave it another look.

Fairly amazing, even by Radway standards. Obviously Junior was a science prodigy. She could picture him clearly, based partly on Liza's description, partly on the slightly pompous language of this report. Small, stiff, tidy, brilliant. Thick glasses and perma-pressed clothes.

Poor Junior. No wonder he hated Tommy Cheatwood, who was stylishly slouchy by instinct. Tommy Cheatwood, who had simply been born cool.

"So what do you think? See a winner yet?" Janice Kilgore, the vice principal, came up behind Molly and peered over her shoulder. "God, not Junior, I hope! If Junior wins another science fair, he won't have a single friend left."

Molly smiled at the other woman, who had called her this morning, begging a favor. The county agricultural agent, who had been scheduled to judge the Earth Science entries this year, had the flu. Would Molly consider being his replacement? Molly had said yes, of course, though she had a million things to attend to at Everspring. In these few short weeks, she had grown quite fond of Janice Kilgore.

"I haven't decided yet. They're all so good." She glanced around Radway's high-tech media center, where scores of entries were on display. "I don't see how I'm going to pick just one."

"Eenie, meenie, miny, mo works, I hear," Jan said, grinning. "Oh, look, there's Ellen. Ellen Fowler, our librarian." She waved vigorously. "Ellen! Come meet Liza Lorring's mother."

Smiling, the librarian made her way toward them, carefully avoiding the posters and pedestals, volcanoes and ant farms and simulated rain forests. She held out her hand.

"Molly Lorring. I'm so delighted to finally meet you." Ellen Fowler was in her late thirties, a beautifully groomed blonde with lovely, serene features. "We're all enormously fond of Liza. But I had another reason for wanting to meet you. I was a great fan of your mother's. In fact, she's probably the reason I became a librarian.''

Molly was intrigued. Her mother had run the Demery Public Library for twenty-five years, so perhaps it wasn't surprising, but still… She would be pleased to think she had left behind such a strong legacy. ''Really? How so?''

Ellen laughed, a soft well-modulated tinkle of sound. ''She was good to me at a time in my life when I was very unhappy. I was thirteen, and my parents were going through an ugly divorce. She seemed to know without my telling her. She took me under her wing—let me be her unofficial assistant.'' The woman smiled. ''I think I've associated peace and comfort with libraries ever since.''

''Not libraries,'' Jan interjected. ''*Media centers.* And there's nothing very peaceful about this one today.'' She sniffed the air suspiciously. ''What on earth is that horrible smell? Oh, no! Is Mason Stewart's volcano erupting *again?*''

Apologizing, Janice bustled back toward the smoking cone of clay, leaving Molly alone with the librarian, who watched the young administrator depart with amused tolerance.

''Yes, she's right. *Media center.* More computers than books in here these days. Makes me long to be thirteen again, shelving novels alongside your mother.'' She looked at Molly curiously. ''How is she?''

''She's great,'' Molly said carefully. ''She's remarried, a great guy named Mitchell, and the two of them are doing a lot of traveling.''

The older woman's eyes lit up. "Don't tell me. The Grand Canyon?" When Molly nodded, she smiled. "She used to talk about it all the time, used to show me picture books about it. She thought it sounded like the most beautiful place on earth. She loved the whole idea of the West. I think she felt a little—" Ellen Fowler seemed to be searching for the right word "—a little confined here in Demery."

Molly didn't quite know how to answer. She fiddled with the blue foam aquifer in Junior Caldwell's project and smiled noncommittally.

"How about you?" The librarian touched Molly's shoulder softly. "I was amazed to hear you were back in Demery. Especially at Everspring." As if she feared that her comment might have lacked diplomacy, she moved on smoothly. "It's such a small town. It suits me perfectly, but I thought you probably hankered for wide-open spaces the way your mother did."

Molly looked up. "I'm only here for a couple of months," she said evenly. "Just until the Everspring renovation is completed."

Ellen Fowler looked surprised. "But Liza—" For the first time, her serenity seemed ruffled. "Liza has been telling her teachers that you'll be staying. That you'll be living in Demery. Just the other day she mentioned that you were going to look for a dog, because you wouldn't be living in an apartment anymore."

Molly felt a sinking deep in her stomach. Staying? Was this Liza's new fantasy? Had dreams of Demery supplanted dreams of the Planet Cuspian? Had she begun imagining herself as the princess of Castle Everspring? And a dog. Liza hadn't begged for a dog in years.

Oh, how terrible to have to disappoint her. And yet it was unavoidable. In two months, three at the most, they'd be returning to Atlanta, to their spacious, eighth-floor condo, which Liza had always seemed to like just fine. But, of course, compared to Everspring...

How could Molly possibly explain that, for them, Everspring might just as well be on another planet?

"I'm afraid she must be confused," she said as calmly as she could. "I have a landscaping business in Atlanta. My partner is running it while I'm away. I couldn't possibly stay beyond the spring."

"I see." The older woman looked tranquil again, her professional poise covering up any uncomfortable deductions she might have made. "Kids are funny, aren't they? You never really know what they're thinking."

"It's just some misunderstanding. I'll talk to Liza."

"Of course. If you think you must. But a lot of people are going to be disappointed. Your mother had a great many friends who were looking forward to seeing you again." Ellen spoke without looking at Molly, apparently focused on straightening an unsteady display of edible plants. "And we could definitely use a good landscape architect around here."

AN HOUR LATER, the first, second and third place winners chosen, ribbons proudly affixed to the displays, Molly headed out to the parking lot. Though it was barely noon, she felt strangely tired. Try as she might, she couldn't stop thinking about the librarian's parting words. *A lot of people are going to be disappointed.*

The woman's suggestion was unmistakable. Molly ought to consider staying, for Liza's sake. Ellen Fowler had wanted Molly to know that the community would support her, that the goodwill people had felt toward her mother would extend to Molly. *We could definitely use a good landscape architect around here.*

How ridiculous to find the suggestion tempting. And yet Molly had to admit that in spite of everything, in spite of the ten years she'd spent building a life in Atlanta, Demery still felt like home. She loved the narrow, oak-canopied roads, the antebellum homes, the quaint main street. She loved the way spring smelled sweet here, without a million cars to fill the air with fumes.

And she loved the tight-knit fabric of the small community. Look how quickly she was being reabsorbed. Only three weeks back and already she was landscaping the new park, judging the science fair. Liza had made a dozen buddies, earned an invitation to join the Girl Scout troop. Just yesterday Molly had run into an old high school friend at the local nursery, and they had planned a catch-up dinner for this Friday night.

But, temping as the homespun package was, Molly had to resist. Demery might have all the charm of a small Southern town, but it had all the dangers, too. Demery society had a long memory, and an intense curiosity about the smallest of its members that simply didn't recognize the notion of privacy. How long before someone began adding up dates, unearthing decade-old gossip? How long before everyone was speculating, investigating, and finally exposing the secret of Liza's birth?

No, she couldn't stay. No matter how much Liza might want to. They would leave in April. That had been her plan, and she would stick to it. She could stay for the azaleas, for the spring tour of homes, for the dedication of Beau's park. But no longer. She would be back in Atlanta before the acres of Everspring daylilies began to bloom in May.

Fortified by this resolution, she walked briskly toward her parking space. She almost didn't see the woman sitting in the beat-up green sedan two cars down from hers. She wouldn't have noticed her at all, except that the sedan's windows were open, and a low rumble of rock music drew Molly's attention.

It was Annie. She undoubtedly hadn't seen Molly go by—she was slumped over the steering wheel, her face completely hidden by her unbound hair. Molly might have been worried, except that Annie was clearly conscious. Her fingers were resting on the wheel, too, and beating a rough counterpoint to the edgy music.

Still, Molly wanted to be sure. She moved to the passenger-side window and bent down. "Annie," she said softly. "Are you all right?"

Annie looked up, and to Molly's surprise she looked as if she might have been crying. Her eyes were red-rimmed and swollen, but when she spoke her voice was as tough and saucy as ever.

"Oh, yeah, I'm just great. Just peachy keen. Thanks for asking."

Molly refused to let the sarcasm get to her. "What are you doing out here? Did you come to take Tommy to lunch?"

Annie snorted. "Yeah, right. Like I've got time for that." She ran her fingers through her hair roughly. "Actually I'm sitting here trying to talk myself out of walking into that classroom, yanking the little darling out by his hair and tossing him straight into military school."

Molly hesitated only a second, then opened the door and slid onto the passenger's seat. She settled herself comfortably, ignoring Annie's surprised irritation. "Is this about the fight the other day? I've been meaning to talk to you about that. Liza said it wasn't Tommy's fault at all."

"The Junior Caldwell thing?" Annie waved her hand dismissively. "Good grief. That's yesterday's crisis. *Today's* problem is the science fair. Tommy told me he'd been doing his project at school, but his teacher called this morning and said he didn't turn one in at all."

"Oh." Molly thought of the rows upon rows of clever experiments she had just judged, all the statistics neatly graphed, all the reports carefully typed. She hadn't seen one by Tommy, but she had merely assumed he had entered another category. "Oh, dear. I'm sorry."

"Yeah. Well." Annie stared at the steering wheel

again, for once disarmingly out of bluster. She sighed. "You want to know the most pathetic part? I'm actually dreading going in there one more time, listening to them patronize me, telling me how smart he is, how he just needs more discipline and structure. Like I don't know what they're really saying. Like I don't know they think it's all my fault."

Molly almost jumped in with a denial, but in her heart she knew some truth lay behind Annie's statements. It was tough being a single mother.

"Sometimes I think he'd be better off in the public school," Annie said after a moment of silence. "At least there they wouldn't look at you as if you had two heads just because you don't live at Mr. and Mrs. Perfect's house."

"That's not such a crazy idea. Liza goes to the public school in Atlanta. It's an excellent school." Molly watched as an orderly line of uniformed children filed across the playground in front of them, heading for recess. Radway did have an elitist atmosphere. You could probably count on one hand the number of children who came from single-parent families. And Annie's little sedan was the only economy car in the entire parking lot. "Have you ever really considered taking him out?"

"Yeah, but—" Annie took a deep breath and tossed Molly a sheepish grin "—I guess I'm just too stubborn to let the snobs drive me away. Kind of dumb, huh?"

Molly just shrugged. What could she say? She had already asked herself several times why she was here. Why had she enrolled Liza at Radway for the short time they'd be in Demery?

It wasn't exactly her alma mater. Though Forrests had been Radway alums for generations, Molly herself had never attended the exclusive private school. Neither had Annie. Public school education had been all their families could dream of affording.

In fact, if Molly's fee from Everspring hadn't been so generous, she wouldn't have been able to manage Radway prices even now. Heaven only knew how Annie was managing to swing it on her salary at the hardware store.

Well…heaven and perhaps Jackson Forrest.

In her heart Molly knew her decision to send Liza there, even for this one semester, had something to do with proving herself as good as the Forrests. As reasons went, that one was embarrassingly shallow, maybe even dangerously vain. At least as dumb as Annie's reason. But true.

And that was why she could never move back to Demery for good. There was too much to prove. And far, far too much to forget.

But while Molly sank deeper into uncomfortable introspection, Annie seemed to be recovering her natural spirits.

"Yeah, I'm pretty stubborn, that's for sure," she said comfortably. "Still, you and I went to the public school, and it didn't kill either one of us." She looked over at Molly and chuckled mischievously. "Of course, we did end up fallen women, didn't we? Not a Mr. Perfect in sight at your house or mine. So…"

Molly opened her mouth, ready to trot out her prefab story of the loving, utterly fictitious dead husband. But then she met Annie's frank, open gaze, and somehow she suddenly just couldn't do it.

Lying was pointless. Annie knew. That look said it all. Annie knew.

So instead Molly just gave her a small, sad smile. "I don't think we can blame that on the public school system, Annie."

Shaking her head slowly, Annie leaned back, reaching forward with one hand to turn up the stereo, which was knocking out an old Melissa Etheridge tune.

"Nope," she said over the throbbing electric guitar. "I think we have to blame that one on green eyes, blue moons—and the amazing stupidity of teenage girls."

## CHAPTER EIGHT

DINNER WAS LATE that night, but no one in the in-
dolent, congenial group of family and friends gathered on the Everspring verandah really cared.

It was a beautiful evening, seeming to promise
that a spectacular spring was only a breath away.
The sky was layered in lavender and peach. The
sunset tinted the white plantation walls in Easter egg
colors. The breeze was gentle, the temperature mild
enough to coax off sweaters.

The porch was crowded. Two of Lavinia's white-
haired, happily foul-mouthed buddies sat at a wicker
table in the corner, playing canasta, the card game
Lavinia had lately introduced them to. They had
tried to persuade Jackson to join them, but he was
half-asleep on the bench swing—or pretending to
be—and couldn't be nudged into activity of any
kind.

Liza was apparently engaged in some important
Planet Cuspian business, training an eager but bewildered Stewball in the subtle art of Mudbluff hunting. The pair skulked by every now and then, and
occasionally Stewball let loose a muffled bark, but
for the most part it was all very cloak-and-dagger.

Molly and Lavinia stood at the top of the steps,

discussing Lavinia's newest brainstorm for the ever-evolving garden. Just this morning she had decided to change the roof of the huge white wooden gazebo that was under construction.

They had already agreed that the gazebo would be erected in the empty spot left by the lost oak. But they had spent the past half an hour locked in happy, heated battle about the exact design of the structure.

"The roof must be pierced," Lavinia insisted. "Open fretwork, lattice, I don't care. As long as you can look up and see the stars."

"But don't you see," Molly argued, "that if the roof is open it provides no protection from the rain? Plus, an open roof will lack mass. It will have less definition when viewed from the house."

"I don't care," the older woman said. "I want it open."

"Be realistic, Lavinia." Molly tilted her head, smiling. "You'd have to be lying flat on your back on one of the seats in order to see the stars from the gazebo you've described."

"So? What's your point?" Lavinia looked disgusted. "Good grief, girl. For a healthy young American gal you have darn little sense of romance!"

Molly felt herself flushing faintly as the two card-players, Grace Pickens and Evelyn Carole, began to laugh. Both women were well into their sixties, elegant and well-groomed, but enormously fond of mint juleps, which over the past hour had made their conversation grow alarmingly risque.

"Lavinia Forrest," Grace called out without even

fully lifting her lips from her drink, "if you're deluding yourself that anybody on this earth is going to take your creaky bag of bones down to that gazebo and—"

"I didn't say it was going to be *me,* you evil-minded old woman," Lavinia retorted. She lifted her chin regally. "But Everspring Plantation has stood for two hundred years, and it's probably going to stand for another two hundred. Don't you think it's possible that somewhere along the way it might host another romance or two?"

With a small huff she turned to Molly, presenting her back to the offending Grace. "That tree saw quite a bit in its day," Lavinia continued, as if she hadn't ever been interrupted. "And so did I. You may not have realized this, but I have a fairly good view of that old oak from my bedroom window."

Molly hesitated. What was Lavinia trying to tell her?

"No," she said carefully. "I didn't realize that—"

Lavinia laughed slyly. "Well, I couldn't see details," she explained, "but I knew when the tree had visitors, and I usually had a pretty good idea who those visitors were. So unless I miss my guess, you looked at the stars through those branches once or twice yourself, Miss Molly."

"Ooh," Grace called out, grinning. *"Busted!"* She slammed her cards down onto the table triumphantly. "Canasta!"

"Damnation!" Evelyn glowered at her partner.

"Blast you, Grace. I think Lavinia taught you how to cheat."

"No one needs to teach Grace Pickens how to cheat," she said indignantly. "But you hush up, Evelyn. The conversation was just getting good. Who took you out to the oak tree and made you see stars, Molly, dear? Was it Beaumont? Or Jackson? Or both?" She made a particularly salacious sound with her tongue against her teeth. "Now that would be a good story. Ha! *Both!*"

Molly instinctively turned toward Liza, wondering what her daughter would make of such comments. But the little girl was on the far side of the verandah, struggling with Stewball, who apparently had lost interest in hunting Mudbluffs. She obviously hadn't heard a thing.

"Well, I—"

But before Molly could articulate an answer, Jackson stirred on the swing. He cast a lazy glance at the older women through half-closed lids.

"Me?" He sounded hugely amused. "Ridiculous. What on earth would make a virtuous girl like Molly give the time of day to a bad boy like me?"

"Oh, brother." Grace rolled her eyes dramatically as she stacked the cards into a neat pile. "I won't even dignify that dumb question with an answer."

Molly smiled gratefully at Jackson. It had been sweet of him to try to deflect the old gossip's attention.

"Maybe a better question," Molly offered, "would be why a highflier like Jackson would ever have wasted his time with a stick-in-the-mud like me.''

"Nope." Grace shuffled the deck of cards crisply. "That's a stupid question, too." Sighing hopelessly, she began to deal a new hand like a pro. "God, Lavinia, why are young people so dense these days?"

"It's called modesty," Lavinia said laconically. "It was around in our day, too, Grace, though you may have missed it."

"Modesty is a bore," Grace pronounced, shaking her empty glass, obviously annoyed at being out of liquor. "And stereotypes are a bore, too. Jackson wasn't such a terrible devil, if you ask me. And Beaumont wasn't always such a saint." She nodded dramatically in slow motion, her head weaving slightly. "No, he sure wasn't, though I know it's the official Demery position to say he was, thanks to you, Lavinia, and your Saint Beaumont Memorial Pavilion."

Unaware of the stunned silence she was leaving in her wake, Grace cleared her throat loudly, picked up her new hand and began scowling at the cards.

"Wasn't he responsible for that fuss over at the country club, the one where all the money went missing? Never did fess up, as I recall. The Lorring fellow lost his job instead."

"Grace—" Lavinia began.

But Grace didn't seem to be listening anymore. She hiccuped slightly. "No sir, no saint," she told her cards confidentially. "Damned fine-looking hunk of manhood, of course. But no saint."

Molly felt frozen in place. She had never heard anyone, *anyone,* speak this way about Beau before. It acted on her like a static shock, making the small hairs at the nape of her neck quiver.

"Grace, dear," Lavinia said slowly and dangerously. 'I'm afraid you've had three or four hundred too many mint juleps."

Grace finally looked up from her cards. "What? Oh. Do I have things mixed-up? Was that you, Jackson, dear? You stole the money? Oh, well. I never was very good at keeping you boys straight."

"What it is," Lavinia answered in a quelling tone, "is ancient history. Quite boring, actually. I'm getting hungry, how about you? I wonder if dinner is—"

"Miss Pickens," Molly interrupted before Lavinia could change the subject. As ashamed as she was of this episode of her father's history, as shocked as she was to discover that it had been common knowledge among the Everspring set, she couldn't allow Beau's memory to be blackened. She couldn't allow him—or Jackson—to take the blame for something her father had done.

"Miss Pickens, it couldn't be Jackson you're thinking about. Jackson never went to the country club. He hated golf. But I am afraid you have your facts confused. It's true, my father lost his job because money was missing from the pro shop. He always contended he didn't take it, though he couldn't ever prove it. But the whole thing had absolutely nothing to do with Beau."

Grace put down her cards and tilted her mint julep

back, obviously stalling, since the glass was quite empty. At long last she looked chagrined.

"Lavinia?" Her voice was unsteady. "I'm sorry. I—I don't know what to say—"

"Then by all means, Grace, dear, *say nothing.*" Lavinia's eyes and tone were frosty. "It's an excellent strategy that you should perhaps employ more often."

JACKSON KNEW Molly had heard him come up behind her. He'd deliberately made plenty of noise as he descended the verandah steps, hoping to give her time to collect herself. But she didn't turn around. She just kept staring down the terraced lawn, down past the landscaping lights, down into the darkness.

"I've been sent to bring you in," he said with a studied levity. "There's good news. Lavinia and Liza have finally managed to console Consuelo, whose sweet potato casserole sank or burned or grew lumps, or some such tragedy. She has found the courage to go on, and apparently there will be a dinner tonight after all."

Still Molly didn't turn around. He saw a tremor pass through her shoulders, and he wondered if she had been crying. *Hell.* He put his hands in his pockets to keep from reaching out and gathering her into his arms. They could be seen from the dining room, and he'd be damned if he'd give Grace Pickens anything else to gossip about.

"Don't let the old witch get to you, M." He tried to communicate comfort through his tone instead.

"She's fifty percent sloshed, seventy-five percent senile and a hundred percent shameless."

"Maybe," Molly answered without turning. Her voice was throaty and strangely rough. Her shoulders rose as she took a deep breath. "But is she *wrong?*"

He shouldn't have needed to hesitate, to buy time before he answered. He had known she'd ask this question. He had seen the way she had looked at Grace Pickens, full of disbelief, rejection and a slowly dawning dread. But he did need time. Though he'd been debating with himself for the past twenty minutes, he still hadn't decided how much to tell her.

Hesitation would eventually become an answer of its own, though, so he forced himself to speak.

"Grace Pickens is the lewdest old busybody south of the North Pole, Molly—you know that. She scoops up every morsel of gossip she finds lying in the gutter. And if that's not repulsive enough to please her, she makes up some more."

Finally Molly turned around. She tried to smile, but, as he had feared, her eyes were bright, shining wetly in the rising moonlight.

"You still haven't answered my question, Jackson. What she said just now about Beau, about my father. Was any of that true?"

He mentally consigned Grace Pickens to hell. "Who knows, Molly? It was what…twelve years ago? I remember Lavinia being suspicious at the time—something about finding cash Beau couldn't explain. But Beau never admitted anything."

"Not even to you?"

"Not even to me. I never even heard about it until months later. I was up at school most of that summer, remember?" But she wouldn't remember, of course. It hadn't ever mattered much to Molly where *he* was, as long as Beau was close enough to touch. "By the time I got home, it had all died down. Your father had a new job—"

"Which Beau found for him," Molly interjected. "Did you know that? Beau helped him get another job."

"Yes," Jackson said slowly. "I knew. As the manager of Touchdown Sports."

Molly's expression was thoughtful. "My father loved that job, and he always said he wouldn't have been hired if he hadn't had a recommendation from the local football hero. I had almost forgotten that. My mother was so relieved." She smiled hesitantly. "So Lavinia's suspicions can't really have been true, can they? Beau wouldn't have bothered to help my father find work if he had been responsible for getting him fired in the first place."

*Unbelievable.* In the face of such resolute naivete, such blind determination to preserve the fantasy, Jackson couldn't quite govern his expression.

*Beau,* he thought, *you slick, incredibly lucky son of a bitch. What did you ever do to deserve this kind of loyalty?* Nothing. His brother had done nothing, and yet this incredible victory had been his, remained his still, ten years after his death.

Molly touched his arm. "What is it?" She looked

at him closely. "You look upset. Was it something I said?"

"Of course not." But Jackson was no saint, either. He was so tempted. Tempted to blast that innocent relief off her face with a few carefully aimed truths. Tempted to knock down all the temples she'd erected in Beau's memory, merely in order to clear the path for himself. He didn't mind waiting for them to crumble under their own weight—if the damn things ever *would.* But Molly wasn't going to allow that, was she? Waiting was a fool's strategy this time. And he hadn't ever been very good at it anyhow.

She moved closer. "What is it, Jackson?"

"I'm just surprised, that's all." He tried to keep his voice neutral. "It sounds as if you would *prefer* to believe that your father stole the money. Looks like you'd rather keep your illusions about Beau intact at any price—even at the price of any illusions you have left about your father. I guess I don't understand that."

She looked at him a long moment. "I guess I don't, either. Not really," she said softly.

He waited. After a few seconds she sighed, crossing her arms as she turned back toward the dark, empty vistas she'd been watching when he arrived. When she shifted, the sweet warmth of her perfume carried toward him like the scent of spring flowers, though no flowers had bloomed yet. Winter might technically be in decline, but it still ruled at Everspring.

"Maybe it's because I haven't had any illusions

about my father in so long," she finally said. "Not since I was a little girl. But Beau—" Her voice caught. "Beau was my magic. I guess I need to believe in that magic."

He closed his eyes. "He was just a man, Molly. Grace was right about one thing. He wasn't really a saint. Surely you know that."

"Of course I do." She sounded sad, but strangely resigned. "I'm not really a fool, Jackson. And I'm not a starry-eyed teenager anymore. Since I've come home, I've seen a lot of things more clearly. I know Beau wasn't perfect. But he was... He's still—" She rubbed her arms with a rough impatience, apparently frustrated by her inability to find the right words. "You see, for me he'll always be—"

Jackson concentrated on breathing deeply, forcing himself to listen.

She shook her head and began again. "I guess I'm just trying to say that Beau will always be a part of me. He left his mark on my life, in so many profound and permanent ways."

"Molly, listen to me," Jackson said darkly, taking her wrist in his hand, as if he feared she would try to bolt. "You have to understand something. You have to accept that Beau was—"

"Mom? Jackson?" The sound of the dining room window being raised stopped Jackson cold. "Are you out there? Lavinia says if you don't come in right this very minute Consuelo is going to quit."

Liza's clear, high voice, floating toward them from the open window, was full of teasing laughter. She sounded so much like Molly that for a moment

Jackson felt hopelessly snagged between the past and the present. Between the sweet, lonely little kid Molly had been, somehow finding magic wherever she could—and the sweet, brave woman she was today, still clinging to the dream that once she had known True Love.

Molly looked up at him trustingly. Her blond hair glimmered in the rising moonlight. "What, Jackson? Beau was what?"

And suddenly he knew he wouldn't tell her. Couldn't tell her the nasty truth—that there hadn't ever been a single ounce of sainthood running through the veins of either of the reckless, willful Forrest twins.

"Mom?"

Jackson swallowed past a jagged rock that had lodged in his throat. *We were bastards, Beau. Both of us.* Yet somehow here was Liza, this laughing, blue-eyed Forrest daughter, who had come into the world with all her mother's purity and none of her father's shame.

And as far as Jackson was concerned, even if he had to cut out his tongue to do it, she was going to stay that way.

"So you do understand why we can't stay, don't you, sweetheart?" Molly put down her red Magic Marker, which she had been using to draw roses all over Queen Willowsong's castle, and gazed somberly at her daughter.

"Sure." Liza was propped up in bed, her sketch pad next to her. She was getting sleepy—Molly could tell by the way she absently twisted a curl of hair around her index finger. "Your clients. And our apartment. And there was something else. Oh, yeah. Robin and Phyllis."

Molly had to smile at the intense oversimplification that could boil a twenty-minute explanation down to three sentences. "Not just Robin and Phyllis," she corrected, picking up a purple marker. "*All* our friends."

"Yeah," Liza agreed. "But my friends in Atlanta wouldn't really *miss* me, you know? Not the way Tommy would."

"Why? Doesn't Tommy have any friends?" Molly looked up, genuinely surprised. "I thought he was like the ringleader of the whole class."

"Oh, he's *popular*," Liza said dismissively. "But that doesn't mean he has any friends. Not real friends. Not friends he can talk to." She set her sketch pad on the floor carefully and snuggled down until she was up to her ears in comforter. She yawned again. "He can talk to me."

"Well, maybe he can come to visit us." Molly was concerned. In a way, this conversation had been less distressing than she had feared. Liza hadn't fussed or complained or begged. She had listened to her mother with her usual sensible equanimity. But Molly had the strange sense that Liza wasn't exactly accepting the inevitability of her decision, either. It was almost as if she were humoring her mother, as Liza believed that fate would somehow step in and see to it that they stayed here in Demery.

"And you do see about the clients, don't you,

honey? The landscaping business in Atlanta is my job. It's how I make the money that we live on.''

Liza smiled, nuzzling herself into a comfortable position on the pillow. ''You'll have clients here too,'' she said reasonably. ''Mrs. Fowler, our librarian at school, said she wished you would help them make the front of the school prettier.''

Molly couldn't help chuckling. Schools were the same all over. ''Yes, honey, but that would be for free. It wouldn't exactly be the kind of client that would pay our bills.''

''I know,'' Liza said, unfazed. ''But other people will look at the school and see what a good landscaper you are. And then *they* will pay you.''

Her eyes drifted shut. Capping her marker, Molly sat a moment just enjoying the sight of her beautiful little girl, who for a nine-year-old actually seemed to have a fairly clear idea of marketing and public relations.

Her heart ached with love for the shining blond hair, the imperfectly scrubbed fingernails, the charcoal-smudged cheek, where Liza had absently touched her pencil as she drew her pictures.

''And we can get a dog like Stewball,'' Liza murmured, already half asleep, but continuing to make her case. ''A dog is a very Willowsong kind of pet.''

Molly smoothed her daughter's hair, drawing comfort from the touch. Liza, her human touchstone. Because of this little girl, Molly would never really lose faith in Beau. He had been spoiled, of course. Selfish, sometimes. A little too arrogant, occasionally manipulative. But never cruel. Never really *bad*.

Could a bad man have produced such a delightful, loving child? Never. Grace Pickens could pull out every shabby scrap of gossip she'd ever invented. As long as Liza's shining goodness was in front of her as proof, Molly would never stop loving Beau.

She knew things about Beau that no one, not even his twin brother, and certainly not that evil Grace Pickens, could possibly know.

Secret things. Gentle things.

She knew that, when he had made love to her that night, he had touched her with a reverence, a humility, she had never seen in him before. She had always known he would be a thrilling, powerful lover, but this—this passionate tenderness had been a stunningly beautiful surprise.

She wished that somehow she could say these things to Jackson. She wished she could make him see that, whatever small flaws Beau's nature had possessed, whatever small wounds he had inflicted on her through the years, everything had been erased that night.

Of course she couldn't tell anyone, least of all Jackson. She didn't even very often let herself think of it. It would be possible to drown in such memories, to sink so deep into the remembered passion that it would be impossible to surface. Impossible to accept love from anyone else.

But tonight, perhaps because of Grace Pickens, she needed to remember. Careful not to make too much noise, Molly put her castle picture on top of Liza's sketchbook and walked to the window.

The three golden moons floated over her shoulder,

swaying slightly as the heater vent blew warm air across their glittering surfaces. Flecks of twinkling gold light moved silently, reflected against the windowpane. Molly touched the cold glass with her fingertips, catching the gold on the backs of her hands.

The sight reminded her of Beau's ring. The Forrest ring, bequeathed to every eldest son for more than a hundred years. She had always loved that ring, not because it stood for wealth, but because it symbolized stability and continuity. It meant that the Forrest family had weathered wars and scandals, financial booms and crashes, births and deaths.

And through it all the ring had made its way unscathed. From father to son, over and over, the promise was unbroken.

Where was the ring now? she wondered. Jackson didn't wear it, though technically it was his. Technically Jackson had become the eldest son.

*Oh, Beau...* She remembered the last time she had seen the ring, its complex facets winking like golden fire from the Cuspian moons. She had pressed Beau's hand against her cheek, begging his forgiveness, and she had felt the carved gold leaves press cold against her tear-warmed skin....

She had almost lost him that night. Back then, they had fought almost every time they met. It was always the same thing. She was too immature, too naive. Too virginal. Or—when he was very angry—too *frigid*.

His contempt bruised her soul. But what else could she have expected? Beau was twenty-two years old, a rich, exciting young man who had just graduated from college. Molly was only eighteen, a little local mouse not quite out of high school.

Oh, he loved her—he had told her so often and eloquently ever since she'd be fifteen years old. But he was a man, with a man's needs. He loved her. He needed her. But it was time for more.

Molly was afraid. Her mother's example was always before her. Molly's mother had, in her own teens, found herself pregnant. In her desperate grasp for respectability, she had married Molly's father, though she knew he had no desire to be a father, no desire to be a husband. No desire to be anything but a boisterous regular at the Proud Lion Pub, found nightly at the bar with a long-neck beer in one hand and long-legged beauty in the other.

And look what had happened to that marriage. Her father had ended up at the bottom of a bottle, and her mother had ended up wedded to resentment.

For years, only the fear of meeting that same fate had kept Molly from succumbing to Beau's expert seductions. She had begged for more time.

But that night she had run out of time.

The evening had started all right. Though he had hated the thought of hanging out with "adolescents," he had finally agreed to escort her to her senior prom, and she was almost sick with excitement.

She would never forget a single detail. She had worn yellow silk—when they danced, it whispered things she couldn't quite hear. When she leaned into him, the fabric slipped across his crisp black tuxedo like liquid gold.

He had bought her a corsage of white orchids with yellow throats and a thick, sweet scent. When he had fixed it to her bodice, right in front of her parents, he had worked slowly, deliberately grazing the sharp point of the long florist's pin lightly across the exposed swell of her breast. The pin had left a small white line and a trail of shivering goose bumps in its path.

She had borrowed her mother's yellow topaz earrings. Once, while they danced, he had nibbled one of the small round studs right out of her ear and then, tossing back his head, he had grinned, displaying it like a pirate's prize, the jewel flashing between his teeth.

Everyone had envied her. Beau was everything the high school girls wanted in a man, everything the high school boys were not. Graceful, athletic, muscular, utterly charismatic. He flirted with all the pretty girls, and then, just when Molly was tense with insecurity, he danced with her. He kissed her neck and whispered how much he wanted her. Only her. But the next dance belonged to some other girl—what was he whispering now?—and fear set in again.

By the time the prom was over, Molly was weak with Beau's special mixture of pleasure and pain. She could see now what she hadn't understood then—that he had devoted the entire night to prepping her for surrender. Deliberately, much the way a chef tenderizes meat.

So sure was he of his technique that when Molly once again said no, he didn't even get angry. This time, he was too clever for that. He knew what would work best.

Instead he killed her with kindness. He apologized for pushing. He knew that he was wrong for her, too mature for her. She needed someone her own age. *Just as he did.* For her own good, he ought never to see her again.

By the time he dropped her at the front door, she was nearly weeping with desolation. She begged, abandoning pride, but he was resolute. For her own good, he was leaving her. It was over.

She had spent two hours paralyzed on her bed, smelling crushed orchids and tasting the salt of her own tears. Through the walls she could hear the nightly argument between her parents, escalating fury on her father's part, dwindling whining from her mother. A pattern so familiar it had become a ritual.

But without Beau, it was suddenly unendurable. It was Beau who had made her feel protected, who had made her feel loved, who had made her believe that there was something worth living for.

Without Beau, there was nothing. Without Beau she couldn't survive.

And then, in one desperate flash of clarity, everything fell into place.

She didn't have to try to live without him.

All he wanted was a real woman, a woman who wasn't afraid to love him. Well, she could be that woman. She wasn't afraid anymore, not of that.

The only thing that scared her then was the idea of living without him.

# CHAPTER NINE

STILL IN HER YELLOW SILK, she climbed out her window, down the thick, rough branches of the tree, and she made her way to Everspring. For once Molly was grateful to have a neurotic mother—she was able to pay for a cab with the emergency twenty-dollar bill her mother always made her tuck into her evening shoes.

But when she arrived, she felt paralyzed, confused, as if she'd awakened from a fugue state to find herself standing in front of Everspring. What now? The formal plantation looked forbidding at this hour, mausoleum gray under the crescent moon. It was too late to ring the bell—what would his mother think?

Then, like a miracle, she spied Beau's little red sports car. He had parked it on the grass, deep in the backyard, under the spreading arms of the biggest, oldest oak tree.

As she drew closer, she could see that Beau lay there, sprawled across the hood. A dozen beer bottles were scattered on the ground beside the car, winking in the starlight. He raised his arm slowly, laying it over his eyes as if the stars had given him a headache. Molly saw the Forrest ring flash, bright and gold and reassuring.

She heard herself emit a small whimper of relief. He was still here—and he was alone. He hadn't really left her, hadn't gone out to find a more willing woman. Thank God, it wasn't too late.

She barely felt her feet touch the ground as she raced toward him. He rose at the sound of her approach, blinking as if he might have been sleeping. His hair was mussed, his gaze muddled from the liquor.

"Molly?" He tried to slide off the hood, but he was awkwardly arranged, and she reached him first.

"Wait. Please wait." She pressed herself close to the car and reached her hands up to his chest, stalling his descent. His legs braced themselves on the fender, on either side of her, and he leaned back on the heels of his hands, steadying himself.

"Molly?" His voice was slurred. "What is it?"

"I'm sorry," she said. "I'm so sorry. I was wrong. You were right." She couldn't think what else to say. She was afraid of words—he was so much better at them. Words had done her no good in the car, when he had been telling her goodbye.

"I love you," she said desperately. "I love you so much." She hated how her voice trembled. She didn't want to sound like a nervous teenager. She wanted to sound like a woman. She stood on her tiptoes and leaned into him, waiting for him to wrap his arms around her.

But he didn't. And she wasn't sure what her next move should be. How embarrassing not to know how to initiate such things. But he had always been the pursuer. She had been focused on how to stop him from going too far.

She kissed him on the lips, hoping that he would understand. Perhaps he would just take over now....

But he was completely motionless, not even breathing. After a moment it felt ridiculous, as if she were kissing a statue, so she pulled back. She could hardly look at him.

"Molly." He frowned, slowly shaking his head. "Molly, you're making a mistake—"

"No, I'm not!" Panic surged through her. Was he going to send her away? Back to that cramped, lonely and unloving house? He didn't understand. He thought it was the same naive little Molly out here, offering him more of her childish kisses, and he simply wasn't interested.

She had to prove that things were different. That *she* was different. Before she could lose her courage, she dropped her hand to his waistband. He had changed into a pair of weathered blue jeans, but he hadn't bothered with a belt, so it was easy to slip free the button and slide the zipper down.

He held his breath, still unmoving, but she knew what these changes in his body meant. She had finally done the right thing. He wanted her to touch him like this. He had often asked for it, but she had always been too afraid.

She was still afraid, but now mixed in with the fear was something that felt more like excitement. Something warm and breathless that made her heart beat very fast.

His breathing was rapid, shallow exhales of sweet, alcohol-tinged warmth, as if his heart were beating fast, too. She could feel his body swelling just under her hand, and, closing her eyes, she lowered her trembling fingers.

He lurched forward, pushing her aside roughly as he staggered down from the car. "No," he said, the sound more moan than word. "I can't let you do this."

He stumbled as far as the tree, pressed his back against the trunk, as if he needed its strength to hold him up, and with a groan slid slowly to the ground. He put his face in his hands. "Go away, Molly," he muttered drunkenly into his fingers. "For God's sake, go away."

Molly knew he didn't mean it. She had felt the hot thrust of his flesh, and she had felt the answering tingle in her own body. He wanted her, *needed* her, and for the first time she, too, understood what need felt like. It had talons, like hunger. Fire, like pain. Ripples, like fear. And a helpless, liquid sweetness, like love.

So she followed him. She knelt in front of him, her gold silk pooling around her on the thick spring grass.

"It's all right," she said softly, kissing his hands, kissing the gold leaves of the Forrest ring. "Don't you see? It's different this time. This time I want it just as much as you do."

He didn't answer. But he didn't need to. She knew what to do, though her hands still trembled as she peeled open the edges of his jeans. As she low-

ered her head to the soft cotton beneath, her breath
came so fast she wondered if she might faint.

But she didn't. She fumbled, but instinct guided
her, instinct she hadn't even known she possessed.
Her lips found him quickly, found the thick, thrilling, musky, rigid power of him. She caught her
breath as she finally understood what was going to
happen to her tonight. And then, breathing his name
in whispering silence, she kissed him.

He shuddered, and one long, low animal sound
tore from his throat. His hands fell away from his
face, and his eyes were feverish in the starlight.

"Tell me I'm dreaming, Molly," he said in a
strange, harsh voice. "Tell me I'm drunk, and I am
dreaming."

She kissed him again, panting slightly against his
skin from the strange, throbbing desire that was rising in her. "But you're not," she whispered without
lifting her head. He groaned once more, clutching
at the soft blades of grass as she tentatively feath-
ered her lips up and down the length of him, learning what made him swell and quiver. "This is not
a dream."

"It is, Molly, it is." His voice was hot, and not
his own. She could feel a thrumming in the muscles
of his legs, as if he fought to maintain balance, as
if he were afraid he might fall from this cushion of
grass into some steep and fatal abyss. "You have
always been my dream, Molly. My first, my last, my
best, most beautiful dream."

The tenderness in his voice drew tears, and they
fell on her fingers as she loved him. And then some-

how, with careful tension, he eased away from her touch. He rose onto his knees, and he touched her, too, gently moving aside yellow silk and ivory lace with reverent, knowing fingers.

For long, elastic minutes they touched, they trembled. His body molded itself to hers with great beauty and brief pain. His breath became hers, his rhythm became hers, and the night sky was barely large enough to contain the sweating, pulsing pleasure of it all.

And finally, arm and legs and silk and tears entangled, on a blanket of grass spread sweetly under the oak tree, they dreamed together as one.

IN HIS ENTIRE CAREER, Ross Riser had never spent more than ten minutes at a stretch inside the Radway art room. And that was not an accident. Ross Riser wasn't the indoorsy type. And he darn sure wasn't the artsy type.

It had always been like that. Although he could shoot a football like an arrow twenty-five yards to a downfield receiver he couldn't even see, although he could thread that spiraling pigskin neatly through the needle's eye of a dozen burly pass rushers, he couldn't take a pencil and draw a straight line on a piece of paper to save his life.

Face it, he was all major muscle mass and bulk energy. He didn't have one single solitary fine motor skill in his whole body.

But look at him now. His fingers were sticky with glue, and he was pretty damn sure he had silver glitter in his hair. *In his hair, for God's sake!* What the hell had he been thinking?

He growled under his breath and fought the urge to kick something.

"Jeez," Tommy Cheatwood said, leaning back in his chair and giving Ross a disgusted glare. "If I'd known you were going to make such a darn fuss about it, I wouldn't have said you could help."

"I'm not making a fuss." Ross returned the black look. "I just said I didn't see what was wrong with your project to start with. It looked okay to me. And considering how late this assignment is already—"

"I told you, I decided I wanted it to be an ice cave instead." Tommy yanked up the tube of glue and squeezed it over the papier-mâché mounds that had just yesterday been a clumsy representation of the Rocky Mountains. The mountains had since been hollowed out into weird, spiky caves.

Tommy's plan was to affix tiny, diamond-shaped rhinestones to the surfaces, creating "ice," and he had been given permission from the art teacher to use her room after school. Ross, stopping in after football practice, had seen Tommy there and, like a fool, had offered to help.

Tommy had seemed grateful, or so Ross had thought at first. But Tommy had put his coach in charge of the silver glitter, which Ross now believed might be part of some diabolical plot to humiliate him. Glitter was the most fiendish, uncooperative substance ever invented. It was like trying to catch smoke and glue it down. The damn stuff went everywhere. *Everywhere.* He'd probably be sneezing glitter for a month.

"Besides, I already missed the science fair, so what difference does it make if I'm late one more day?" Tommy grimaced as the glue refused to squirt. He squeezed harder, grunting irritably. Suddenly the top of the tube popped off under the pressure, and about a cupful of thick, oozy paste flooded out like white lava.

"Damn!" he said explosively. It was all over his fingers. He wiped them on his blue jeans, smearing glue everywhere.

"Watch your language," Ross cautioned automatically, but when he reached over to help, he knocked the shaker of glitter in his lap. *"Damn!"*

The two gluey, glittery, exasperated males glared at each other across the table. For a moment the art room was as cold as any ice cave ever discovered. And then Tommy began to laugh.

"Man, you look pathetic," he said. "You've got glitter all over your ears."

Ross grinned. "You look pretty stupid yourself, Cheatwood. Your hair is glued to your eyebrow."

Tommy reached up, found the mess, and made a retching sound. "Jeez. What a couple of losers we are."

Ross tried to shake the glitter from his fingertips, but the stuff wouldn't budge. "I tell you, Tommy, I'd rather be *lost* in an ice cave than have to make one."

"Think so? Ice caves are pretty dangerous," Tommy said with a macabre glee in his voice. "And freezing cold. They're actually inside glaciers, you know.''

Ross raised one eyebrow. ''Yeah. Well, I'd still rather be lost in one.''

''Oh, yeah?'' It had become a contest of wills. ''Well, you could get impaled on a stalagmite. And sometimes the cave walls are too thin, and they come crashing down, burying you alive.''

Ross grinned. ''Still.''

''Yeah, well, you know these caves were carved out by glacier meltwaters, and the water is still in there.'' Tommy's eyes grew theatrically wide. ''Sometimes there can be flash floods, and if you're in too deep you can't get out.''

''Hmm.'' Ross pretended to consider. He knew better than to express any amazement that Tommy knew all the glaciological terminology. Clearly, for once, the kid had actually done some research. ''Well, at least you don't die of shame. At least you don't die covered in silver glitter.''

Tommy laughed out loud and nodded, tacitly acknowledging defeat. ''You got a point there, coach. You do look pretty dopey. I guess you wouldn't want my mom to see you now.''

''No, and you'd better not tell her about this, either, young man,'' Ross said, pointing a silver finger at the little boy. Tommy just made a wrinkled, noncommittal face and tilted his head mischievously. But that was okay. For the first time, Ross felt absolutely no antagonism coming from the kid. That was real progress. It was worth filling every exposed orifice with glitter. Almost.

"So what got you interested in ice caves?" He tilted his chair onto its back legs and eyed Tommy comfortably. The kid had already resumed his work, placing rhinestones onto the cave walls as carefully as his ten thumbs would allow.

"I don't know. Liza was talking about them the other day. You know Liza Lorring? She gave me the idea, I guess." Tommy scrutinized the caves, choosing the spot for his next rhinestone with the intensity of a surgeon deciding where to make his next cut. "I thought I might give it to her after I get my grade. That's why I'm using so much glitter. Liza is like *in love* with glitter."

*Ahh.* Ross finally understood. "So you and Liza are friends?" He made the question very casual, looking up only briefly, concentrating on picking tiny silver flecks out from under his fingernails. "She's a pretty cool kid?"

Tommy shrugged. "Well, she's a girl. But I guess she doesn't *completely* stink."

Ross chuckled. "Except for the glitter."

Looking up, Tommy offered Ross a man-to-man grin—and, for just a second, in that extraordinary smile Ross could glimpse the charismatic young heartbreaker Tommy was destined to become. Five years, maybe? God help the girls then. And every other boy who tried to compete with this cocky little charmer. Oh, yeah. Ross knew all about that.

"You got that right, Coach." Tommy offered Ross a sticky silver high five of mutual machismo. "The glitter stinks big-time."

WHEN MOLLY PASSED by the art room after picking up Liza's science project from the media center, she glanced absently in through the open door. Two seconds later, she did a double take.

Backing up slowly, she peeked around the door frame. Yes, that's what she had thought she saw. Ross Riser and Tommy Cheatwood darting absurdly around the room, laughing and tossing a football back and forth. Or *was* that a football? It looked kind of like...well, like a football trailing a tail of—

Of flowers? She kept staring. Yes, the "football" clearly was made of a foam ball they had pulled out of a flower arrangement, and it still had a couple of silk roses attached. When they tossed the ball, the flowers flew along behind like a comet's tail. How very strange.

And something even stranger... Molly blinked hard to be completely sure her eyes weren't fooling her. No, it wasn't a hallucination. It was true.

Tommy Cheatwood and Coach Ross Riser were twinkling all over, like Las Vegas showgirls.

Ross saw her first. He froze comically in place, and in his sudden distraction he completely missed Tommy's incoming pass. The football thudded against Ross's shirt, then fell to the floor with a splat, knocking loose one of the roses.

"Hi, Molly," Ross said with a sheepish grin. He touched his silver ear self-consciously. "I was just helping Tommy with his science project."

She smiled back. "Testing the maximum hang time of various football materials?" She glanced down at the dented foam oblong. "I don't know, though. Do you suppose the flower tail will ever catch on in the NFL?''

''Ms. Lorring. Hi. Coach and I were just goofing around a little bit,'' Tommy added quickly. ''We already finished my project.'' He sauntered over and picked up the ball, stuck the loose rose back in, then replaced the whole thing casually into the empty vase. ''We didn't hurt anything.''

Tommy went over to stand next to Ross, and he gazed back at Molly stubbornly, as if daring her to object. Molly realized with some surprise that he wasn't seeking support—he was giving it. Though it was camouflaged nicely by his usual ultracool nonchalance, Tommy was actually sticking up for Coach Riser.

How sweet. And how eerily familiar.

A bad boy with a soft streak he'd rather die than reveal. Apparently Tommy's similarities to Jackson were more than skin deep.

''So what was your project?'' She looked both of them over carefully. ''Would I be right if I guess it involved silver glitter?''

''Yeah,'' Tommy answered smoothly, doing an admirable job of pretending he didn't care that his hair was twinkling. Ross was less blasé. He kept plucking at his ears and trying to brush the glitter from his chin. It was hopeless, which Tommy obviously understood, choosing instead to project a sublime indifference.

''I did a project on ice caves,'' he explained, sharing a glance with Ross. ''Things got pretty messy. We decided glitter stinks.''

"It makes a lovely fashion statement, though."

Jackson's lightly teasing voice came from behind Molly's shoulder. She turned and smiled a welcome. Jackson, too? This was a pretty busy schoolroom so late on a Friday afternoon.

"Hi, there, M." He touched her cheek gently, then turned to Tommy with a grin. "Go wash up, twinkletoes. I've got to take you home in my car, and I'd rather you didn't sprinkle pixie dust all over everything."

"Oh, yeah? Well, that's just too darn bad for your precious old car, isn't it?" Tommy retorted sarcastically. "'Cause soap won't help. It's gonna take a blowtorch to get this crummy stuff off me."

"Watch it, smart mouth." Jackson chuckled. "That could be arranged."

Ross seemed to be watching the interplay carefully. It was obvious to anyone that as soon as Jackson had entered the room, Tommy's allegiance had shifted. He had even physically switched places to stand nearer to Jackson. Ross had become a third wheel, at best. At worst, completely invisible.

But now he spoke up. "I could take Tommy home in my truck," he suggested. He gestured to his own sparkling blue jeans. "It's doomed to be covered in glitter as soon as I put one foot into it anyhow."

Jackson's expression was flawlessly polite as he appeared to consider the idea. And in that moment, watching the subtle barrier created by that cold courtesy, Molly remembered the lesson she had learned long ago, listening to Beau and Jackson banter mercilessly. For some men, trading insults was a form of expressing affection. Paradoxically, the absence of casual abuse was the real insult here.

"Thanks, Riser," Jackson responded with a chillingly civil formality. "But I promised Annie I'd do it, so I suppose I'd better follow through. Good of you to offer, though."

Ross's posture stiffened almost imperceptibly. "No problem."

Jackson turned once more to Tommy. "Come on, then, champ. Maybe I can strap you to the roof." He put his fingertips on Tommy's head, avoiding the gluey wads of glitter, and guided him toward the door. He paused by Molly. "Need a ride, M?"

"No, thanks," she said, self-conscious about witnessing the subtle yet complete put-down he had just delivered. She didn't want Ross to think she shared Jackson's somewhat bewildering contempt for him. "I think I'll stay a few minutes. I've got my car here."

"Okay. See you back at the house."

When they were gone, Molly turned to Ross, who was carefully rearranging chairs and tables, putting things back in order. He didn't look up, and she didn't speak right away. Instead she pitched in with the cleanup, finding the whisk broom to sweep away the worst of the glitter.

She stopped beside the ice cave, which actually looked pretty good, all things considered. "Wow. This is impressive. Is this Tommy's project?"

Ross nodded, glancing up from a hunk of sculpting clay, from which he was scraping a thin layer of glitter. "Yep. The ice caves. Not bad, considering about half the decorations ended up on us."

Molly walked around the table, studying the project from all sides. "This is quite a coincidence. My daughter is writing a story where the hero is lost in some ice caves. I think the poor man is in big trouble." She smiled. "Something about flash floods."

Ross finally quit picking at the clay and sat down on the nearest chair. "I'll bet that was Tommy's idea," he said thoughtfully. "He learned about flash floods in his research. Did you know he's planning to give this ice cave to Liza after he turns it in?"

"No." Molly was quite surprised. "Gosh, she'll be thrilled."

"He likes your daughter a lot. I think his exact words were that, for a girl, 'she doesn't *completely* stink.'" He plucked once more at the glitter on his chin, then, heaving a deep sigh, he seemed to abandon the effort. "Aw, heck. I give up."

"Don't worry," Molly said sympathetically. "Most of it will come off in the shower. Take my word for it—I have a lot of experience dealing with glitter disasters. It's Liza's favorite interior design technique."

Ross nodded, smiling. "So I heard."

"You did? Tommy must have really opened up to you this afternoon." From the pleased look on Ross's face, she deduced that a good relationship with Tommy was something he longed to achieve. "From what I've seen of Tommy, that's pretty unusual. You two must be very close."

"I wouldn't say close." He shrugged. "But we

did okay today. A lot better than usual. He's a tough kid to read, you know? He's got that cool, sardonic thing going almost all the time. At only nine years old, can you believe it? And yet sometimes I think we'd do pretty well, if it weren't for—''

He stopped abruptly, shifting uncomfortably on the child-size chair. Molly found his awkwardness endearing. No wonder he was intimidated by Tommy's "cool, sardonic" thing. Ross Riser didn't have it, not an ounce of it. He seemed to be unusually honest and open, simple and fair.

What a great guy. However, it was clear that, in a confrontation like the one she had just witnessed, Ross's straightforward style would be no match for the subtle Forrest rapier, which was often quicker than the eye, and almost always fatal.

He tried again. "I mean if it weren't for—''

"If it weren't for what?" He might as well go ahead and say it, she thought. He had come so close—what was the point in turning back now? "If it weren't for Jackson?"

"Well, yes, to tell you the truth. I do mean Jackson." He began clumsily picking at the glitter again. His hands were large, thick-fingered, kind: perfect for throwing balls and petting dogs and pushing lawn mowers. Another difference between Ross and Jackson, she thought irrelevantly. Jackson's hands were just as large, but with long, elegant fingers, more finely tuned, as if they had been designed for precision tasks.

It was only natural, perhaps, for the two such different men to have trouble bonding.

"If it weren't for Jackson, I honestly think I could make some headway with the kid. When we're together at soccer practice, we work well together. He doesn't really hate me, you know. He just pretends to sometimes, because Jackson does."

She shook her head. "You can't mean that. Jackson doesn't *hate* you."

He raised his eyebrows eloquently and tucked one corner of his mouth in wryly. "He doesn't?"

"Well, why would he? What did you ever do to him? Hatred is an awfully strong emotion."

"So is jealousy," Ross said concisely. "One can lead to the other pretty easily."

That stopped her. For a moment she wondered whether she really wanted to press on with this. She had no right, of course, to pry into Ross's affairs. And in spite of their years of friendship, she didn't have the right to dig for any of Jackson's secrets, either. She had no claim on him.

One kiss—that was all they'd ever shared. Just one kiss, which had probably meant less than nothing to him. It gave her no rights at all.

Still, for a quick, one-sided kiss, it had been strangely haunting. It had opened a door in her mind and offered her a glimpse of mysterious vistas beyond. She couldn't bring herself to pull the door shut again. She wanted to understand her feelings for him. She wanted to understand *him.*

And talking to Ross might help.

"I'm not sure I know what you mean," she said carefully. "Who is jealous? You or Jackson? And of what?"

"I know what you're thinking. Sure—*I'm* jealous of *him*. Look at him, for God's sake. He's ten years younger, and women swarm around him like the bugs around my patio light. And hell, you could fit my whole bank account into one corner of his checkbook. But that's not what I mean. Believe it or not, I'm pretty sure he's jealous of me, too. He's jealous of every hour I spend with Annie." He gave her a straight look. "And every second I spend with Tommy."

"But why?" She knew the old lawyer adage: never ask a question if you don't already know the answer. You might not like what you hear. But common sense wasn't in charge right now. "Is there some—" Oh, great. How was she going to put this? "Is their relationship—"

*Get the words out, Molly,* she ordered herself. It wasn't as if this hadn't occurred to Ross before. Anyone who had ever seen Jackson and Annie together must have entertained the possibility that they were more than friends.

"Is their relationship serious?"

"Serious?" Ross looked faintly amused. "Hell, what does *serious* mean to a man like Jackson Forrest?"

"Ross," she began.

He held up his glittering hands. "Sorry. I know, I know." He looked at her with something that closely resembled sympathy. "Look, Molly, I really do know what you're trying to ask here. I know what's worrying you. But what am I going to say?

What *can* I say? I'm not really the guy who ought to be answering these questions, am I?''

She took a deep breath. ''No,'' she said, ashamed. ''No, you're not.''

''So maybe you should just take the bull by the horns, huh? If you really want to know what's going on with Annie and Tommy and Jackson, maybe you ought to just ask the old bull himself.''

''You're absolutely right,'' she said. ''I'm sorry, Ross. Of course I'll do that. I'll ask Jackson.''

Ross grinned suddenly. He put his big hands on his knees and hoisted himself out of the awkward little chair.

''Great,'' he said. ''And hey—when you find out, would you please tell me?''

## CHAPTER TEN

THE MORNING PARLOR had always been Molly's favorite room at Everspring. Floor-to-ceiling windows took up most of three walls, and by 11:00 a.m. on a clear day the sun came pouring in like honey. It caught on the gold-toned fabrics, the gilt picture frames, the bronze vases full of yellow roses, until the whole space seemed alive with light.

Molly and Lavinia sat in the parlor now, having coffee and discussing the day's landscaping chores. As usual, they were arguing. Molly had long since discovered that Lavinia loved to argue.

"I wish I'd never asked you to do the park project," Lavinia grumbled as she bit into a buttered croissant. "I want you to stay at the house today and supervise the pruning. Bad pruning will ruin everything, you know."

Molly leaned back and, closing her eyes, enjoyed the feel of the spring sunshine beating down on her hair. "I know," she said calmly. "But no one is going to do any bad pruning." She peeked at Lavinia, who was still chewing. "Mel, the person I'm leaving in charge of it, is an absolute magician with a pair of shears."

"But suppose I get a yen to do some pruning

myself," Lavinia said mischievously. "If you're over at the park, who'll be here to stop me?"

"Did I mention that Mel the magician weighs three hundred pounds?"

Lavinia pursed her lips. "But, Molly, I think I've found an old map of the gardens from 1799, and I was hoping we could look over it together. Why do you have to be at the park?"

Molly sat up and gave the older woman her sternest stare. "Because we're only two weeks away from the park dedication—and we've got two and a half weeks of work left. Because they're erecting the pavilion today, and I want to be sure they don't trample the azaleas. Because I've got a bunch of newbies planting the ornamentals, and I don't trust them to do it right. Because the fountain is still splashing all over the roses, and we'll end up with mildew everywhere if I can't get it fixed."

Lavinia twitched irritably, but Molly went on. "Besides, if we start tearing up our plans now, just because you've found another historical map, the gardens won't be ready for the Tour of Homes, which is also in only two weeks." She raised her eyebrows. "Is that enough reason for you?"

"Oh, all right. You don't have to get an attitude about it." Lavinia sipped her coffee peacefully. One of her nicest qualities was that she never minded losing her arguments. "You young people always adopt such annoying attitudes. Do you know I still can't get Jackson to agree to make the dedication speech? I don't know what's wrong with that boy."

Molly had been wondering about that, but she'd

been reluctant to bring it up. Since the day at the park, when Lavinia had first broached the subject, she hadn't heard anyone mention it. She had just assumed that Lavinia had prevailed, as she so often did. Molly found it hard to imagine Jackson denying his aunt much of anything.

"What reason does he give for refusing? Is it some kind of scheduling conflict?"

Lavinia shook her head. "No, it's some kind of bullheaded stubbornness." She put down her cup and looked out the window at the Ballerina roses that stood in white clay planters all over the patio.

She suddenly looked tired, though it was not yet eight o'clock. Molly could tell that she wasn't teasing anymore. Jackson's refusal really bothered her.

"But why?" Molly was perplexed. "Surely he's the natural choice, as Beau's twin. No one knew Beau better than Jackson. As you pointed out when you asked him, no one *loved* Beau more."

Lavinia kept staring out into the garden. "Maybe," she said pensively, "that's the problem."

Molly frowned. "What on earth does that mean?"

The older woman turned, and her gaze was still cloudy and contemplative, her thoughts still tuned to some deep internal frequency.

"It means that maybe Jackson hasn't really come to terms with his brother's death yet. Maybe he doesn't want to get up in front of the whole town and talk about it, because he still feels too guilty."

Molly leaned forward. "Guilty? But that's ridiculous!"

Lavinia smiled. "The fact that something is ridiculous hasn't ever kept it from being true." She twisted her no-nonsense pearl stud earring thoughtfully. "I also suspect he's still too angry with Beau over the accident. Beau was driving like a maniac, you know. Almost a hundred miles an hour, the police said. He could have killed them both, but instead he left Jackson behind, to carry all the guilt alone."

Molly didn't know how to respond. Though the logic was obviously flawed, still she could see a basic human truth in Lavinia's analysis. That didn't surprise her. She had always known that Lavinia was wise about people. She used to think it came from studying family history so much. Lavinia had seen it all, one way or another, on the page or in the flesh.

"Okay," Molly said, accepting the premise for the moment. "If that is true, why try to make him do it? Why not just find someone else?"

"Because it would be good for him," Lavinia answered flatly. She gave her shoulders a small shake, as if throwing off the cobwebs of such an unusually long bout with introspection. "He needs to face down the past and get it over with. Everyone should do that occasionally, you know. Builds character. Clears the debris off the highway, so to speak. Then you can travel faster to your next life destination."

She reached for a lump of sugar. "Speaking of which... Did you decide to accept the offer those thieves made on your house or not?"

Molly didn't have any trouble following *that* little piece of logic. "I take it Jackson told you how low it was. No, I didn't accept. I made a counteroffer, but the buyers weren't interested."

She bit her lower lip, remembering the ambivalence she'd felt when she realized she'd lost her first and only chance to unload the house. "I guess Jackson is right. If I want to get even a fraction of what it's worth, I may have to make some improvements."

"Doesn't sound like a bad idea," Lavinia, said, nodding slowly. "One of our ministers used to say that a person should always try to leave a place a little nicer than he found it. It's good for the spirit. And besides—"

Molly smiled. "It'll clear some of the debris off the highway?"

"You always were a smart little thing." Lavinia reached over and gave her hand a warm squeeze. "But actually I was just going to say it will be nice to have you around a while longer. We've missed you. You've been gone far too long."

They both looked up as a low rap sounded on the French doors that led to the family garden in back. Through the sparkling panes, they could see that a slim young woman in dungarees and a baseball cap stood on the brick patio, looking intensely worried.

"Mel!" Molly stood and hurried to meet her employee. Mel wasn't ever exactly a barrel of laughs, but that expression was grimmer than usual.

Lavinia snorted behind her. "That's Mel the three-hundred-pound magician? My, my, I'd like to have her diet secrets."

Ignoring Lavinia's babbling, Molly opened the

French doors. "Mel? What is it? Is everything okay?"

"No, ma'am, it sure isn't," the young woman responded, her head shaking like a metronome set for a funeral dirge. "You'd better come on down. The azaleas are here, and I'd say we're in a heap of trouble."


LIZA GOT HOME from school early, because Jackson had picked her and Tommy up right after class. She loved it when that happened. She could feel the other kids, the ones waiting in line for the school bus, watching them walk to the parking lot. She hoped maybe some of the kids thought Jackson was her father. They were both blond and kind of tall, so maybe it didn't seem impossible.

And even better, Jackson had an adventure planned. He was going to take them to the airport. He had to charter a flight to New York for tomorrow, he said, and if they went along he would let them sit in one of the planes, right where his pilot friend usually sat.

She was so excited she didn't even think about the Planet Cuspian once on the whole ride home. Today, Planet Earth seemed even cooler.

But as soon as she saw her mother, her hopes flickered. Her mom was upset. Molly was standing out in the Everspring garden, talking on the cell phone in that very stiff, very quiet way she did when she was really, really mad. It was almost as if she were afraid to talk above a whisper, for fear she might start yelling and not be able to stop.

"There is *no* adequate excuse for sending plants in that condition," her mother was saying as they walked up. Her voice was so cold that Liza instinctively felt kind of sorry for the person on the other end. "And if your plants have infected even one blade of grass here at Everspring, you can be sure we'll be sending you a bill for treatment."

After a couple more minutes of talk like that—during which Liza, Tommy and Jackson all exchanged awkward glances—her mother hung up. She stared at the telephone sadly, her anger seemingly all spent.

Instinctively, Liza went up and put her arms tightly around her mother. When things were bad, everybody needed a hug, even moms.

"What's wrong, M?" Jackson's voice was the talking equivalent of a hug, and Liza was glad he was the kind of man who would understand. He really was the perfect King Willowsong, she thought, leaning her head against her mother's arm. Had her mom noticed that? "Did someone send you some bad plants?"

"It's the azaleas and the rhododendrons for the west drifts," Molly answered, and her voice sounded kind of numb. "Two hundred of them. All diseased. I couldn't even let them off the trucks."

"Wow." Jackson groaned sympathetically. "What a disaster."

Even Tommy looked impressed. "Two hundred sick flowers? And they could have given it to the other flowers, too? It's like the plague, like in history class. What did they have? Was it gross?"

"What *didn't* they have?" Molly ran her hand over her forehead, as if she couldn't believe the information herself. "Whiteflies, spider mites, leaf gall—"

"Thrips?" Liza remembered once when some plants got thrips at her mom's business in Atlanta. She remembered because the word was so funny.

*"Thrips?"* Tommy repeated it incredulously, and Liza could see he was about to break into laughter. She gave him a look that said, "Don't."

Luckily he understood. "Oh, that would be bad, huh? Thrips?"

"That would be bad." Jackson had his hand on Tommy's head, probably warning him not to laugh, too. Jackson was so smart about things, Liza thought. Things always went better when he was around.

He turned to Molly. "Where does that leave the landscaping, M? Can you get replacements?"

"I don't see how," she said wearily. "With the Tour of Homes coming up, every house around here is sprucing up, and the nurseries are depleted. That's why I used these people to begin with. Ordinarily I avoid them because they run a shoddy operation. But I needed so many. I was desperate."

She took a deep breath and for the first time seemed to realize that it was odd for all three of them to be standing together in the garden a full half an hour before the bus usually arrived.

"I'm sorry," she said, summoning a smile that didn't look quite natural. "I was so wrapped up in my little melodrama that I didn't even think. What's up? How'd you get home so quickly? Is everything okay?''

"Jackson was going to take us to the airport to look at the planes," Liza said, trying to hide her eagerness just like her mom was trying to hide her frustration. ''But don't worry, I won't go if you need me here.'' She swallowed hard. ''Jackson and Tommy can still go. But I'll stay here if you need me.''

For just a moment, her mother's eyes met Jackson's eyes, and something soft passed between them, something that felt very Willowsong, even though Liza only half saw it. She suddenly felt happy again, in spite of the thrips.

Her mom ruffled her hair. ''Let's see. If you stayed here, sweetheart, could you make two hundred azaleas magically appear?''

Liza smiled up at her mother. ''No. I bet there are two *million* flowers on the Planet Cuspian, but I don't think that's going to help you much.''

Her mom's answering smile looked more natural. 'Well, then I guess I don't need you to stay. You go ahead with Jackson and have fun.''

Liza took her mom's hand. ''Are you sure?''

"I'm sure. And don't worry, sweetheart. Things will work out about the flowers, I promise.''

''Actually, Liza, I think your mom's right,'' Jackson said. He had a twinkle in his eye that Liza loved. She was going to try to draw that in King Willowsong's eye the next time. ''I think everything really *is* going to be fine. Tell me, M, what are you doing just before dawn tomorrow?''

Molly laughed. "Stealing azaleas off your neighbors' lawns?"

Jackson shook his head. "No, I think you're going to be with me. I've got a plan."

"I don't need a plan, Jackson," Molly said, sighing as she scanned the empty yards of naked beds. "I need a miracle."

"No problem." He grinned. "I've got one of those, too."

THEY HAD BEEN DRIVING for half an hour, and the whole time Jackson had refused to tell her where they were going. They were heading east, she knew that. The most dazzling sunrise she'd ever seen was unfolding itself in front of them. Small, puffy clouds, tinted a dozen shades of red and pink, jumbled together like an overstuffed bouquet—like a sky full of the azaleas she couldn't find.

The beauty of it almost distracted her from her worries, which had kept her up half the night, trying to figure out alternatives to her original design. There were always alternatives. The worst was that Lavinia would be terribly disappointed. Lavinia adored azaleas, and would happily wait all year for their few weeks of glorious bloom.

It wasn't until Jackson made one sharp left turn, away from the sky show, that Molly even realized they had arrived at Blossom Hill Nurseries.

Her heart fell. She had already tried Blossom Hill Nurseries. Like everyone else, they didn't have a single flowering shrub of any description left in their inventory.

"Oh, Jackson," she said mournfully, as sorry for him as she was for herself or Lavinia. He had seemed so excited about his "miracle."

"Is this where we're heading? I should have told you—I called them weeks ago. They're completely out."

His smile didn't fade a single millimeter. "Really?" He pulled the car into the empty parking lot and shut off the engine. "I guess you must have forgotten to say the magic word."

"What?" She nudged his elbow. "I resent that. I *always* say *please*."

"I'm sure you do." He looked smug as he disengaged his seat belt. "But in this particular case, the magic word is *Virginia*."

She shook her head, confused. "Virginia?"

"Well, I suppose *Kentucky* would have done. Or *Delaware*. You just needed another state. And of course, it helps to add the words *overnight express*."

She stared at him, not quite believing her ears. "You had the plants shipped here overnight?" She glanced at the quiet nursery incredulously, then looked back at him. "Impossible. Or almost impossible. I'll bet you had to throw in a couple of other words, too. Like *unbelievably expensive?*"

He tssked disapprovingly. "You know, Molly, when you're given a gift-wrapped miracle, it's tacky to look at the price tag."

She bit her lower lip. "It's just that I can hardly believe—" She touched his sleeve. "Are you serious? You really had two hundred plants shipped here from Virginia?"

"Two hundred and fifty, actually. I thought you needed a cushion." He grinned. "You know, in case a couple of them had a galloping case of thrips."

Molly tightened her grip on his forearm. "Hey, don't think I didn't see you guys out there yesterday, laughing about the thrips. I'll have you know, mister, that having thrips is not funny."

His grin broadened shamelessly. "Sure it is, M. Hear it? *Thrips.*" He put his hand on the door handle. "But are we going to go in and pick out some plants or not?"

She didn't let go of his arm, but with her free hand she gestured toward the darkened building with its silent acres of greenery stretching out behind. "It's not even open."

"It is for us." He dangled a single gold key toward her. "My misspent youth has finally paid off. I just happen to be old drinking buddies with the owner."

And somehow the sight of that silly little key finally convinced her that he wasn't joking. "Jackson," she said, leaning toward him, her hand softening on his arm. "What can I say? How can I thank—"

He put his two fingers gently over her lips. "Shhh," he said with a smile. "Come on. Let's go buy some flowers."

*Let's go buy some flowers....* What an understatement that sentence turned out to be.

When they entered the nursery, it was like walking into the sweetest scented fairyland she had ever imagined. The Planet Cuspian couldn't be more magical, she thought, staring at the long tables of velvety African violets and deep-blue pansies, the hanging baskets of shyly blooming lily of the valley, the long lines of potted phlox in all colors of the rainbow.

Perhaps it was just the dusty streams of dawn-pink light that made everything seem so perfect. Or perhaps it as the eerie knowledge that they were the only humans here in this world of silently growing things.

Or perhaps it was simply the sweet awareness that Jackson had worked a little miracle—and he had done it just to make her happy.

But, whatever the reason, even Molly, who worked every day with plants, who combed nurseries daily searching for merchandise, was moved by the extraordinary loveliness of this place.

"Come on," Jackson said. "Our plants are out back."

She was surprised to hear him speak in a normal voice. She had half expected him to whisper, as if she were in church. "Okay," she answered softly. "Lead the way."

He walked briskly through the narrow aisles. Occasionally his broad shoulders would brush an overhanging blossom, and the gentle perfume he released would float toward her. Now and then she fell behind, unable to pass some particularly beautiful daffodil without pressing a finger to its golden throat.

He would turn, arch an eyebrow at her, and she would begin moving again, guiltily aware that he was on a deadline. He had told her that his charter plane was due to take off from Demery's executive airport in only a couple of hours.

The plants he had ordered for Everspring were massed just outside the main building. It was an impressive sight; dozens of ten-gallon containers of rhododendrons that were just beginning to bud, and dozens more of azaleas that were already bursting into color.

She scanned, making a quick mental inventory. Pink Countess of Derby for a large drift just outside the carriage house. Lavender Grandiflorum, which would grow as tall as a tree, to frame the back door. Small, purple Besse Howells, which would always hug the ground, to border the brick steps leading down to the fountain.

They were gorgeous. They were everything the rejected plants had not been: thick, healthy, glossy and heavy with buds.

Jackson leaned patiently against the wall, watching with a smile as she examined them carefully. It was slow, but she was glad he didn't mind, because she loved this work. She loved feathering her fingers through the leaves, looking for tiny signs that could mean big trouble later.

Were there any small, watery brown spots on any of the blooms that had already appeared—the dreaded petal blight? Mildew, fungus? Or, God forbid, whiteflies? Leaves that were too small, too yellow, too curled in on themselves, or gnawed by bugs?

But, one after another, she found that the plants were fine.

Finally she stood, rubbing the small of her back to ease the burning from so much bending and squatting.

"I can't believe how perfect everything is," she said, suddenly overwhelmed by that very perfection. "It *is* a miracle. How could you have known exactly what I had ordered without looking at my plans?"

"That was the easy part. I called the other nursery, the shoddy one. They faxed me a list."

He made it all seem so simple. Just as he always did... She brushed her hands against her jeans and walked over to him.

"Thank you, Jackson." She placed a kiss on his cheek. "Thank you so much."

Still standing in front of him, she turned to admire the plants one more time. She reached back, asking for his hands, and when he put them in hers, she wrapped his arms around her waist comfortably and leaned against him.

They had stood this way a hundred times, back in the old days. Often, huddling on the sidelines of the football field watching Beau loft flawless passes, Jackson had sheltered her from the autumn winds just like this. His girlfriends had frequently complained—lusting powerfully after Jackson themselves, they had been skeptical that any female could really love him only as a brother. But Jackson had never given any girl the right to dictate his behavior. They all knew they had to back off or lose him completely.

"Look," Molly said contentedly, looking at the sea of greenery through half-closed lids. "Look how beautiful they are."

"Nice plants," he said blandly. He blew teasingly into her hair. "You're cute when you're overreacting, did I ever tell you that?"

She tilted a look at him over her shoulder. The rising sun was behind him, creating a nimbus around his hair. She caught a glimpse of his smiling eyes, so mocking and yet so gentle.

"You know, as we were driving here, I remembered something," she said. "Something you did a long time ago."

He groaned. "Lord. Can a man never outlive his sins?"

She patted his hand reassuringly. "This wasn't a sin, silly. I'm much too polite to bring those up right now." She smiled, turning her head toward the plants again. "It was just a little thing—you probably don't even remember it. It happened when I was about fifteen. Beau and I had just started dating. He was supposed to pick me up after school, but he forgot. I waited there almost an hour, and I was getting nervous, because I knew I was going to be in trouble at home. And then you came."

He shifted, as if to dismiss any impending compliments, but she went on in spite of his obvious reluctance to be cast as a hero.

"It wasn't the first time you saved me," she said, choosing her words carefully, "and it certainly wasn't the last."

She could feel him shaking his head behind her.

"You never needed me for that, M. You were always capable of saving yourself. Even from the dreaded thrips." She knew that sound—she knew that a one-sided smile was tugging at his lips. "I'll bet you even had a backup plan for the landscaping, didn't you? You're just carrying on about this to humor me."

"Don't change the subject." She squeezed his hands reprovingly, pressing them against her stomach. "I have an important point to make." She took a deep breath. "Ever since I've come back home, I've been seeing things so much more clearly. Things about Beau, I mean. And I've realized that I never really noticed how careless Beau was. Careless with me, with my feelings. And do you know why I didn't notice?"

His hands twitched almost imperceptibly. "Because you were crazy in love with him and blind as a newborn?"

"No." She shook her head. "I didn't notice it because of you. Because you were always there to keep his promises for him."

"Molly," he said stiffly. "Molly, that's nonsense."

"Don't worry, I'm not going to 'carry on' about it," she promised, leaning her head back against his shoulder. "I just wanted to say thank you. Thanks for looking out for me. Today, and all those days so long ago."

He took a long time answering. And in that space of time, with her body resting against the safe wall of his chest, she became acutely aware of the world waking up around them.

Only a few feet away, in one of the sweet olive trees, a mockingbird had begun an erratic, piercing song. On the highway that ran alongside the nursery, the trickle of traffic had thickened into a steady flow of groaning motion. And somewhere completely unseen a nursery worker must have arrived. Someone was digging rhythmically, shovel pounding against earth with a steady vibration that Molly felt in her veins.

Even her senses were waking up. Suddenly she could smell the sweet sunshine of Jackson's crisp cotton shirt, which had been line-dried in the kitchen garden at Everspring. She could feel the warmth of his skin through the shirt. If she held her breath, she could even sense the steady beat of his heart against her shoulder blades. Instinctively she pressed back, just a little, so that the rhythm was clearer.

When she began again to breathe, her lungs felt tight, as if she couldn't quite get enough air. She tingled strangely all over, especially where her body met his. She felt like one of the buds on those azalea bushes herself—folded tightly in a cocoon of green, but swollen and strangely expectant, ready at the slightest touch to burst into rich, flagrant color.

And suddenly she understood that she no longer saw Jackson as anyone's brother. Especially not her own.

"I've been wanting to tell you something else, too," she said carefully. "When I kissed you the other day…"

"Yes?"

She took a shallow breath. "It was wonderful," she admitted. "I haven't been able to stop thinking about it."

"Really?" She felt his breath warm against her hair. His arms tightened around her, and his hands began to move on her stomach, making slow circles with his fingers. "What do you think about, M?"

Her body responded instantly, and it became even more difficult to breathe. "I think about you," she said shallowly, closing her eyes as his thumbs drifted up toward her rib cage. "About how you tasted. About how you made me feel."

His hands kept moving, slowly, confidently, until they grazed her breasts. She made a small sound and let a wave of rippling shivers wash over her.

And suddenly, from somewhere deep inside the nursery, someone flicked a switch. Just above the flower-laden tables beside them, a long silver system of pipes bubbled and hissed. She watched, mesmerized, as the pipes finally erupted, shooting cool, clear water over a thousand thirsty plants.

Within seconds, the air was filled with moisture. Rainbows and sunlight danced in the misty spray. The morning breeze carried it the few feet toward them, and she felt her face growing damp. She looked down, and his tanned hands sparkled with the mist.

"And how do I make you feel, Molly?" As if he hadn't even noticed the sprinklers, he unbuttoned her wet shirt slowly and slipped his damp fingers inside.

She couldn't answer him then. The water was cold, but his fingers were hot, and they moved slickly over her. Her lips opened slightly, letting the mist find its way in, tiny, cool needles of moisture against her tongue.

"How, Molly? How do I make you feel?" He whispered the words against her neck. But she didn't remember words. Oh, she had been right about his hands—they were designed for precision. Deftly, delicately, his fingers turning and touching with easy authority, he brought her to a trembling spike of desire.

"Jackson." She put her hands up. She touched his wet, silken hair. She pressed back, looking for more. And she found it. His familiar, comfortable body was newly contoured, carved hard and powerful with desire. He pressed, too, and she moaned in the mist.

"Oh, my heavens. I didn't know anyone was in here!" The voice behind them seemed to come from another world. There was an awkward, scurrying bustle, and suddenly the world stopped dancing with rainbowed mist. The sprinklers subsided. And within seconds, only the slow, hollow plopping of the last drops of water remained.

Somehow, in those crazy seconds, Jackson had managed to button up Molly's shirt. He moved away smoothly and greeted the newcomer.

"Hi," he was saying with complete aplomb, apparently unfazed by the fact that his shirt was plastered to his chest and his hair shone wetly in the sunlight. "I'm sorry. I'm Jackson Forrest. Brad ordered some plants for us, and we've come to collect them.''

The small, tidy woman still looked distressed. ''I wouldn't ever have turned on the irrigation system if I'd known you were out here. I'm so sorry.''

Jackson reassured her, and finally Molly gathered her wits enough to turn around and give the woman a smile, too. ''Hi,'' she said politely. ''Don't worry. We're fine.''

''Oh, my dear, you're soaked!'' The woman reached behind the main counter and pulled out a soft cotton rag. ''Here, this may help dry you off a little.''

While Molly dabbed at her face with the rag, and the woman kept repeating her abject apologies, Jackson calmly explained that their trucks would be arriving soon for the plants. He gave her the key, and finally his gentle assurances seemed to soothe her embarrassed misery.

She turned to Molly, who hoped she was looking a little more presentable now, thanks to the miraculously absorbent rag. ''Let me make it up to you, dear,'' the little lady said somberly. ''I know! Won't you take a flower home? We've a great many lovely things here, as you can see.''

''Yes,'' Molly said, ''you have a magnificent selection, but really there's no need—''

''Please,'' the woman urged. ''It would make me feel much better. And Brad would want you to go away happy.''

Molly flushed, and somehow managed not to look at Jackson. ''All right. Thank you,'' she said, glancing around. "Actually, it would be nice to have some memento of your beautiful nursery, and the lovely time we spent here."

But what? Out of these thousands of exquisite flowers, which one would best symbolize the burgeoning excitement, the sensual awakening, the pure misty romance of it all?

Of course. An orchid. One small display of pink and purple orchids stood on the corner of the table nearest to Molly. She moved toward it as if led by a thread.

"How about this one?" She touched a small cattlyea, not the most expensive by far, but the one that seemed to call to her. So strangely delicate it didn't seem real. So fragrant, so blatantly sensual that it made her tingle all over again. "I've always loved orchids. Somehow they've always symbolized romance to me."

She looked up. The woman was smiling, delighted with the choice. But Jackson's face was blank. Completely, alarmingly empty.

Molly felt the blood rush out of her. She had done something wrong. Something terribly wrong. She looked at the orchid, then back at Jackson. What was it? Had he not wanted her to accept a gift?

"You know," he said with an equal emptiness in his voice. "We've taken somewhat longer here than I had expected, and I'm in danger of missing my flight. Would you mind driving the car home by yourself, Molly? I think I'd better just take a cab straight to the airport."

"Oh, dear, I'll call one right away," the woman

said, still eager to atone for her earlier mistake. She picked up the telephone and began to punch buttons.

"Thank you." Jackson turned back to Molly. "You're all right, then? You can find your way home?"

"Of course," she answered numbly. "But I had hoped—"

"After all, it's not as if you'll really be alone," he observed pleasantly. "You'll have your orchid. And, as always, you'll have your memories of Beau."

# CHAPTER ELEVEN

"LEAVE IT ALONE, LAVINIA." Jackson was too damn tired to have this argument now. His charter from New York had touched down less than an hour ago, and he was halfway up the stairs, still lugging his garment bag over his shoulder. It was nearly one in the morning, and he just wanted to go to bed. "You don't understand."

"Well, of course I don't understand," Lavinia retorted somewhat acerbically. She stood at the bottom of the stairs, her hand on the newel post as she looked up at him. "That's because you refuse to explain it to me."

Only ten more stairs. If he had just climbed a little faster, he could have reached the peace and quiet of his bedroom before she waylaid him. But he'd been movingly slowly, physically exhausted from the nonstop meetings of the past two days. And mentally exhausted, too, from wrestling with himself about Molly.

Wrestling with himself—and losing.

Much as he wanted to think he and Molly could someday make it work, he'd finally accepted that it was impossible. Yes, there was a physical attraction, but that wasn't enough. The lines between the past and the present, between truth and lie, between memory and reality, were all too hopelessly tangled.

In the end, it didn't even matter how much he cared about her. He was the one man she could never really love—because he was the one man who couldn't ever really exist for her. He would always live in her mind merely in some distorted relation to Beau.

His kisses would either be comfortingly like Beau's, or they would be strangely different from Beau's. His voice, his laugh, his touch—the true north on her compass would always be Beau, and Jackson would be only some deviation, for the better or the worse, from that point.

But it wasn't until she picked up that orchid, cradled it reverently in her hand, that he had realized how hopeless the situation really was. How entwined the two brothers would always be in her psyche.

Just moments before, Jackson had held her. He had put his hands on her skin, as he had dreamed of doing a thousand restless nights. Hell, he had come within a sinful inch of making love to her among the drenched flowers.

And, then, when invited to choose a memento of that occasion, she had picked the orchid, the symbol of Beau's love. The flower Beau had pinned to her heart a dozen times, including the last night of his life.

"Well?" Lavinia sounded irritated, and he realized he must have been losing track of the conversation. "Explain it to me."

"Vinnie," he said as calmly as he could. "I have explained it. You've just refused to listen."

"I'm old." She stood there, implacable and unmoving. "I'm senile. Tell me again."

He shifted the garment bag to a more comfortable spot on his shoulder. Who would have thought that one suit, three shirts and a razor could weigh so much? Who would have thought one little trip to check out a building site could leave him so depleted?

"I don't suppose you'd consider postponing this nag-a-thon until the morning?"

"No," she stated flatly. "I wouldn't."

"All right. One more time." He draped the garment bag over the stair rail. "Though I'm delighted that you've decided to donate land to the city for a community park, I have never liked the idea of naming it after Beau. And because I don't think it's a good idea, I refuse to participate in it."

Lavinia waved that away with one flash of her hand. "Your education cost your mother a fortune. Looks to me as if she could just as well have thrown that money into the compost heap. Don't they teach any logic classes at Yale? 'I don't want to because I don't want to' is just about the simplest example of circular logic I've ever heard."

"You don't want me to be more specific," he said through a clenched jaw. "I'm too damn tired to be diplomatic."

"Good," she said, settling herself on the bottom step. "Maybe for once I'll hear the truth, then. Forget diplomacy. Tell me why don't you think we should name the park in Beau's memory.''

"Damn it, Vinnie." Why couldn't all this remain unspoken? He didn't want to articulate this. He didn't even want to think about it. "Grace Pickens said it about as well as it can be said, don't you think? You're erecting the Saint Beaumont memorial pavilion. You say I knew him better than anyone else in the world. Well, you're right—I did. And one thing I know, goddamn it, is that he was no saint."

"Of course he wasn't, dear." Lavinia didn't look disturbed by his profanity—or by his pronouncement. "But no one is, at least no one I know. Luckily, you don't have to be a saint to be loved. You don't have to be a saint to be missed. You don't even have to be a saint to be honored in such a way."

She met his gaze squarely. "If we had lost you that day, Jackson, instead of Beau, we would be building the pavilion just the same."

He sighed, exasperated. "Is that what you think this is about, Vinnie? You think I'm just jealous of Beau?"

"I don't know," she said. "Is it? Are you?"

"No. Damn it, no." He came down the steps slowly and sat wearily on the tread just above her. "Look, I'll admit it was difficult at first, knowing that everyone was saying that, in a just world, the good brother would have lived, while the bad brother—"

Lavinia looked at him unflinchingly. "Not everyone," she corrected matter-of-factly.

"Hell, I even felt that way myself," he said, ignoring her. "I lay there in that godforsaken hospital bed for two solid months, wishing I could trade places with him. But at the end of the two months, I was still alive. And Beau was still dead. So I learned to deal with it."

"All right." Lavinia folded her hands in her lap patiently. "And? I'm not sure your logic is getting any clearer, dear. You learned to deal with it... and?"

Her tone broke through the last of his reserve. Maybe she was right. Maybe he wasn't making sense. But it was complicated—layered with secrets he couldn't tell, secrets that weren't his to tell. But the secrets couldn't stay hidden forever. Already they were taking shape, a visible, undeniable human form that no one could ignore forever.

Demery loved a scandal, and setting Beau up as the town hero would guarantee that any scandal about *him*—or about his surviving twin brother— would be the biggest, juiciest story of all. A great many innocent people would suffer.

"Jackson? Help me out here. You learned to deal with it...and?"

Why couldn't she just let him be? He was tired, and he was angry and he was sick of the whole subject.

"And I guess I just think the rest of the world should learn to deal with it, too." He stood. "Get someone else to deliver your speech, Vinnie. Someone who still thinks Beau was perfect. Why don't you do it? Or get Molly—she's still completely bewitched." He rose quickly up the stairs and grabbed his garment bag roughly. "But you ought to accept that Beau's gone, damn it. He's dead. Erecting a shrine to him, either in the park or in your heart, won't bring him back."

Lavinia looked disgustingly smug, as if she'd been trying to make him say those very words all along. "Are you sure you're really talking to me, Jackson? Are you sure you're not talking to someone else?"

He shook his head, defeated. "Apparently," he said flatly, "I'm just talking to myself."

AFTER SCHOOL on Tuesday, Tommy and Liza spent two hours at Everspring, tracking Mudbluffs in the lower forty. Stewball helped, sometimes—when he wasn't being lazy.

Finally Tommy and Liza were tired, too. They joined Stewball on the sunny side of the riverbank and began eating the cookies Lavinia had given them.

Tommy glanced disgustedly at Stewball, who had collapsed in a heap and was snoring contentedly. "When I get a dog, I'm going to get a puppy," Tommy announced around a mouthful of gooey carrot-cookie. "Old dogs just want to sleep all the time."

Liza's eyes widened. "But my mom says people who live in apartments can't have pets. Is your mom really going to let you get a dog?"

"Sure she is." Tommy made a face at his cookie

and began crumbling up the rest for the birds. He didn't meet Liza's eyes. "Someday, anyhow."

"Oh." Liza settled back, disappointed. She knew what *someday* meant.

They sat in silence for a few minutes. Tommy had gathered a few small stones, and he was working at skipping them across the river. He was showing off, Liza knew. But he was pretty good at it.

Finally he consented to notice her again. "If you really were going to get a pet," he asked, "what kind would it be?"

Liza closed her eyes, which made it easier to see pretend things. She loved this kind of game. "It would be a big, white, furry dog. Snow-white. So big I could ride him. But very gentle. And I would call him Franics."

*"Francis?"* Tommy twisted his face. "You'd better get a girl dog, then. Francis! Yuck."

"I like Francis. I read it in a story." Liza refused to speak for a few seconds, but she wasn't very good at staying mad, so in a minute she asked him, "What about you? What kind of dog would you—I mean, *are* you going to get?"

"A collie," he said promptly. It was obvious he'd thought about this a lot. "They're very smart. But I darn sure won't call him a sissy name like Francis."

Liza tossed a bit of her cookie at him. "No, you'll probably call him something stupid and mean, like Killer. Or Fang."

"Probably." Tommy lay back, closing his eyes against the sun. "And I'll train him to keep all girls away."

Liza made a small harrumphing sound. "That won't be very hard. Girls hate mean dogs named Fang and they hate dumb, stuck-up boys named Tommy, too."

Without opening his eyes, Tommy chuckled. "Whatever. Now what about a house? If you could live anywhere you wanted, what house would you buy?"

She was glad he wasn't watching, because she couldn't keep her gaze from drifting back toward Everspring. The plantation was the most beautiful home she had ever seen, and she loved it here, loved it fiercely. It was the only place on earth that made her feel as happy as the Planet Cuspian did.

But she knew Tommy would make terrible fun of her if he knew she dreamed of staying here. So she crossed her fingers and lied.

"Maybe a little house like the one my mother grew up in. And I'd plant Ballerina roses everywhere. That's what Aunt Lavinia has on the side patio. Don't they have the most beautiful name?" She repeated it with feeling. "Ballerina roses."

"Not me! I'd have a big four-story house," Tommy said. "Like Junior Caldwell's, only bigger. And I'd have one whole giant room just for video games and TVs and stuff."

"Cool," Liza agreed, though she mentally added Ballerina roses to that picture. She lay back, then, too, and stared into the afternoon sky, which was loaded down with clouds. From this angle, it was easy to imagine herself flying up there, in the clouds.

"And what if you just absolutely *had* to have a

father?'' Tommy was chewing on a straw of grass, and his voice was all fakey bored, like he didn't care about the question at all. ''Who would you want?''

She closed her eyes and pictured King Willowsong. ''I would want my real father, of course.''

Tommy shifted on the grass, as if he were annoyed that she didn't know how to play the game. ''Well, if he's actually dead, you can't have him. So say someone else.''

''I don't know,'' she said nervously. He might not like her answer. He might think she was trespassing on his territory. ''I'm not sure. Maybe Jackson.'' She rolled over on her side and looked at Tommy, hoping he wasn't mad. ''How about you? Who would you want?''

''You mean if I *had* to have a father?'' He didn't look mad, but he gave her a tense look, as if daring her to misunderstand this conversation. ''Because dads are a pain in the butt. I'd a whole lot rather not have anyone bossing me around at all.''

She nodded. ''Right. I mean if you had to.'' She threaded her fingers together. ''Would it be Coach Riser?''

''I don't know.'' He tossed his blade of grass aside. ''He might be all right. Or I guess I could stand Jackson.''

She felt a ridiculous panic, as if this silly game were going to decide something important. ''But that's not really fair,'' she said carefully. ''I mean, you could have either one of them. They both like you a lot. But Coach Riser would never take me, because I'm a girl, and I can't play soccer or football with him. Jackson is the only one who might ever want to be my dad.''

Tommy raised himself up on one elbow. ''Do you really think Coach Riser likes me that much?''

She nodded. ''I know he does.''

Tommy smiled, and it looked like a really happy smile. But then he caught himself and went back to being cool. ''Oh, you just want me to take Coach Riser so you can have Jackson.''

She shrugged, hoping she didn't look too pitiful. ''It's just—that's really the only way it would work, don't you think?''

He watched her for a long time. About a million thoughts seemed to be going through his mind.

''Okay, then,'' he said at length. ''I guess you can have Jackson.''

She looked down at her hands. ''Thanks,'' she said. ''I mean—I know we're just goofing, but...''

''Hey,'' he interrupted, jumping to his feet. ''I've got an idea! Let's go to the crook in the river. I know a place that we can pretend is King Willowsong's ice cave.''

She looked up, grateful that he had changed the subject. Talking like that had been kind of confusing, and strangely sad.

''Okay,'' she said, climbing up. ''That sounds great.''

Rousing Stewball, Tommy darted off immediately, going much faster than she could hope to follow. After a minute, he came back and walked more slowly.

''And look, don't worry about that father thing,''

he said casually. "Coach Riser doesn't really stink, I guess. Although, like I said, all dads are a royal pain in the butt."

WITH AN EXHAUSTED sense of satisfaction, Molly packed the earth down around the last of the abelia she had chosen as a border plant for the park pavilion.

Beau's pavilion was finally finished—and it was huge. It had taken fifty abelias to surround it. The plants weren't very impressive right now, just a thick, glossy ribbon of green around the lovely white pavilion. But just wait until June—the shrubs would be covered in a soft blanket of small white flowers. By then the azaleas, which always occupied center stage in spring, would have faded, and the abelia would take the spotlight.

Not that she would be here to see it. She and Liza would be long gone by then, back in Atlanta, designing the other gardens, other parks. But summer would come to Demery whether Molly was here or not. The abelia would bloom according to the dictates of the seasons, not the desires of her heart.

Though it was almost six, time to go home, she knelt there at the last plant, too tired to stand. As she always did when she was unhappy, she had worked herself to death these past few days. She had forced thoughts of Jackson out of her mind, replacing them with thoughts of site measurements and grids and sketches, brick walkways, iron fences, truck schedules, fertilizer formulas and a thousand wholesale orders. She had planted, transplanted, pinched and pruned, until both the Everspring garden and the city park had begun to take on their final shape.

But now, with the bulk of the work done, it was harder to keep from thinking about him. Hard not to remember his kisses and his hands. Hard not to lament what a fool she had been, choosing that small purple orchid at the last, disastrous moment.

It had taken her a ridiculously long time to figure out what she had done wrong. Jackson had already sped off in his taxi, rushing to make his plane. And she was in his purring Thunderbird, heading back toward Everspring with the orchid propped beside her on the passenger seat. It was a spunky little plant, giving off perfume enough to fill the whole car.

It was the scent that finally made her understand. Whenever their date called for formality, Beau had always given her an orchid corsage. Always. The orchid scent was the perfume she associated with Beau to this day.

And Jackson knew it.

Subconsciously, at that critical moment in the nursery, she had been thinking of Beau. Jackson knew that, too.

It had been stupid of her, and inadvertently insulting. Somehow she had to make Jackson forgive her. She needed to make him understand. She had for so long associated sex, love and romance all with Beau—it would take a while to reroute such a deeply ingrained emotional pattern.

But she was ready to begin. She was ready to try.

When Jackson had touched her that day, it was the first time she had ever felt true, overwhelming desire for anyone but Beau. It was the first time she hadn't wanted to pull away, to retreat into her memories.

It was a beginning. Could Jackson settle for that, at least for now?

But, deep in her heart, she knew he wouldn't. Jackson had never been the kind of man who settled. And that was why she had been burying herself in work, pruning thoughts of him from her mind while she pruned dead canes from the glorious Everspring roses.

Now, though, she had to go home. She needed to get dinner for Liza, and probably for Tommy, too, if Annie hadn't picked him up already. Dinnertime was like the summer—it arrived on its own schedule, not yours.

Suddenly she felt the ground vibrate under her knees as someone came running toward her. Who was it? Was there some new problem? Welcoming the diversion from her harried thoughts, she rose quickly, pulling off her gloves.

It was Jackson, his long runner's legs easily covering the distance between them. When he reached her he wasn't even slightly breathless.

"Molly," he said without preamble. "Have you seen Liza or Tommy? Are they with you?"

Molly froze, her glove half on and half off. "No," she said, staying calm as best she could. Tommy had probably just forgotten to tell his mother where he was going. "They're back at the plantation. Tommy came over to play, and Lavinia is watching both of them.''

She caught the dark flicker in Jackson's eyes, and like a fire spreading, it ignited a small panic in her own body. ''What's wrong? Have you already been to Everspring? Doesn't Lavinia know where they are?''

''I'm sure they're fine.'' He took her hand in his, holding it hard. ''But apparently they've wandered off. They were playing by the river, and they were supposed to tell her if they wanted to go anywhere else. But when she went to look for them they were gone.''

Molly pulled her hand away and used it to tear off her other glove. Tossing both of them onto the ground, she began to walk swiftly toward his Thunderbird. He kept pace easily, accepting without question that she would go with him and not in her own car.

''We'll find them, M.''

''Of course we will. Kids do things like this,'' she said, and it was clear, even to her, that she was trying to reassure herself. ''They just got carried away playing some game. When Liza is pretending she's on Planet Cuspian, she forgets everything else.''

He opened the passenger door for her. ''I'm sure that's it,'' he said evenly.

But when he climbed in beside her and flicked the key quickly into the ignition, she saw that tension still tightened the edge of his jaw.

''You're worried,'' she said, and, though she

hadn't intended it, the sentence came out like an accusation. She had expected him to tell her she was overreacting again. Instead, his concern seemed to say just the opposite. "Why? Don't you think I'm right? Don't you think they've probably just lost track of the time?"

"Probably," he said neutrally. He glanced over at her, as if deciding how much to say. "I'm not really worried, M. I'm just a little concerned. This isn't like Tommy."

"It isn't?" She stared at him, surprised. "I would have thought he did things like this all the time. He seems so—" What was the right word? "Willful."

"He is willful. Very." Jackson kept his eyes on the road. "But he's not cruel. That's what makes me wonder. He knows this would distress his mother, and he loves her too much to do that deliberately. Besides, he knew she was coming at six, and he's always eager to see her. With her working such long hours, they don't get enough time together as it is."

She tried to reconcile his description with the cocky little boy she'd seen—but it was difficult. "No one would guess that, just judging from his attitude. You obviously understand Tommy pretty well."

"Having attitude and having common sense are not mutually exclusive," he observed dryly. "Tommy talks tough, but he knows where the boundaries are."

He sounded so sure. It was hard to doubt the accuracy of his analysis. But if Tommy wouldn't worry his mother deliberately... What scenario did that leave? She tried to swallow an ever ballooning sense of panic.

"All right," she said, struggling for calm. "So what do you think has happened?"

"I don't know." Jackson was driving safely, but very fast. His hands were gripping the wheel hard, his knuckles and fingertips pale against the leather. "We've already called their friends. Annie and Lavinia are looking around Everspring. Ross may be there by now, too."

What did that leave for them? Molly searched her mind, but came up with nothing. Liza didn't do things like this. Not ever.

"Maybe..." Jackson narrowed his eyes thoughtfully. "What about Cuspian? You said Liza gets caught up in her Planet Cuspian games. Tell me about the planet. What does it look like? What games does she play?"

Molly didn't really understand what he was getting at, but she didn't waste time with questions. She began to describe the planet, its three golden moons, its trees with rainbow-colored leaves. Its Mudbluff marshes and its Willowsong mountains. And, of course, the newest addition, the ice caves in which poor King Willowsong was currently trapped.

Jackson listened attentively, his face revealing nothing until she began to describe the ice caves. When she got to the part about Tommy's science project, about how fascinated the boy had seemed by the whole ice cave phenomenon, Jackson glanced over at her, his face suddenly alert.

"Of course." He thumped at the steering wheel once, and immediately began to guide the car into a sharp left turn. "It's worth a try."

"What?"

"There's a small cave carved into the bluff not far from where they were playing. The little fool just might have been dumb enough to take her there."

"A cave?" The word sounded dark and fearful, a labyrinth of danger and desolation. Molly made fists in her lap. "Surely he wouldn't take her into a cave."

Without taking his eyes from the road, Jackson put out his hand and grazed her cheek with the tips of his fingers. "It's just a little cave, M. Just a little hollow in the bluff. They couldn't really get lost in there."

She tried to take comfort from that. But if it was just a little cave, if they couldn't get lost in it...

Then why hadn't they come home?

# CHAPTER TWELVE

THOUGH JACKSON DIDN'T waste a second, driving with a ferocious concentration and efficiency, it still took them almost half an hour to reach the crook in the river.

By then it was nearly six-thirty. Thanking heaven for whoever invented daylight savings time, Molly noted gratefully that the sun was only now beginning to sink. The clouds in the west had turned a color that she would always think of as Cuspian gold.

Shock and fear made the next few minutes rather a blur.

Thinking back on it all later, Molly would only hazily remember getting out of the car, or following Jackson across the bluff to where he thought the cave might be. It had been years since he'd played there, and the bluff was notched with a dozen potential "caves." She knew that she had stood there, calling Liza's name, while Jackson roamed farther downriver, calling Tommy, but she didn't really remember it. She had only a fuzzy recollection of the cool evening wind blowing across her face, and being afraid that it might blow away the sound of her voice.

But mostly all those moments were like a half-remembered dream. The first thing she would clearly recall was the small, sweet sound of Liza's voice.

"Mommy?" The sound was too faint for Molly's conscious mind to be absolutely sure it was Liza. It could have been a bird. Or the wind. But Molly's body knew instinctively. At the reedy sound of those two syllables, Molly's whole being felt washed with an incredible gush of relief.

"Liza!"

"Mommy? We're down here."

She called Jackson, and obviously he could tell from the sound of her cry that she had found them. As he came loping back, his face mirrored the same flooding release that she felt.

"Both of them?" he asked as they ran.

"I don't know," she said. "I heard Liza, but I don't know."

Together they picked their way down the slope toward the little voice, Molly calling encouragement every step of the way, and Liza calling back, guiding them to the depression in the cliff wall where she waited for them to find her.

Molly tried not to ask herself why Liza didn't come, didn't run to show herself, to meet them, to help them find the way. It was enough that Liza's voice, though clearly frightened, sounded strong and normal. That was enough for now.

Finally they saw her. Liza sat cross-legged in the grass, just outside the cave entrance. She sat so close to Tommy that her knee was touching his shoulder. He seemed to be sleeping. His face was dirty and bruised, and his leg was tilted at a weird and terrible angle.

Liza leaned forward, her hands outstretched, her whole body straining to her mother, but she didn't leave her spot at Tommy's side.

"Mommy!" she cried, tears of relief flowing freely now, now that the grown-ups were here, and she didn't need to be quite so strong anymore.

Jackson ran faster than Molly ever could, again the eighteen-year-old sprinting champion he had once been. He reached the children first, and he gathered Liza in his arms even while he bent toward Tommy.

"Stewball ran home, but I promised Tommy I wouldn't leave him," Liza said, choking now on the sobs that seemed to come faster than she could absorb them into her breathing. "I think he was scared to be alone. But I knew you would come." She lifted her drenched face to Jackson with a reverent adoration. "I knew you would find us."

Jackson pressed the little girl against his chest tightly. "Of course we would find you, sweetheart," he said huskily. "You can always count on that. Can you tell me what happened, honey? Can you tell me what's the matter with Tommy?"

Molly had finally reached them. Now that Jackson had arrived to stand guard over Tommy, Liza was free to throw herself desperately into her mother's embrace. And from the safety of that spot, she answered Jackson's question.

"We were having a pretend fight on the cliff," she said. "We were fighting Mudbluffs. But Tommy slipped, and he fell down here by the cave. I'm pretty sure his leg is broken. I think it hurt a lot, because a little while ago he passed out.''

"But he didn't pass out right when he fell? He was talking for a while after that?'' Molly marveled at how calm Jackson sounded. She watched, her heart in a slow stall, as his gentle hands moved over the little boy while he talked.

"Yes, he was talking. He said his leg hurt really bad.''

Now that she was calm enough to focus clearly, Molly could see that Tommy's chest rose and fell with a reassuring regularity. Broken, then—but alive. She offered a short, intense sentence of gratitude to Tommy's guardian angel.

"Why didn't you come to get someone, honey?'' Molly stroked her daughter's tangled hair over and over, as if she had to convince herself that Liza was real. "Don't you know the way back to Everspring from here?''

"I know the way," Liza said, still allowing the pent-up tears to fall unchecked down her stained cheeks. "At least I'm pretty sure I do. But Tommy was afraid. He didn't want me to leave him alone. He made me promise.''

She had finally pulled herself together a little. She wiped her nose bravely. "I knew I would have to go get help, if you didn't find us," she said. "But I was going to wait a little bit, in case he woke up and got scared. I was going to wait until the sun was actually touching the trees.''

They stopped talking then, and watched while

Jackson lifted Tommy into his strong arms. They held their breath, as if Jackson needed complete silence for such a delicate operation.

Though Jackson was infinitely tender, the little boy roused at the painful movement. He winced as his leg shifted, but then he saw Jackson, and he smiled a dirty, blissful smile.

"I guess you really are King Willowsong," he said groggily, letting his head fall limply against Jackson's chest. "She told me you would come."

"GO HOME, JACKSON. It's late. Tommy's fine. I'm fine. Go home."

Jackson looked up at Annie, who stood in the doorway of her son's room, scowling at him, with one hand cocked on her hip for emphasis.

He didn't rise from his seat on the edge of Tommy's bed. He merely gave her a smile that said she didn't scare him. She talked tough, just like Tommy, but Jackson knew that the events of this afternoon had terrified her. Here it was almost nine o'clock, and she still hadn't taken off her orange Low Country Hardware apron. He guessed she'd probably sleep in it. She'd probably sleep in here, on the chair. She had no time for anything but Tommy tonight.

But what a trouper she was! At the hospital, he had offered to stand by while the doctor set Tommy's leg—he remembered from his own reckless youth that bone setting wasn't pretty—but Annie had insisted on doing it. She had exited the emergency room looking a rather strange shade of green, but she hadn't said a single word about it. She'd even waved away a cup of water, as if only a sissy would need such a thing.

Yeah, there were guts to spare in this family. Jackson looked back at Tommy, who was a little pale—just a couple of shades warmer than his off-white cast—but otherwise remarkably unscathed.

"So I guess the dragon is kicking me out," Jackson said. "You okay? You need anything?"

Tommy grinned at him. He pulled a sad puppy-dog face. "Well, now that my leg is broken in *three* places, and I can't get outside, or walk or *anything*—" he blinked in tragic innocence "—all I have is my hands. I guess I could play video games or something. If only I had any good ones…"

Jackson chuckled. "Which ones do you want?"

Tommy abandoned the pitiful invalid routine immediately, and sat up straight, his face eager. "How about Vampire Blaster? Or Blood and Guts 3-D? Of course, I'd need that new video system to play it—"

Jackson started to nod, but Annie moved in and pinched the back of his neck threateningly. "Do it," she rasped, "and you die."

"Ow." But Annie didn't let up, and finally Jackson shrugged helplessly. "Sorry, champ. The dragon has spoken."

"Jeez." Tommy flopped back in disgusted defeat. "What a loser. Afraid of a girl!"

"I'm not a girl, Thomas Cheatwood. I'm your mother. And Jackson is smart to be afraid of me. *You* would be smart to be afraid of me. If you ever pull another stunt like the one this afternoon, I'll—"

She frowned fiercely, obviously trying to think of something bad enough. "If you ever scare me like that again, I'll—"

And then to Jackson's surprise, Annie's eyes were suddenly shining. He stared, unable to remember ever seeing Annie in tears before, not even at the worst moments of her life. She obviously hated it. She made a strangled, furious sound, waved her arm over the two of them in a universal sign of profound frustration, and then stalked out of the room.

The two males exchanged a glance that spoke volumes. Patting Tommy's head in a silent goodbye, Jackson followed Annie out to the small living room.

She had her back to him. "Go home, Jackson," she said grimly. "I want you gone and him asleep so I can fall apart in privacy."

"I'm leaving," Jackson said softly. "But promise me you'll call if you decide you need anything."

She nodded without turning around. "Now go."

He went. But at the door he stopped. "Anything," he repeated. "Promise me, Annie. Call if you need anything."

Finally she looked at him. Her eyes, her brave brown eyes, were now completely dry. And in them he read the same lonely fear and the same stubborn pride he had seen there that terrible day ten years ago, when she had come to him to announce that she was pregnant.

"I need you to go," she said. And so, once again, he went.

MOLLY SAT at the kitchen table with Liza, trying to get her interested in drawing a picture of a Cuspian castle. She had brought out markers in all the colors of the rainbow—and about a hundred more—to tempt her. She had even brought out the glitter. But for the first time in her life Liza simply wasn't in the mood.

"Why can't we call Tommy's house?" she had asked this question four times already. That was unlike Liza, too. She was never the type to whine and beg once she had received an answer. "I just want to know if he's okay."

"Honey, they probably aren't even home yet. It takes forever in the emergency room." Molly didn't add that she, too, was fighting the urge to call. It was horrible not knowing. "And if they are home, they probably have a million things to do, getting him settled. We mustn't pester them."

With a heavy sigh, Liza left the table and moved to the couch. In the tiny carriage house, the living room and the dining room were really the same space, so it was more a comment than a real transition. She curled up on one edge, her nightgown tucked up under her feet, her head resting against the arm of the couch.

Her face was so empty and sad that Molly could hardly bear to look at her.

"Jackson will call," Molly said, hoping it was true.

But would he? Molly and Liza weren't really family, in spite of Liza's special friendship with Tommy. And in spite of any feelings that Molly might be discovering for Jackson himself. Even in spite of any steamy episodes under the nursery sprinklers.

In reality, they were just visitors—here today and gone next month. The hired help, in brutal fact. They had no legitimate role in this drama.

Still. Somehow she had an irrational faith that Jackson would sense Liza's misery. And that he would not abandon her.

"As soon as he has a minute, I promise you Jackson will call."

Liza perked up slightly at that, obviously accepting her mother's promise as gospel. She ate a little— a very little—of the casserole Molly had prepared, and then she settled down with a book, though she gave the phone a dirty look every five minutes or so just for good measure.

When, at nearly ten o'clock, footsteps sounded on the stairs, Liza bounded off the couch and flung herself toward the door with such excitement that Molly could only watch and hope that it actually was Jackson.

It was.

"Jackson!" Liza's happiness transformed her. "I knew you'd come."

Molly cringed inwardly to hear that sentence again so soon. It implied a world of great need and blind faith. She stood in the kitchenette, a dish towel in her hand, and watched as Jackson scooped Liza up in his arms for a bear hug.

The picture tugged at her heart. Had she made a mistake, staying at Everspring this long? She had realized she was risking her own heart—and she had been willing to take that risk. But why hadn't she seen that Liza's heart was in jeopardy, too? She had known for months now that Liza longed for a daddy. Why hadn't she anticipated that Jackson Forrest would look like the perfect candidate?

She hoped he didn't hear all the unspoken expectations that lay behind that short, heartfelt sentence. She jumped in, trying to mask the moment. "Liza has been worried sick about Tommy," she explained. "We've been hoping to get news."

"He's fine." Putting Liza down, Jackson let her lead him by the hand toward the sofa. "His leg was broken in three places, but he has already figured how to play it for maximum sympathy. When I left, he was trying to wheedle a new video game out of me."

Liza nodded knowingly. "Vampire Blaster, I bet. He wants that really bad. Junior Caldwell has it. His dad gave it to him, and he's always bragging about it."

"That's the one," Jackson agreed. "But Tommy's mom says no, so I guess that's that." He looked at his watch. "Have you been waiting up to hear about Tommy? I'll bet it's past your bedtime."

Liza looked worried. She glanced toward her mother anxiously. "Yes, but I can't go to bed, not now that you've come. I have a lot more questions about Tommy."

"Liza—" Molly began.

"I have an idea," Jackson interjected. "How

about if I tuck you in, and instead of telling you a bedtime story, I tell you all about Tommy?''

''You don't have to do that, Jackson,'' Molly said quickly. He looked tired himself, and he probably needed to get home. Or back to Annie's house... ''Now that we know he's all right, Liza can wait until tomorrow to find out—''

''Mom!'' Liza's voice was horrified. ''I can't. I really can't.''

''It's okay, M. I'd like to.'' Jackson stood, and he gave Molly a small smile over Liza's head. ''It's been a tough day. We could all use a little extra TLC tonight.''

IT WAS THE longest hour of her life.

She scrubbed the dishes. She folded laundry. She sent an unnecessary fax to her partner in Atlanta, and she paid seven bills that weren't due until next month. She straightened the cushions on the living room sofa, and she stared blindly at her Everspring plans.

But through it all, her heart was in the bedroom with Jackson and Liza. She heard the sounds of laughter, and she longed to know what the joke had been. She heard the murmur of voices, and she yearned to know what secret had been shared.

As she put away laundry, she passed Liza's room more times than were strictly necessary, just for the bittersweet pleasure of seeing Jackson sitting on the edge of her daughter's little bed.

She tried to stop herself. What kind of fantasy tableau was this? Had she grown as unrealistic as

Liza? But Jackson looked so right there, with the restless Cuspian moons throwing golden sparks across both sets of silken blond hair.

So right to see Liza chattering merrily, Jackson listening with a smile. He was so perfectly at ease. So comfortable. Just like a father. As if he tucked nine year olds into bed all the time.

Which, she reminded herself, forcing herself to move away from the door, was quite possibly the case. For all she knew, he tucked Tommy Cheatwood in bed with stories and laughter every night of the little boy's life.

And then...did he join Annie in her bed?

Though the thought had crossed Molly's mind at least a hundred times before, this time it took root, like some poisonous weed. It crowded out all other thoughts. No matter how she tried, she couldn't dislodge it.

She didn't really care that Jackson and Annie shared a past. She didn't even mind about Tommy, though it was obvious that Jackson was his father. She had faith in Jackson, and she had seen the work he put into caring for Tommy. He was doing his best. Someday perhaps he would trust her enough to explain, but until then she would trust him.

No, the *past* wasn't what bothered Molly. What Molly dreaded was the present. She hated the idea that today, tonight, tomorrow night...Jackson might *still* be Annie Cheatwood's lover.

She didn't want him to belong to someone else. Their episode in the nursery hadn't been some strange aberration caused by the seductive scent of flowers. It had been the moment of truth. The moment at which she had to admit she desperately wanted to make love to Jackson Forrest.

Why had it taken her so long to face it? It was perfectly natural, perfectly human. Jackson was not only a breathtakingly attractive man, he was a good man, as well. And Molly was a woman. Though she had, for the sake of her daughter, pretended for the past ten years that she was a mother and nothing else, Molly knew it was not true.

In Jackson's hands, she was once again a woman.

And so, abandoning all pretence of busy work, Molly sat silently on the couch, waiting for him to return to her.

He entered the room softly, as though reluctant to disturb Liza's slumber. He must have forgotten what Molly had told him the last time he was here. Once Liza was unconscious, a Broadway chorus line could tap dance across her headboard, and she would sleep through it.

Molly had hoped he would sit beside her on the sofa, but he didn't. With his hands in his pockets, he leaned against the door frame, like a well-mannered guest, comfortably poised to exit before he overstayed his welcome. He looked wonderful, she thought. His green-and-gold-plaid flannel shirt was unbuttoned over an ivory T-shirt, and his jeans were dark and soft.

"Liza seems fine," he observed. "How about you, M? Are you okay?"

The question was polite, too. Nothing more. It

was as if they, who had once been the best of buddies, had become courteous strangers.

"I'm fine," she said. "Really I am."

He smiled. "Good."

"I'm glad you came tonight, Jackson," she said, hastening to begin, before she lost her nerve. "I've been wanting to talk to you. There's something very important I need to tell you."

He raised his eyebrows. "Okay."

She drew in her breath. "I just wanted to say that I know why you were angry with me, back at the nursery. You thought that my choosing the orchid meant I was still thinking about Beau, longing for Beau. Even after we—"

"Yes. Even after we." He shifted. "But that's okay, M. I should have known it would be like that. It always has been, hasn't it?"

"No. That's what I'm telling you. You were wrong, Jackson. You were completely, one hundred percent wrong. I wasn't thinking about Beau. I was thinking about you."

He gazed at her, unblinking. "I would like to believe that," he said neutrally. "But experience argues against it."

"Well, you *can* believe it," she said. "You *must* believe it, because if that woman hadn't arrived like that, I would have—"

Somehow she stopped herself. Before she could admit how much she wanted him, she had to ask about Annie. She couldn't enter into a relationship with him if he had given another woman any kind of vow.

"But I'm glad we were interrupted. Before we begin anything that serious, we have things that need to be discussed. I need to know—I need to be sure—" She started over carefully. "Is there any reason why we shouldn't be together that way?"

He tilted his head stiffly. "What do you mean?"

"I want us to be honest with each other, Jackson. I don't want to take you away from…anyone." She looked down at her hands. This dancing around the subject was ridiculous. She was an adult, and so was he. It was time to speak frankly. "You don't have to tell me everything. I know that Tommy is your son, and I know that you love him very much. I'm glad of that, and I would never want to interfere with it. But what I don't know is whether you and Annie—whether she might think—whether she might hope—"

And abruptly, midsentence, she ran out of courage. There simply was no good way to say such things. She looked up, hoping that he understood.

For a moment, he looked completely blank. His eyes were just a shadowed emptiness. And then, to her astonishment, he began to laugh. It wasn't, somehow, a very happy sound.

"What is it?" She drew her arms across her chest instinctively, as if his strange laughter were some kind of weapon, as if the sound could hurt her. "What have I said that's funny?"

"You know Tommy is my son?" He threw his head back and laughed that black laughter one more time. When he lowered his head, his face was a cold collage of inexpressible disappointment and disgust.

"You *know* Tommy is my son? How exactly do you *know* that, Molly?"

"I—" She had expressed herself badly. She hadn't meant to accuse him of anything. She had only hoped to get the fact out in the open. She had merely wanted to start their new relationship with as few secrets and lies as possible.

"I don't really *know,* of course. But it's hardly much of a secret, Jackson. You couldn't be closer to him. And it would be obvious anyhow. Anyone can see—"

"Anyone can see what?"

This was foolish. Was he really going to deny the evidence of those extraordinarily green Forrest eyes, that arrogant Forrest profile? That long-limbed, bright and beautiful little boy might as well have his heritage printed on a sign and hung around his neck.

"For heaven's sake, Jackson," she said softly. "Be reasonable. Look at him. Look at his eyes. That particular shade of green is—"

"Ahh. His eyes." Jackson's smile was bitter, his tone icily sarcastic. "My God, to be convicted by one minute, utterly random spin of the color wheel."

"It's not random," she said stiffly. "That particular shade of green might as well be a fingerprint, and you know it."

He made one mirthless, scoffing sound. "Can you honestly tell me, Molly, that I am the only man in Demery, South Carolina, with eyes that 'particular' shade of green?"

She lifted her chin. She didn't like being lied to,

especially in that nasty tone of voice. "Yes," she said flatly. "As a matter of fact, you are."

He stared her across the ever widening gulf.

"But what about ten years ago, M?" His smile was as deadly as winter. "How many of us were there then?"

## CHAPTER THIRTEEN

"IT WAS REALLY thoughtful of you to bring my little darling a nice, wholesome vampire video game," Annie said, putting her feet up on her scarred patio table and taking a noisy sip of hot cinnamon tea. "But somehow I'm getting vibes that this little visit isn't entirely a mission of mercy. Somehow I just get that feeling, you know?"

"You do?" Molly flushed uncomfortable. She leaned back in her chair. "God, I must be the world's most transparent liar."

Annie chuckled. "Well, yeah, actually you are." She crossed her feet at the ankles, balanced her teacup in her lap, and grinned at her guest. "But also I had a little help. My good buddy Jackson called last night."

"Oh." Molly stared at Annie, at a loss to decide what the appropriate response was at such a moment. But she should have expected this. It was so like Jackson to know what she would do long before she did it. "What did he say?"

"Just that you might be paying me a little visit. And that you might have a few minor questions about the statistical probability of inheriting eyes in a particular shade of green."

Molly stirred her tea carefully, finding its warmth bracing. As though Annie had anticipated that they would need privacy for this conversation, she had led Molly out to a small patio behind her apartment. Unfortunately, the weather this morning was chilly, more kin to winter than to spring. Molly had been up at dawn, checking the park plants for frost damage. But then, she hadn't been to sleep all night anyhow.

"And did he tell you why I'd be asking those questions?"

"Yeah, he told me why." Annie laughed. "Because he's a sorry son of a gun who can't keep his mouth shut, that's why. He could at least have warned me before he started spilling the beans."

"Annie," Molly said, distressed and embarrassed almost beyond endurance. "I'm so sorry. I know this is a dreadful intrusion. I know I'm asking a lot. But I just have to know..."

Annie's eyebrows went up, and Molly paused, struggling to be totally honest. "No, I don't *have* to know. And you don't have to tell me. But I *want* to know. I want very much to know the truth, and I'm hoping you will help me."

She met Annie's sardonic gaze somberly. "I understand that you don't want the identity of Tommy's father to be public knowledge. I want you to know I will respect that. I will never tell another soul anything you—"

"Enough, enough." Annie waved Molly's protestations away with both hands, as if she were shooing out a roomful of annoying pests. She leaned her head back and sighed loudly.

"Aw, heck, what's the use?" She twisted her mouth wryly. "I'll be honest with you, Molly. I don't mind that you've found out. I actually thought you should be told, given the situation. But I had hoped to keep this from Tommy as long as possible. I didn't see any point in letting him get an attitude, you know—letting him get above himself, thinking he's something special. But hell, apparently Forrest men are born with attitude. Nothing you can do to stop it."

She grinned. "Besides, obviously we aren't really fooling anybody. No offense, kiddo, but you're probably the only person in town who hadn't figured it out already."

"No offense taken," Molly said humbly. "I'm aware that I've been almost unbelievably dense."

"Yeah, well, you can blame Jackson for some of that. I kept telling him he ought to let you in on the joke, but he's got this whole too-noble-to-live thing going. He seemed to think it wasn't quite kosher for him to stick a pin in your little fantasy Beau bubble, seeing as he had an itch for you himself." She rolled her eyes. "Not to mix my metaphors or anything."

Molly sat very still, very stiff, as if she were holding the pieces of herself together. "So it really is true, then?" She put her teacup carefully on the table. "Tommy and Beau—? I mean, you and Beau—?"

"Yeah," Annie said, her voice suddenly just a

tone softer. Her eyes were softer, too. "Me and Beau." She shrugged. "Sorry, kiddo."

"It's okay." Molly stood, suddenly unable to sit quietly any longer. "Really. It's okay."

But even after hearing it straight from Annie's mouth, she still could hardly believe it. *Annie and Beau.*

*And Tommy.*

She had been up all night, doing the calculations again and again like some overheated computer. Even allowing for slight errors, it always added up the same. Tommy had been conceived no more than a few short weeks before Molly had given herself to Beau out on the soft, green Everspring lawn.

For some reason, that was the most difficult element of this whole travesty. *God.* It made her out to be such a fool, all gussied up in her yellow silk dress, racing across town with her tears and her terror.

And the most beautiful memory of her life... What had that become? A joke. A dirty joke—one that, except for the intervention of fate, would have provided Beau with some great locker room smut. Her prissy virtue had been notorious among their friends. How he would have loved to boast of her surrender!

And the act that she had believed was a sacred experience, a shared moment of rare bliss and mutual commitment... It had merely been another studly roll in the hay for her beloved Beau.

"Don't let it hit you so hard, sweetie." Annie

sounded affectionately amused. "Take it from me. The boy didn't deserve you."

Molly just shook her head, unable to speak without fear of breaking into tears, which she absolutely refused to do. Not in front of Annie. Not ever, if she could help it.

"I'll tell you what a louse he was," Annie continued. "When he first started coming around, he was pretending to be Jackson. I think he did that a lot. Guess he figured Jackson's reputation was already shot to hell, and a few more sins would hardly even show."

Molly looked at her, incredulous. "Did you believe it? Did you really mistake him for Jackson?"

Annie shrugged. "For the first few minutes, maybe. Those boys really were two peas in a pod, you know. And of course he was always careful to leave the Forrest ring at home—that would have been a dead giveaway. But I'd seen that trick before. Married guys do it all the time, hoping you won't notice the little tan-free line on their ring finger. They must think girls are really dumb."

Molly smiled. "Some girls are, I hear."

"Yeah, well, not this girl." Annie patted her chest emphatically. "I knew what was going on."

"So, if you knew it was a charade, why did you let him—"

Annie grinned sheepishly. "Well, now, sweetie, I may be smart, but I'm still human. You know how sinfully sexy those Forrest boys were. I'm not sure there was a female on the entire eastern seaboard who would have said no to either one of them." She wrinkled her nose. "Well, except for you. But frankly we weren't ever sure you *were* human."

Molly laughed softly. "Gee, thanks," she said. "That makes me feel *much* better."

"Well, you're laughing, aren't you?" Annie patted her shoulder. "And you should laugh, kiddo. You should just give that memory one big belly-aching laugh goodbye. The boy didn't treat you right, and that's a fact." Her gaze sobered for a fleeting second. "I didn't treat you right, either. I'm sorry about that, Molly. I really am."

"I know," Molly said gently. "I know."

After that, there didn't seem to be much to say. Molly bent to gather up her purse and keys. "I guess I should get back out to Everspring," she said awkwardly. "There's a lot left to do before Saturday."

"Okay." Annie didn't try to stop her. Maybe she realized that Molly needed time alone. That she needed time to adjust to this new view of the past. "But if you decide you want to talk some more, I'll be around. I can't go to work, because His Highness in there needs someone twenty-four-seven to tote and fetch. At least until he gets used to his crutches."

"Thanks." Molly knew that Annie was right. The time might well come when she would want to know more. How often had Annie and Beau been together? Where? When?

But not yet. Right now she had all she could absorb.

"Thanks, Annie. I mean that sincerely. I appreciate your honesty."

Annie lifted her cup in a wry salute. "Well, better late than never, I guess, huh?"

At the last moment, Molly turned back from the door. "You know," she said slowly, "the ironic thing is, it never once crossed my mind that you—that you and Beau..." She lifted her shoulders wearily. "Even back then I always thought Jackson was more your type. I thought you had kind of a—a weakness for bad boys."

"I did, God help me. I did." Annie gave her a small half smile, and for the first time Molly glimpsed the wounded vulnerability beneath the brassy facade. "Don't you get it yet, sweetie? Boys didn't come any badder than Beau."

LIZA WAS SO EXCITED she could hardly concentrate on her math. But her mom had a very strict rule about weekend homework: do it first thing after school Friday, or there would be no Saturday adventures.

So Liza pulled out a piece of scrap paper and doggedly began scribbling her first long division problem—415 divided by 72... She wiggled her pencil and thought hard.

This weekend, of all weekends, she couldn't let anything go wrong. So many cool things were happening. The grand opening of the park began at noon tomorrow and went on all day, right up until dark, when there were going to be fireworks. Liza loved fireworks. On the Planet Cuspian, the sky just naturally erupted in golden fireworks every single night.

And tonight was going to be wonderful, too. Her mom had somewhere to go, so Aunt Lavinia was coming over to baby-sit. Just thinking about that made Liza feel as if she had breathed in a little bubble of happiness. Aunt Lavinia was so much fun. She had promised to bring over stuff to make Cuspian cookies. Liza could hardly wait to see what a Cuspian cookie would look like.

Best of all, her mom was finally acting happy again. For the past couple of days, Molly had been kind of quiet, a little bit sad. Liza had begun to worry, but Aunt Lavinia had said it probably was just all the pressure from the landscaping jobs, which had to be finished by tomorrow.

Aunt Lavinia must have been right, because today, when Molly came in from her final checkup at the park, she had been smiling in a very special, very Willowsong sort of way.

"Would you mind if Aunt Lavinia came over to play with you tonight, sweetheart?" Molly had been busy peeling off her dirty jeans, as if she were in a hurry, but she had blown Liza a kiss in the mirror. "I need to go out for a while."

Something wonderful was going to happen. Liza could feel it. And then, a few minutes later, she had heard her mother humming in the shower. That was a very good sign. Liza began to wonder where her mother was going.

When Aunt Lavinia arrived, Liza asked her if she knew.

"Well, she just said she needed to talk to Jackson. That's all I know."

Molly appeared in the hall doorway, wrapped in her blue terry cloth robe. "Hi, Lavinia," she said, wrapping a big towel around her wet hair with two quick twists. "Thanks so much for helping out. I won't be late, I promise."

Lavinia smiled blandly. "I'm sure you won't, dear." She chuckled and patted her large handbag. "But I brought a toothbrush and my best flannel nightgown, just in case."

Molly gave Lavinia a stare that was half a frown, half a laugh. "Good grief, Lavinia," she said, cutting a quick glance in Liza's direction. Liza bent over her long division, trying to look invisible. "What ridiculous ideas you get."

Lavinia moved toward the kitchen and began depositing her containers of dough and decorations on the counter.

"I don't know what you mean, dear. I just believe in being prepared." She looked up with a wide-eyed, innocent expression. "And may I say, I hope that's one lesson you've learned in life yourself?"

Molly laughed, a small flutter of surprised amusement. When Liza peeked up at her, she saw that her mother was blushing.

"Lavinia Forrest, you are positively incorrigible," she said in a funny voice, tightening the belt of her robe. "I'm going to get dressed now."

Liza looked up at that. "Are you going to wear your Willowsong dress?" Of all her mother's dresses, that was Liza's favorite. It was long and loose and soft, not a party dress really, but kind of fairy-princessy anyhow. And it was the most Willowsong shade of blue she had ever seen.

Molly paused. "I hadn't planned to," she said. "I was thinking about my green skirt and sweater."

"Oh, Mom, no," Liza pleaded. "You look so pretty in your Willowsong dress."

"What nonsense," Molly muttered. "It's much too warm for that dress. You're *both* completely incorrigible."

Liza wasn't sure what that meant, but after a long while Molly came back out, looking for her shoes, and she was wearing the Willowsong dress. Liza didn't say anything. She just stared at Molly, amazed, as she often was, that such a beautiful, perfect Queen Willowsong could actually be her own mother.

Her hair was pulled back in a soft French braid that fell halfway down her back. She was wearing perfume. When she walked by, lifting the ruffle of the sofa to hunt for her shoes, Liza caught a faint whiff of spring flowers.

Curious, Liza looked more carefully. Molly was even wearing lipstick. *Wow*. Her mother almost never wore makeup. She always laughed and said it was too much trouble, and besides, it clashed with the dirt. But Liza thought it was because her mom didn't need it. Her mom was just naturally beautiful.

So something really, really special must be happening tonight. Liza held her breath as the most marvelous thought occurred to her. Maybe Jackson and her mom were going to go to a dance. Maybe they would waltz and kiss and fall in love, and then they might start talking about getting married.

After that, Liza couldn't do a single one of her long division problems. The numbers just kept jumping around. Her heart was beating so fast she wondered if her mom and Lavinia could tell.

Finally Molly found her shoes, and, slipping them on, she frowned at herself in the mirror. She touched her hair nervously, and then she slid her hands down the front of her dress, as if she were afraid it didn't look right. But it did. It looked wonderful. Liza was so proud. She just knew that Jackson would fall in love with her tonight. Anybody would.

"Stop fussing, Molly. You look fine," Lavinia said. "The poor man doesn't stand a chance." She took a can of rainbow-colored sprinkles out of her paper bag and set it on the counter. "So. Do you have everything you need?"

Molly nodded. "Yes," she said. "I do."

Lavinia unearthed a roll of Saran Wrap. "Everything?" she repeated with a heavy emphasis on the word.

Molly made a small growling sound. "Yes, Lavinia," she said tightly. "I have *everything* I need."

Lavinia smiled. "Good. Because when I left him, the poor boy was down at the gazebo, and he was looking mighty down in the dumps, so I doubt he's made any preparations at all for your arrival. In fact, I think he's going to be extremely surprised to see you."

Molly bit her lower lip, hesitating. Liza watched

curiously—she had never seen her mother look so uncertain.

"Happily surprised, do you think?" Molly fingered the large mother-of-pearl button at her throat nervously. She caught her lower lip between her teeth again, and Liza was afraid she might bite off all her pretty lipstick before Jackson ever saw it.

Lavinia must have been thinking the same thing, because she suddenly made an impatient tsking sound.

"For heaven's sake, Molly my dear, how would I know?" She tossed a subtle wink toward Liza, who bent back over her homework quickly. "Why don't you just stop stalling and go find out for yourself?"

HE WAS STANDING at the open gazebo door, casually dressed in jeans and sweatshirt, staring out toward the starlit darkness. His golden hair fell softly onto his forehead, teased by the cool spring breeze. As her shadow fell across the doorway, he looked over at her.

He didn't show even the smallest sign of welcome.

"Hi," she said diffidently, gripping the freshly painted gazebo frame with one hand. "Lavinia told me you were here so I thought maybe…"

"I'm here," he said. His face was studiously blank. "What do you want?"

She hesitated. "May I come in?"

He was going to say no—she could feel it. She could even see it in the sudden tightening of his shoulders, in the way his fingers clenched around themselves, whitening the knuckles.

"Jackson? Please?"

"What do you *want*, Molly?" He moved to one side harshly, leaving just enough room for her to enter without brushing against him. "What more do you want from me?"

"I want to apologize," she said, still hovering at the doorway, as if it were some magic line, as if she needed his spoken permission to cross. She summoned her well-rehearsed speech. "I want to tell you how sorry I am. Annie has told me everything, about Beau and how he—"

"Apology accepted," Jackson ground out tightly. "Is there anything else?"

In the face of his curt impatience, she faltered, but she went on. The speech was already written. "I know there's no excuse for the unfair assumptions I made. To accuse you of—" She shook her head. "It was insane. You are one of the most noble, generous men I've ever—"

"*Noble?*" He uttered a low syllable of profound disgust. "For God's sake, Molly, you'd better go home. You're delusional. You're just trading one preposterous fantasy for another."

"No," she said. "I'm not. I am finally facing the truth. Beau was never what I believed he was, while *you*—"

"Forget *me*." He slashed at the air disparagingly with one hand, cutting off the thought. "I haven't got the slightest interest in stepping up to take

Beau's place now that he has toppled off your pedestal.''

She flinched slightly from the force of his sudden attack. ''That's not what I'm saying—''

''Sure it is. You're still looking for a hero, aren't you? Well, look somewhere else. He may not have been Saint Beau, but I'm damn sure not Saint Jackson.'' He laughed harshly. ''Hell, I'm not even King Willowsong. Fathering Tommy may not be on my list of sins, but I do have a list. And it's just as long. It's just as black.''

She didn't know what to say. Of course he had sins. Who didn't? Her own list was long enough to cause many a sleepless night. But how could she prove to him that she wasn't looking for perfection? She had ceased to believe in that weeks ago, as she slowly faced little truths about Beau. This new, larger betrayal was just the final awakening.

She watched him for a moment. She studied the long, tapered grace of his strong back. And his hair, which seemed almost white gold tonight, as if it had caught the starlight in its strands. His face was harshly beautiful, his jaw etched in silver, his angles well defined by moonshadows.

''Do you know how I felt,'' she asked him suddenly, ''when I found out that Beau had been cheating on me? When I found out that he had even created a child with someone else?''

''Yes. I know,'' Jackson said. ''And I'm sorry for it.'' He lifted his head wearily. ''But I can't glue your heart back together anymore, Molly. Beau was what he was—I can't change that. Frankly, I'm tired of trying."

"But you obviously *don't* know. Because what I felt was *relieved.*" Her voice gathered strength. "That's all, Jackson. *Relieved.*"

He looked at her, darkly contemplative, as if he were trying to read the nuances of her face through the liquid moonlight.

"Am I supposed to believe that?"

Finally releasing the door, she took one tentative step into the gazebo. The paint still smelled sharp and new. Freshly cut wood gave off its cedar scent.

"Yes," she said flatly. "Because it's true. I was relieved because if Beau was Tommy's father, that meant that you were *not.* It meant that Annie had no claims on you."

She moved closer.

"It meant," she said, stopping just behind his shoulder, "that she couldn't take you away from me."

"Molly—" He started to shift, as if to escape the nearness of her, or perhaps to flee the implications of her words. But though the gazebo was of typical, generous Everspring proportions, it still wasn't large enough.

He closed his eyes briefly. "I think you should go away. You're emotional right now. You're vulnerable, and you're looking for something to hang on to...."

Frustration tightened inside her. What more could she say to convince him? She looked at his remote profile. They stood skin to skin, and yet there was a cavern gaping between them. How was she ever going to bridge it?

She took a deep breath. Perhaps, she thought, there was no bridge. Maybe there was only courage, and the one great leap of faith.

"I can't go away. I can't go because I want you." She touched his arm. "It has nothing to do with Beau or Tommy—or anything except that I want to make love to you. I want it so much I'm nearly sick with it."

His gaze met hers again, and for the first time his green eyes seemed truly alive. They glittered in the moonlight.

"I don't want to live in the past anymore," she said. "I want the present. I want now." She moved behind him again and leaned forward, letting her body mold itself softly, like a moth's wing, against his. "I want you."

"No, Molly," he said, his tension a steel thread holding his words together. "We can't. We still need to talk."

"I'm tired of talking." She pressed harder, breathing deeply of him, resting her cheek against the warm cotton of his sweatshirt. She put her hands on his shoulders. "We just go around in circles. And none of it matters anyway. Please, Jackson. Please. No more talking."

"Molly, I—" His voice was hoarse. A small shudder ran from his shoulders down the long arc of his back. "Listen to me. I've never been very sensible where you were concerned. I've never been very strong. And this—"

He stopped, strangling a moan as she wrapped her hands around his waist.

"No more talking," she repeated. She slipped her hands up under the sweatshirt, splaying her fingers against the rigid ribbons of muscle that formed the beautiful and complicated patterns of his torso.

Her face was against his shoulder, and her breath came warm and shallow against his back.

"If you don't stop now," he said, throwing his head back and training his eyes on the stars that moved slowly across the sky, "I'm not going to be able to resist you. And then tomorrow, when you decide it was a mistake, when you decide I'm not so noble after all, then this will be just one more entry on my miserable list of sins."

She lifted her head slowly at that.

"Do you want me?" she asked, as if that was all that mattered, as if he hadn't spoken at all.

She waited. It was such a simple question. And yet everything, from the spinning of the universe to the continued beating of her heart, seemed to hang on his answer.

He dragged in one long, jagged breath.

"Only my whole life long," he said.

Molly felt something tight and cruel loosen its grip inside her. *Thank heaven,* she thought, exhaling the last of her fear against his skin. In spite of her mistakes, in spite of her ridiculous, childish clinging to the past, miraculously she hadn't lost her chance.

"Then turn around, Jackson, and kiss me," she said. "We've waited for each other long enough."

It must have been the right thing to say, because

almost immediately she felt his shuddering surrender. Resistance gave way to a flaring desperation. Murmuring her name thickly, he turned and took her into his arms. They kissed with blind abandon, with wild, whispered words, and hard, roaming hands. And somehow they found their way to the cushioned bench.

She had vowed that she would not think of the last time, that she would not think of Beau. But a small remnant of fear had haunted her. That night with Beau had been her only other act of love. And it had been here, in this same place. How could she help but compare the two?

But when Jackson had slowly unbuttoned her blue dress, he lowered his lips to her breast with a gentle fire that ignited her whole body in a blinding instant. And she knew there would be no comparisons.

The last time, she had made love in fear and defeated submission, to a young, angry man clumsy with beer and rushed with frustration. Tonight was completely different. It was everything that first night could not have been.

Jackson was the perfect lover—patient, exotic, intense, aware. He knew things about women, and about himself, that no twenty-two year old could ever understand.

His hands were gifted. His lips were wise. His body was strong as he rose over her, powerful as he moved in her, and beautiful as he answered prayers she wasn't aware of praying.

"Open your eyes," he said as he brought her toward the final moment. "I want you to see me. Really *see* me."

She obeyed, and with an almost hypnotic focus he refused to let her gaze flicker, even when the hot waves of climax began to wash over her.

"Jackson," she murmured weakly. Reality began to slip.

"Molly, look at me." And somehow, because he willed it, she did. He owned her consciousness, kept her focused on his fiercely tender face. He never allowed his rhythm to falter, even when she couldn't do anything to help, when she couldn't do anything but accept the driving pleasure he brought her.

She called out, half-frightened by her own helplessness, but his eyes, his beautiful green eyes, were always there.

And then, when she thought she could bear no more, she heard his voice.

"I love you," he said, as if in pain, and then he, too, was lost to anything but pleasure.

For a long time after, she lay in his arms, drenched, exhausted and more at peace than she remembered being ever before in her life. She gazed up at the silver stars sewn like sequins on the black velvet sky and thought how wise Lavinia had been, insisting that the gazebo's roof be left open. It would have been a shame to miss such beauty.

But eventually Molly's eyes drifted shut, and she drowsed, maybe for an hour, maybe for just a few floating minutes. When she awoke, he was watching her with something that looked both infinitely tender and strangely sad.

She touched his cheek, wondering how sadness could possibly have entered this blissful place. "I never dreamed," she said sleepily, "that anything could be like this."

He tilted his head, and he looked down at her with such a somber intensity she felt suddenly awake and a little bit confused.

"I did," he said. "I've dreamed it a million times. You have always been my dream."

She felt a small hitch in her breathing, just a tiny, flickering awareness, like the subtle flash of lightning in the half-seen distance.

"What did you say?" She let her hand fall slowly from his cheek.

"You heard me, Molly." His answer came with a grave and conscious dignity. "I said you have always been my dream. My first, my last, my best, my most beautiful dream."

## CHAPTER FOURTEEN

HE WATCHED IT SINK IN.

He saw the confusion, the doubt, the instinctive rejection. She shook her head, frowning, but the truth was like a storm surge, washing over her, and her struggles were no match for it.

"It was you?" Her voice was a whisper, as if she had forgotten how to form normal words. "It was always you, even then?"

She looked so lost. He hated himself, just as he had known he would. Just sixty seconds ago, she had been happy. She had been the ultimate innocent, clinging to her precious notions of his own nobility—and to her one last untainted memory of Beau. Now, like a bully, Jackson had kicked her beautiful castle of cards into a fluttering heap of rubble.

He stood, turning his gaze away from her stricken face, and began carefully rearranging his clothes into some semblance of normalcy. His conscience, he suspected, would take somewhat longer to fix.

"It can't be true." She seemed to be talking to herself, her voice numb and toneless. "It can't be."

He was such a coward. Even now, if he could have taken back the words, he would have. *No,* he wanted to say, cradling her in his arms, *of course it isn't true. I could never have done such a thing. I could never have let you offer your innocence to me under false pretenses. I could never have been such a selfish, deceitful bastard.*

But he couldn't say that. Because he had been.

And not just once.

Twice.

Letting her make love to him tonight without knowing the truth was just as bad as what he'd done ten years ago. Worse, because back then he had been drunk, drunk enough to think, for the first few critical moments, that she was merely a phantasm of the alcohol, a lovely hallucination come to him as the embodiment of a dream.

"But how could I have been so wrong?" Like a tired child, she had drawn her legs up under her and was sitting cross-legged on the cushioned bench. Her head was bent, and he could see that her soft blond hair was snarled slightly from their encounter and fell in a tousled veil around her face. She held her dress together with one white-knuckled fist, her fingers tangled in the soft blue fabric.

She looked up, brushing her other hand across her forehead and then into her hair, trying to tame the mess. "How could I have thought that you were—?"

"You didn't look at me very much," he said succinctly. "You seemed...uncomfortable with the role of seductress. My memory of the early moments is a little blurred, actually, but it seems to me that you didn't let your eyes meet mine any more than you had to."

She nodded slowly. "That's true. I was afraid. I—" She swallowed awkwardly. "Beau had been furious that night. I was terrified that he might reject me." Her eyes took on a remote expression, as if she had entered an interior world. "But then he was so gentle. He was so good to me—"

He set his jaw as she blinked the memory away. "Not Beau," she said, reminding herself. "You."

"Yes."

She nodded. And then, following an internal argument only she could hear, she began to shake her head instead. "You must have thought I was very stupid."

"I thought you were magnificent."

But she didn't seem to hear him. She was frowning, still shaking her head with a numbed sorrow. "I can't imagine what you—" She closed her eyes. "You must have thought I was.... You must have thought that Beau and I—"

"I was there, Molly. I knew you had never been with anyone before." He tightened his throat, closing off a groan at the memory, which was suddenly so intense it had a physical quality, a touch and scent and sound. "Not even Beau."

She looked up at him. "Did you tell Beau?" For the first time, her eyes seemed to shine with the threat of tears. "Did he die that night thinking I had betrayed him?" She inhaled brokenly, as if a new thought had slid under her ribs, like a blade. "Oh, God. Did that have anything to do with what happened? With the accident?"

Jackson knelt quickly, gathering up that first, evil

germ of guilt before it could lodge itself in her mind. He knew all about guilt, and he would not allow it to infect her.

"No, Molly," he said softly. He reached out, pried her hands from her dress, and began to slowly close up the cool mother-of-pearl buttons. "He never knew. He wasn't thinking about either one of us that night. He had been with Annie, and she had just told him she was pregnant. She had waited several months, until it was too late for him to suggest anything—"

He hadn't meant to use this speech to further blacken Beau's name, so he caught himself and started again. "Beau was shocked, and he was angry. He was probably scared to death. It made him reckless."

"I see." She watched his hands passively as he completed his task. She touched the fourth finger of his right hand and looked at him quizzically.

"You had on the ring that night," she said. Her voice was not accusatory. Merely curious. "The Forrest ring."

"Yes." But that was all he said. He wouldn't make this any worse. He wouldn't defend himself further at Beau's expense.

He didn't need to. She sighed deeply, and nodded again, as if it were finally beginning to come clear. "Annie told me that he would leave it at home when he visited her. He pretended to be you, hoping that he could commit all his sins in your name. One of the advantages, I suppose, of being an identical twin."

He just looked at her, thinking how it must look to her. The identical Forrest twins—what a pair of spoiled, black-hearted young bastards they had been. After that night, Jackson had never worn the ring again. It had sat in a small black box on his bedroom dresser for ten years, gathering dust. But there wasn't enough dust in the world to bury the shame of what they had done.

"Maybe that's why you made love to me." She tilted her head, searching his face, and he forced himself to let her. "I can almost understand that, I think. If Beau was out there pretending to be you— perhaps you decided it would be fair revenge if you pretended, just that once, to be Beau."

He stood. "No," he said. "That wasn't why."

"Then why?" Her lips were parted and her face was wan in the starlight. "Why didn't you just tell me who you really were?"

Looking down at her, he chose his words carefully. "Because I wanted you. Because I had wanted you for years. It's as simple, and as ugly, as that. I was drunk and I was half out of my mind with wanting you."

"You wanted me." Molly repeated it strangely, as if she were still trying to find her bearings in this new emotional landscape. "You said that before, that you had wanted me all your life."

He moved to the open door of the gazebo, breathing in the cold night air as deeply as his lungs would accept it.

"Yes," he said with his back to her. "And frankly, I would have pretended to be the devil himself that night, if that had been what it took to get you.''

LIZA WAS PUTTING the finishing touches on King Willowsong's golden crown—a bigger, fancier crown, which she had designed for him just to-night—when she heard her mother come in the front door.

She was supposed to be asleep. Stuffing the picture under her pillow, she flopped down, peeking quickly at her bedside clock. Ten-thirty.

She looked again. Ten-thirty? She wrapped her fingers around her crayon, trying to hide it, and told herself not to worry. She mustn't, as her mother always lectured her, go jumping to conclusions.

But only ten-thirty? If her mother and Jackson had been falling in love, wouldn't it have taken longer than that?

''Molly!'' Aunt Lavinia, who had been sitting in the little living room reading a book, sounded surprised, too. ''What on earth are you doing back already? Did you and Jackson quarrel?''

Apparently it was all right for grown-ups to jump to conclusions.

Liza strained to hear her mother's answer. She even held her breath, hoping she could make out some of the words. But her mother talked so softly that all Molly could hear was a low murmur.

Aunt Lavinia spoke again, but now she had lowered her voice, too. They were like two people talking at a funeral.

It was so frustrating. Liza debated the idea of getting up and going out there, pretending she wanted a glass of water, or a trip to the bathroom, or something. But somehow she just didn't do it. She lay under her covers, watching as the light from her nightstand lamp caught the glow of the Cuspian moons and scattered it like magic fire all over the walls.

She wasn't going to be sad about this. Maybe it wasn't as bad as it looked. Probably there was some other explanation. Liza was usually pretty good at finding another, happier way to explain things.

Sure! She had an idea! Probably her mother and Jackson had seen right away that they should get married, and her mother had rushed home to tell Liza all about it. She was probably terribly disappointed that Liza was already asleep. Liza should get up right now and run out there to hear the happy news.

But Liza didn't move. She didn't exactly believe that new idea. It didn't answer all the questions—like why her mother and Lavinia were talking so low and serious. If your new idea was going to work, if it was going to make the sad thoughts go away, it had to answer all the questions.

"I'm fine, Lavinia. I just need to get some sleep." Liza's mom was standing near the hallway, close enough for Liza to hear. "There's so much to do in the morning."

Well, that might be true, Liza thought. Her mother did sound very tired. Liza raised herself on one elbow, and through the crack in the door she could see her mom and Lavinia both, standing close together.

Molly was still wearing her Willowsong dress, but her hair needed brushing, and her lipstick was completely gone. She held her shoes in her hand, as if she'd just taken them off. She was smiling politely at Lavinia, but her shoulders sagged a little.

Her mother wasn't making that up—she really was terribly tired. But somehow that didn't make Liza feel any better. She wondered how the fresh, laughing woman who had left this house at eight-thirty had become so exhausted in less than two hours.

While Molly and Lavinia said their goodbyes at the door, Liza lifted her pillow and looked at her picture. She had done a pretty good job of drawing King Willowsong this time, she thought. Drawing was a lot harder than people understood. You had to see things very clearly. That twinkle in King Willowsong's gaze, for instance. At first she had thought it would be done with little gold flashes in his eyes. But it wasn't. After a lot of tries, she had discovered that it was the result of a certain tilt to his head, a tiny dimple at the corner of his smile, a deeper curve at the upper edge of his cheek.

She had finally caught it, though. She looked down at it now, feeling strangely betrayed. How could a man who smiled like that have made her mother look so sad and tired tonight?

She heard the front door close. Sweeping the picture back under the pillow, Liza hustled into her best sleeping position and shut her eyes. A small, soft sound told her that Molly was standing at her door, checking on her, as she did every night.

Now was her chance. She could sit up, look sleepy, and ask her mother how things had gone on her date. And her mother would come in, sit on the edge of her bed, and tell her all about it.

But Liza couldn't make herself do it. If things were bad, she didn't want to know it yet. She wanted to keep hoping, to keep trying to find another idea, one that would answer all the questions....

Molly shut the door quietly, and her bare footsteps moved lightly away, toward her own bedroom. And then, through the wall that separated the two little rooms, Liza heard the rare and disturbing sound of her mother's muffled weeping.

She listened for a few minutes. It was a terrible sound. It made something swell and ache in her chest the way your toe might throb if you stubbed it on a chair.

After a short time, though, the crying stopped. Liza lay there for a moment and then, sliding her hand under her pillow, she touched her best-ever picture of King Willowsong.

She wrapped her fingers around it slowly and squeezed, crumpling it into a tight, ruined ball in her fist.

IT WAS SATURDAY MORNING, the day of the park dedication. But Ross wasn't going to the dedication. He was going to Everspring. He idled his car in the front driveway with a touch of silent defiance.

He knew that most Forrest friends—and all the

Forrest family—used the back driveway, the one between the plantation and the carriage house, but he didn't care. This was a formal visit, and he'd be damned if he was going to come in through the back door, his hat in his hand, as if he were a workman begging favors.

This time he wasn't begging. This time he was demanding.

He refused to be intimidated, though the house looked more grand than ever this morning, all spruced up for the Tour of Homes, no doubt. And the grounds seemed to have exploded into color since the last time he was here.

He wasn't much for that stuff. He knew what a rose looked like, because, hell, everyone did. And he knew what a camellia was because once he had been playing football in the yard with his brothers, and his mother had come out waving her hands and yelling, "Boys! No! My camellias!"

But, though that was the extent of his acquaintance with landscaping, he knew when something looked good, and the yard here looked good. Ross had automatically assumed that Lavinia had hired Molly Lorring purely for old times' sake. But maybe not. The kid had obviously grown up to be mighty good at her job.

He reached the front door, and, ignoring the small button for the electric bell, Ross lifted the gleaming brass knocker and rapped it firmly three times. He wasn't requesting admittance, he reminded himself. He was demanding it.

But nothing happened. The house seemed as

empty as a stage set between shows. He scanned the windows, frustrated. Surely they were still here. The dedication ceremony didn't begin until noon, and it was only nine now.

He knocked again, louder. He'd knock all day if he had to. He wasn't going away until he'd said what he came to say.

After another minute, though, Jackson finally opened the door. He had clearly been dressing. His white shirt, though perfectly ironed to a crisp knife-edge along the sleeve, was unbuttoned at the cuffs and hadn't yet been tucked into his expensive wool slacks. His tie, the official muted stripe of the good-old-boy fraternity, hung loosely around his open collar.

Ross refused to let any of that bother him. Jackson's University Club tie didn't make him any more of a man, and Ross's department store flannel shirt didn't make him any less of one. And actually, now that he looked closer, Ross thought Jackson's eyes looked a little bruised around the edges, as if he hadn't slept well.

"Riser?" Jackson raised one eyebrow in a manner completely consistent with his tie. So much for the momentary hallucination that he was just another guy with ordinary problems that kept him awake at night. "Something I can do for you?"

"Yeah," Ross said, feeling himself getting a little hot under his flannel collar at the supercilious tone. "Actually, Forrest, there is."

"Okay." Jackson waited. But Ross wanted to

calm down first, so he waited, too. They stared at each other across the threshold.

After a few seconds, Jackson began buttoning his cuff. He smiled at Ross. "Do you want me to guess? It would be fun, of course, but it might take a while, and I do need to be at the park by noon—"

"Stop talking, Forrest." Ross took a deep breath. "I'll tell you what I want you to do. I want you to be quiet and listen, just listen, while I tell you how things are going to be."

"All right," Jackson said, his cool voice revealing only a pleasant measure of curiosity. "I'm listening."

"Okay." Ross twisted his neck, listening to the tension crack in the small bones, and took another deep breath. "Well, the first thing I wanted to say is that I'm sorry. I'll never be able to tell you how bad I feel about asking Beau to help me throw that game. I know I've implied before that it was partly Beau's fault, but it wasn't. I was young for a couch, but still, I was the adult. I was supposed to teach and guide him. And instead I led him into that mess. I'll never forgive myself for it, and I don't expect you to forgive me, either."

He paused. But if he had expected Jackson to jump in, to fall all over himself accepting the apology and offering absolution, he was wrong. Jackson merely continued to stand there, sliding the button on his other cuff closed with long, sure fingers.

"Okay, that's the first part. But there's more. I want to tell you that I actually do understand why you're worried about my spending too much time with Tommy. I know I've had problems.''

He stopped, took yet another deep breath—what was wrong with the air out here?—and forced himself to rephrase it. ''No. I had—I *have*—an *addiction.* And just because I haven't gambled in fourteen years, just because I've spent about a million hours in meetings working on it—well, that doesn't mean I'm cured. I know that.''

The cuffs were finished, and Jackson, without taking his cool, steady gaze from Ross's face, began deftly shoving his shirt inside his waistband. Still he didn't utter a syllable.

''Fine. So I'm not cured. But I *am* handling it. I have controlled it for fourteen years, and I can control it for fourteen more. And fourteen more after that. And, when I marry Annie and become Tommy's father, I'm perfectly capable of protecting that little boy from it, too.''

This was where Ross really did expect Jackson to jump in, unable to tolerate the very utterance of the phrase *Tommy's father.* But again the other man surprised him. He calmly picked up the edges of his tie and began wrapping one end around the other, swiftly creating a complicated, elegant knot.

''And I *am* going to marry Annie, Forrest. If she'll have me. That's what I'm here to tell you.''

Jackson slid the tie's knot up to the top in one smooth motion.

It annoyed the hell out of Ross. Was the man even human? How could he look so suave and poker-faced, so unmoved by anything?

"Don't you understand me, Jackson? Do you even hear what I'm saying? I'm going to marry Annie. Don't you have anything to say about that?"

"Sorry." Jackson smiled. "I didn't realize it was my turn yet."

"It's not." Ross knew he was behaving like an ass, but he just couldn't seem to stop himself. "Oh, hell. Maybe I'm not making any sense. But I'm angry, Jackson. I'm damned angry. It isn't all your fault, of course. I've been a fool, and a miserable coward, too. I'm ten years older than you are, and yet I've spent fourteen years under your thumb. I've spent fourteen years knowing you could destroy me with one sentence, and instead of just standing up and taking my lumps like a man, I've spent those fourteen years more or less hiding under the covers, wondering when you were going to do it."

Jackson's smile had faded. "And now?"

"And now I'm sick of it. Now I'm finished with hiding and being ashamed." Ross moved closer, close enough to be absolutely sure Forrest understood that he was willing to back up his words if necessary. "You can tell anybody you damn well please about my problem, Jackson. You can stand up in the Beaumont Pavilion and announce it over the microphone this afternoon if you want to. Because by then I will already have told Annie about it. And I don't think she's going to care. I think she's going to marry me anyhow. After that, I don't give a damn *what* you do."

He stopped then, aware that his breath was coming too quickly. He hadn't meant to be brutish. He had only meant to be irrefutable.

"That's all, then," he said roughly. "Now it's your turn."

Jackson looked thoughtful. His golden hair gleamed in the morning sunlight, and, now that he was fully dressed, he looked every inch the son of privilege that he was. Ross braced himself, knowing that the handsome, pampered man before him was clearly as ready to scorn, as quick with contempt, as ever.

Except for his eyes.

Jackson's startling green eyes were touched at the edges with shadow—and with something that might have been respect. The shadows had been there all along…but had the respect just emerged? Or was it something that Ross, in his fever to proclaim his independence, had stupidly missed?

Jackson seemed to come to a decision.

"I've got something to give you, Riser." Jackson stood back a little from the door. "Make that *two* things. Would you like to come in while I get them?"

Ross frowned. "No." He didn't trust this strange calm. "No, thank you. I think I'd better wait out here."

Jackson shrugged. "Suit yourself."

He disappeared then, into the elegant, spacious interior of a house Ross had never entered. For just a moment, doubt scratched at Ross's conscience. Was he doing the right thing? Could it possibly be the right thing to deny Tommy and Annie a life of grace and comfort inside this extraordinary house? Could Ross Riser's brand of simple love ever make up for eight thousand square feet of luxury and history?

Especially if that history was Tommy's birthright.

Stoically, Ross brushed away the doubt. It would be Annie's decision to make. All he could do was present her with the choice.

Jackson took longer than Ross had expected, but he finally did return. And he was holding two peculiar items—a sports magazine and a small, dusty black velvet box.

He held out the magazine, a football periodical with a famous helmeted quarterback smiling out at them from the cover. "Tommy has a friend whose father reads football stats to him at night, in lieu of a bedtime story." Jackson smiled. "Sounds supremely dull to me, but apparently Tommy thought it was cool."

Ross took it cautiously. "Football stats?"

"I couldn't believe it, either, but that's what he told me." Jackson lifted that eyebrow again, but this time Ross could see the humor in the glance beneath. "And one more thing—this won't score any points with Annie, but apparently he's pretty hot for a dog, too."

"A dog." Ross nodded stupidly, momentarily overwhelmed at the prospect of taking on a wife, a son and a dog. And bedtime stories...

"Why are you telling me all this, Jackson?" He eyed the other man suspiciously. "I thought you didn't want me near him. I thought you couldn't get past my sins—I thought you were determined to make me pay.''

Jackson laughed softly, almost to himself. And when he did the shadows around his eyes grew even more pronounced.

"Maybe," he said, "I've decided we've paid enough."

Ross looked at him hard. *"We?"*

"Yeah. You. Me. Beau. The whole sorry lot of us." He held out the dusty black box and looked at Ross over it with an expression more serious than the other man had ever glimpsed on his rakishly handsome features. "Here. I want you to give this to Annie. And I want you to tell her something for me, okay?"

Ross took the box. "Okay."

"I want you to tell her…" He paused. "Just tell her I'm ready whenever she is."

"Ready for what?" Ross wished he weren't so confused.

"She'll know." Jackson grinned. "Annie is an amazingly smart lady, haven't you noticed that yet? She'll know. Just give her the box, and tell her what I said. And then you'd better stand back, Riser, because things are going to get worse in this gossiping little town before they get better."

Ross gripped the box, suddenly anxious. "Is this about Tommy?"

"Annie will tell you." Jackson put a fraternal hand on the other man's shoulder, the first such gesture of their lifetimes. "Right now I have to go give a speech."

## CHAPTER FIFTEEN

AUNT LAVINIA was so cool. She didn't act like it was one bit weird when Liza asked if they could stop by and see Tommy Cheatwood before they went to the grand opening of the new park.

Liza was glad her mom had already headed over to the park, to check on any last-minute problems. Her mom would have asked a zillion questions. *Why Tommy? Why now?* Liza wouldn't have wanted to try to make up answers.

But Aunt Lavinia didn't ask anything. Liza loved that. She loved everything about Aunt Lavinia, actually. She wasn't pretty, exactly, with her short, straight white hair and her strict brown suits, and she certainly never fussed and cooed over you.

But she was smart, and she told great stories about the Forrest family way back in the sixteen hundreds. And most of all she was easy to be with. She seemed comfortable with herself, and that made you comfortable with yourself.

Liza had to swallow hard, thinking about when she went back to Atlanta, how much she was going to miss Aunt Lavinia.

"It's too bad Tommy won't be able to come to the party in the park," Aunt Lavinia said as they drove up to the redbrick apartment complex where the Cheatwoods lived. "I'll bet he's disappointed."

Liza nodded. "Yeah, but it's not just his broken leg. He cut his other foot pretty bad that day, too, and it had to get stitches. He says that one hurts even more than the broken one. He can't even walk yet."

"Well, tell him we'll bring him some cotton candy and a big pretzel tomorrow. The food's the best part of these celebrations anyhow."

"And the fireworks." Liza had really wanted to watch the fireworks with Tommy, so that they could pretend they were on the Planet Cuspian. Some of her other new friends would be there, too, but she hadn't told any of them about Cuspian yet.

And now she never would. Molly had seemed so quiet this morning. Liza had finally had to accept that nothing wonderful had happened with Jackson last night. And she knew what that meant. As soon as the school year was over—in just a few short weeks—they would be packing up and returning to Atlanta.

And she'd have to start looking for a new King Willowsong.

That was the saddest part of all. Because deep in her heart, Liza knew she would never find one.

Annie looked surprised but happy to see them. She took Liza right back to Tommy's room, where he was playing Vampire Blaster. That made Liza feel a little better, because she and her mother had given the game to him. That way he'd always have something to remember them by.

He paused the game and turned toward her. He seemed even thinner than ever, she thought. And his mouth looked kind of pinched, as if he hurt quite a lot.

But he smiled, obviously pleased, before he remembered to be too cool to care that she had come.

"Hey," he said, fiddling with his pillows to sit up better, "how come you're not at the park?"

"We're going there next," she said. "I just wanted to talk to you first."

"Oh, yeah? Why?" Then, raising his eyebrows, he made a knowing O with his mouth. He leaned forward and lowered his voice. "What? Did it happen? Did he ask her?"

Liza tried not to look too sad. "No," she said. She and Tommy had talked on the telephone last night, and they had discussed Molly's date. Both of them had agreed that the perfume and lipstick had sounded very promising. "Nothing good happened at all. She came home early, and she cried in her room when she went to bed."

"Man!" Tommy thumped the covers. "Don't you just *hate* it when they do that?"

"Yes." Liza hated even remembering it. She gazed at Tommy helplessly. "I think maybe something really bad happened. I think maybe they had a fight."

For a minute Tommy looked worried, but then his face cleared. "Oh, well, that's okay. People in love fight all the time. You should hear my mom and Ross go at it sometimes."

Liza braided her fingers in her lap. "Yeah, but my mom doesn't, remember?"

"Oh, yeah." Tommy looked frustrated, and a little defeated, as if he had just run into a dead end he couldn't see his way out of. "Jackson doesn't either, now that I think of it. They're so, I don't know, kind of all held in, aren't they?"

"I guess so." Liza hoped she wasn't going to start crying. She didn't want Tommy to remember her as a sissy. "So what about *your* mom? Has Coach Riser come by or anything?"

Tommy shifted the video game controller around on the bedspread pointlessly. Liza knew it was just something to do so that he wouldn't have to look at her right away. "Naw. Not that I care." He raised his eyes suddenly, and Liza saw that he had recovered a portion of his usual cocky bravado.

"But who needs them anyhow, right?" He nudged Liza's knee with his elbow. "You remember what I said about dads, don't you?"

She nodded.

"What? What did I say?" He was grinning, egging her on, daring her to show the same spunky indifference he always had.

"I remember." She smiled sheepishly. "But I'm not allowed to say that word."

He rolled his eyes, as he always did when she was too prissy. "Man! You're such a *girl!* My mom and Lavinia are in the other room, you wuss. They can't hear you. Now tell me. What did I say about dads?"

Liza chewed on her lip, astonished that it felt so

strangely exciting to be just a little disobedient. Maybe this was why Tommy was always getting in trouble. Maybe he liked the way it felt kind of courageous, not quite so weak and vulnerable.

"They're all," she said bravely, though she couldn't help lowering her voice to its tiniest whisper, "a royal pain in the butt."

Tommy grinned at her proudly. "See? And the world didn't end, did it?"

But at that exact moment, a crowd of grown-ups appeared at the doorway to Tommy's room, as if they had all magically heard her being vulgar and had arrived to mete out punishment. Liza held her breath.

Tommy looked up, too. It was his mother, Aunt Lavinia, and one more, unexpected, person. Coach Riser.

Tommy and Liza exchanged silent glances.

"We need to go now, honey," Aunt Lavinia said to Liza. "Tommy and Annie have more company, and I need to get to the park. The dedication speech starts in less than an hour."

"Hi, Liza," Coach said, smiling.

Liza smiled back. And then she saw what he was holding in the palm of his big hand. A small, black velvet box.

Liza's heart thumped twice, heavily. She knew what that was. A jewelry box. The kind of box the hero in the movies always brought when he asked the heroine to marry him. The kind of box that always had a diamond ring in it.

She saw Aunt Lavinia noticing it, too. And Tommy.

Tommy's mouth was hanging open. He looked at Liza, completely unable to be cool.

She smiled, suddenly very happy. This was good, so good. If her own dreams weren't going to come true, at least maybe Tommy's would. That would be something to hold on to.

"Well, bye, then, Tommy," she said, standing up from the chair. "I hope your leg feels better. Because I think maybe you're going to start hurting in a brand-new place."

He screwed up his mouth, trying to hide his smile.

"Shut up, Liza," he said, but anyone could hear that the words lacked his usual sting.

TOMMY WAITED almost an hour while Coach Riser and his mother talked alone out in the living room. It seemed like forever—he even got bored with Vampire Blaster. Then he began to worry, because his mom had made him take his pain pill, and that always made him sleepy.

What if he fell asleep before he could find out what was going on?

Just when he thought he'd go nuts, though, Coach poked his head in the door.

"Mind if I come in?"

Tommy shrugged. "I don't care," he said.

Coach sat on the same chair Liza had used, but he looked way too big for it. He looked downright uncomfortable, as a matter of fact, and Tommy got the idea it wasn't just the chair.

"I wanted to talk to you about something important," Coach said.

Tommy turned off the video game. "Yeah?" He noticed the Coach wasn't holding the little black box anymore. That seemed like a good sign. "What?"

Coach shifted on the chair. "You know I've been dating your mom a lot." *Well, duh.* Though Coach paused, Tommy didn't bother to answer that. He couldn't expect Tommy to walk him through this whole conversation. He was just going to have to spit it out.

"Anyhow, we've been talking, and we decided that we might like to get married." Coach looked at Tommy, and it was clear that he was big-time nervous. "I thought I'd check with you, to see how you felt about that."

Tommy pretended to think it over. "I guess it would be okay," he said finally.

"Well, good." Coach's face looked tons more relaxed, but he was still talking pretty goofy. "Good. That's really good."

"Sure. It's good," Tommy agreed. "So. You'll be…you'll be like my dad, or what?"

Coach hesitated. "I'd like very much to be," he said. "If it's okay with you. I'll never be your real father, of course. Your father was a very special man. I think your mom is going to tell you a lot about him after I leave. But I don't want you to worry that I'd ever try to take his place."

Tommy laughed, more like a snort, really. "He doesn't *have* a place. He doesn't even have a name, or a face, or anything. He's nobody."

"Well, I'll leave that to your mom," Coach said slowly. "Maybe you'll feel different when she's told you all about it. But anyhow, the part I wanted to straighten out with you was just...I wanted to be sure you're okay with my marrying your mom. With my becoming, you know...like your dad."

He looked kind of sweet, Tommy thought. As if he really cared. For a minute, Tommy considered telling him how much he had been wanting a dad, how happy it would make him to finally get one. Especially somebody like Coach Riser, somebody who was big and strong and always on his side.

But Tommy pulled himself back from the brink at the last minute. *Whoa!* That must have been the pain pill making him weird. He darn sure wasn't going to start admitting any sissy stuff like that.

Not yet, anyhow.

"I told you," he said, letting himself slide a little farther down under the covers. The pain pill was really making him sleepy. "It'll probably be okay."

"Good." That seemed to be Coach Riser's only word. But that was okay. Tommy knew what he meant.

"So you need a nap right now, or what?"

Tommy tried to keep his eyes open. "It's just the darn pills," he said irritably. "They always do this. I would be fine without them. I'm not scared of hurting. But mom makes me."

Coach smiled. "Moms are like that," he said. And then he pulled a magazine out of his jacket pocket. "I brought a copy of *Quarterback* with me.

What do you say? Want me to read some of the stuff in here while you rest?''

Tommy just nodded. "That would be okay, I guess," he said, letting his head drift down onto the pillow.

Coach began to read. He read for several minutes, a bunch of stuff about some quarterback's career statistics. Passing yards. Passing yards in one game. Passing yards in one season. Tommy lost track, but he loved the sound of Coach's voice. He hadn't ever noticed before, but Coach had a nice, deep voice. A safe voice.

"Good grief. This magazine is three months old," Coach said suddenly, and Tommy heard the sound of rustling paper as Coach folded the magazine shut. "It doesn't even have the stats from the Super Bowl, when he threw for another 310 passing yards. And four touchdowns, which puts him in the top three in the Central Division—"

Tommy tried to open his eyes. He wanted to tell Coach how cool that was, that he didn't even need the magazine. He knew more in his own head than Junior Caldwell's dad could find in a hundred magazines.

But Tommy's eyes wouldn't open. His mom's little white pain pill and the comfort of Coach Riser's voice had finally put him to sleep.

JACKSON LOOKED OUT at the sea of faces in the crowd gathered at the park, waiting for the dedication ceremony. Mostly familiar faces. If you lived your whole life in a city the size of Demery, you pretty much got to know everybody.

And everybody knew you.

They knew about the time you brought home the gold for Radway in the district track-and-field competition. And they knew about the time you got caught putting a black lace bra on the statue that stood in the middle of Milton Square. They knew you had a B.A. from Yale, and they knew your back porch swing had an intractable squeak. They knew you had never had the chicken pox, or a blind date, or a decent singing voice.

And they knew you had nearly died of grief because you had not been able to save your brother, when he drove like a madman through the night.

So what exactly had he thought he was hiding? There probably wasn't a single thing he could get up here today and say about Beau that this close-knit community of Demery didn't already know.

Except that he forgave him. And that, even more difficult, he forgave himself.

Jackson saw Lavinia, stolid and comfortably predictable in her no-frills brown tweed suit, readying her notes, preparing to deliver the speech. He made his way up to the dais and, when he reached her, he held out his hand.

"Maybe I should do that," he said.

She hardly skipped a beat. She pressed the speech into his hands and smiled. "What an excellent idea," she said. "Why didn't I think of that?"

But when he arranged the pages in front of him

on the podium, he saw that they were all completely blank.

He glanced up, caught her eye, and shook his head softly, accepting that he had been outmaneuvered. She had known all along that he would do it.

He turned to his audience. He waited until they were all listening politely, and then he switched on his microphone.

"My brother Beaumont died when he was only twenty-two," he said. "On his way to becoming a man."

The faces were quiet. Interested. Sympathetic, even. He took a steadying breath.

"Beau wasn't perfect. Not even close. But he was trying. He was learning a little more every day. A little more about life, about truth, about responsibility and about love."

He saw Molly, standing apart from the rest. Liza was at her side, leaning into her mother with a slightly lost look in her eye. Jackson had always intended to keep his speech short—but the expression on Liza's face made him more determined than ever.

"And so," he finished, "we dedicate this pavilion to my brother, not because he was a gifted athlete, or a charming young man, or a beloved brother, nephew and son, though he was without question all of those things. We dedicate it to him because he was human. Because his struggle to be better is the same struggle we all take on every day."

He felt the spring breeze touching his face like understanding fingers. He gave one quick glance toward the memorial plaque that had been attached to the pavilion wall.

"The Beaumont Forrest pavilion doesn't stand for perfection, or for sainthood. It stands instead for hope." His voice was giving out on him. He could hear the thickness that threatened to break into an emotion he couldn't hide. "It stands for the hope that we'll all cherish every day of life that we're given. The hope that we'll use each day to love ourselves, and to love one another, just a little more than we did the day before."

He stopped. Only Lavinia seemed to realize that he was finished. That was all he was going to say. As he gripped the podium, trying to control his face, she began to clap. Her lone applause was like a small, rhythmic cracking in the air.

And then slowly, catching on, the others joined her, swelling to a crescendo that he had never expected. It moved him, and yet, even as he stood there, washed by the surprising outpouring of emotion, he scanned the crowd for Molly.

But she had moved away. He could no longer see her. He smiled automatically at well-wishers, shook hands and answered questions, struggling through the voices and the commotion, until somehow he was able to make his way down from the dais and into the park.

It wasn't a very big park, really. So he found her quickly, over by the fountain, where a Girl Scout troop was selling cotton candy. She and Liza were standing at the front of the line, paying for their treat.

He held back briefly, just looking at them—his own kind of treat. Molly wore a long, loose yellow jumper that somehow was the essence of spring. Liza was in blue, the color of her eyes. Even from the back, with their blond hair streaming loose down their long, slim backs, anyone would have known they belonged together.

Liza saw him first. She turned, looking at him over a big pink cloud of cotton candy. "Hi, Jackson," she said quietly, watching him with somber eyes.

Molly turned, then, too. And her cheeks were suddenly as pink as her daughter's candy.

"Hi." She slipped her change into her pocket awkwardly, then looked up at him again. "It was a beautiful speech," she said. "I was surprised to see you up there. I had thought Lavinia was going to—"

"No," Liza interrupted. "Aunt Lavinia said that Jackson would do it. She told me that this morning."

"Liza—" Molly looked chagrined.

"She's right," Lavinia said, coming up from behind them with a smile. "That's exactly what I told her, and that's exactly what happened, wasn't it, honey?" She reached down and gave Liza a big hug. Then she straightened and looked at her nephew.

"Well done, Jackson," she said matter-of-factly. "I knew you had something to say. And you kept it short, that was the best part. No point forcing these folks to listen to a lot of claptrap when all they really want to do is eat hot dogs and candy till they get sick or pop.''

Liza giggled, her mouth already pink with cotton candy.

"Which reminds me," Lavinia continued, looking down at the little girl. "You and I had a date with a couple of funnel cakes, didn't we, young lady? Maybe we should leave your mom and Jackson alone while we explore the food situation around here.''

She winked broadly at Liza, who had begun to smile. "If we're going to get to the popping stage by fireworks time, we'd better get started.''

Liza looked over at her mother eagerly. Molly nodded, avoiding Jackson's gaze. "You might want to consider stopping just short of popping, though, sweetheart," she said, giving her daughter a warm goodbye kiss that probably smelled of pink sugar.

"Okay," Liza said agreeably. She turned to Jackson, her expression sobering again. Something, some subtle yearning in her face, made him want to take her in his arms and kiss that expression away. "Will I see you later, do you think?''

"You can count on it," he said firmly, touching his knuckle to her cheek. He turned to his aunt. "Take good care of her, Vinnie.''

Lavinia wagged a finger in his face. "Ditto, my boy. If you know what I mean.''

And then he was alone with Molly. As if by mutual, unspoken decision, they began to walk slowly, following the wide brick path that had been laid here only last week, weaving among the bright-fuchsia azaleas she had planted with her own hands only yesterday.

He didn't speak. It was up to her to begin. Last night, when he had left her, she had said she needed time to think. How much time, only she could say. He might be pressuring her by doing even this much, by being this close. But he knew that his good intentions would take him only so far. He couldn't wait forever. He'd done too much waiting already.

"She loves you," Molly said suddenly, reaching out to pinch off a fading bloom from one of the azaleas. "You know that, don't you?"

"Of course." He smiled. "I am King Willowsong. All my subjects love me."

Molly found another blossom that needed to be removed. She was so focused on her task that he might have believed it was the only thing on her mind, except that he could see the flush on her cheeks, the tension in her shoulders.

"But Liza isn't your subject." Molly looked at him, finally, her palm full of wilted flowers. "You know that, too, don't you? She's..."

Her voice faltered, so Jackson finished for her.

"She's my daughter," he said softly.

Molly just stared at him helplessly. "How long have you known?"

"From the first moment I saw her, in the maze at Everspring." He felt again the stunning shock of that moment, when she had barreled into him, and he had for the first time understood that he had a child, a beautiful, breathless being of sunshine and laughter. "I knew you had a daughter, of course.

Lavinia told me. But I was quite sure she couldn't be mine. Until I saw her.''

Molly looked at him curiously. ''Why were you so sure? You knew we had made love....''

''Because I went to see you,'' he said. ''As soon as I was able to get around on my own, about eight months after the accident, I went to Atlanta to see you. I wanted to be sure that there had been no...consequences from that night.''

''Oh.'' She looked pensive, as if she were remembering that time in her life. As if it had been far from easy. ''Eight months. Liza had been born by then. She was six weeks premature. But you probably already know that, don't you?''

''I do now,'' he said. ''She told me about it that day when we were out fishing. It explained, she said, why you were so protective of her. But I didn't know about that back then. So when I saw you—'' He paused, seeing her once again in his mind, slim, beautiful, dressed in winter black, like a widow.

Mourning Beau, he had understood. Still mourning Beau after eight long months.

He shook away the picture. ''You were coming out of the local technical college, where you'd been taking landscape design classes. You were with another man. You were most definitely not pregnant with my child. And you looked happy, happy enough, anyhow. I knew I had no right to step in and risk destroying that first step toward happiness. I had no claim on you—I never had. So I decided to do what I should have done all along—to leave you alone and let you get on with your life. To leave your memories of Beau intact. I never tried to contact you again."

She was studying his face. "Even though you still cared for me? Why? Was that part of your punishment? Your punishment for being alive when Beau was dead?"

"No," he said, choosing his words carefully. "It had nothing to do with his death. It was my punishment for betraying him while he was still alive. For stealing something beautiful and rare that should have been his, something that was never meant to be mine."

She looked indescribably sad, but she didn't turn away. She met his gaze with eyes of such gentle liquid blue that he almost had to look away himself. No one should be that beautiful, he thought. No wonder they both had loved her.

"And so you missed ten years of your daughter's life," she said. "And she missed ten years of you. What a waste."

"Yes," he said. Almost unendurable to think of it.

"And now is that enough, Jackson?" She shook her head sadly. "Do you finally believe you have been punished enough?"

He set his shoulders. "That's a decision you'll have to make, Molly. What do you think? You know all my sins now. Can you ever forgive me?"

She smiled, just slightly. "For what? For making love to me that night? Or for letting me spend so many years mourning the wrong lover?"

"For all of it." He watched her eyes. They were

soft now, glowing with something he thought he recognized, though he was almost afraid to hope.

"Can I forgive you? Well, it depends," she said, thoughtfully. "Can you forgive me for being such a fool? For not realizing that the memory I cherished from the past and the love that I was discovering in the present were one and the same? For not realizing that only your hands, only your lips, could have introduced me to love in such a tender, unselfish way?" She touched his arm. "Well, Jackson? Can you forgive me for being so blind?"

"Yes," he said, his voice husky with relief, deep with the love he'd always felt but had spent so many years denying. "For all of that and more."

She smiled and held out her hand. He took it, feeling his whole life come to a complete, safe circle in the joining of their fingers.

"Good," she said, a small tremor shaking the borders of her words. "And now let's see... Do you vow to always be my most devoted King Willowsong, and live with us happily on the Planet Cuspian forever?"

He grinned, and he took her in his arms, where she belonged. "I do."

She held back a little, her lips quirked into a teasing smile that did hot and wonderful things to his blood temperature. "And do you swear that you will never, ever make wild, passionate love to me without my being fully aware of it?"

Now that was an easy one.

"My lady. By the three golden moons of Cuspian," he whispered, lowering his lips to hers. "I do."

# EPILOGUE

THE FIREWORKS were spectacular. They shot like exotic flowers across the clear spring sky, red and green and gold and blue and beautiful.

But Liza wasn't enjoying them quite as much as she had expected to. She and Aunt Lavinia were sitting on the best, most comfortable park bench together, trying to decide whether to get sick or pop.

Liza decided it might be better just to go to sleep. It was late, and it had been a long day. She was up to her eyes in candy apples, funnel cakes, cotton candy, popcorn and pretzels. Aunt Lavinia wasn't very good at saying no, Liza thought sleepily. She should take some lessons from her mom.

But in spite of the queasy, overstuffed ending, it had been a good day.

The very best day.

This morning, less than an hour after they had gone off together, her mother and Jackson had come back to them, hand in hand.

Liza had known immediately that everything was going to be all right. Her mother's lipstick was all fuzzy, and Jackson even had a little of it on his own lips.

Like bad children acting up, Liza and Lavinia had

begun to laugh. It was just that they were both so relieved, Liza knew. That was what had made it seem so wonderful and funny.

They had spent the whole day together. Though Liza and Aunt Lavinia had wandered off occasionally to indulge in some sugary or deep-fried snack, the four of them had never been far apart.

Even now, as Liza lay there, with her head in Aunt Lavinia's lap, they could see Molly and Jackson, standing shoulder to shoulder in the distance, looking up at the sky, which was full of streaming, glittering, exploding colors.

"Well, would you look at that," Aunt Lavinia said softly. "Three golden fireworks at once, Liza. Just like the Cuspian moons."

Liza peeked up sleepily.

And it was true. Her mom and Jackson were kissing, kissing with such a sweet, clinging happiness that Liza knew she would never forget the sight as long as she lived. And in the sky above their heads three golden fireworks hung like Cuspian moons, magical, shimmering balls of electric glitter.

She shut her eyes again.

"Aw, darn, you missed them," Aunt Lavinia said, disappointed. "They're already gone."

Liza smiled into Aunt Lavinia's skirt as she felt herself drifting off into a warm and peaceful sleep.

"That's okay," she murmured. "I don't really need them anymore."

Daddy's little girl... **THAT'S MY BABY!** by

# Vicki Lewis Thompson

Nat Grady is finally home—older and wiser. When the woman he'd loved had hinted at commitment, Nat had run far and fast. But now he knows he can't live without her. But Jessica's nowhere to be found.

Jessica Franklin is living a nightmare. She'd thought things were rough when the man she loved ran out on her, leaving her to give birth to their child alone. But when she realizes she has a stalker on her trail, she has to run—and the only man who can help her is Nat Grady.

## THAT'S MY BABY!

On sale September 2000 at your favorite retail outlet.

**HARLEQUIN®**
*Makes any time special* ™

If you enjoyed what you just read,
then we've got an offer you can't resist!

# Take 2 bestselling love stories FREE!

# Plus get a FREE surprise gift!

Clip this page and mail it to Harlequin Reader Service®

| IN U.S.A. | IN CANADA |
|---|---|
| 3010 Walden Ave. | P.O. Box 609 |
| P.O. Box 1867 | Fort Erie, Ontario |
| Buffalo, N.Y. 14240-1867 | L2A 5X3 |

**YES!** Please send me 2 free Harlequin Superromance® novels and my free surprise gift. Then send me 6 brand-new novels every month, which I will receive before they're available in stores. In the U.S.A., bill me at the bargain price of $3.80 plus 25¢ delivery per book and applicable sales tax, if any*. In Canada, bill me at the bargain price of $4.21 plus 25¢ delivery per book and applicable taxes**. That's the complete price, and a saving of at least 10% off the cover prices—what a great deal! I understand that accepting the 2 free books and gift places me under no obligation ever to buy any books. I can always return a shipment and cancel at any time. Even if I never buy another book from Harlequin, the 2 free books and gift are mine to keep forever. So why not take us up on our invitation. You'll be glad you did!

135 HEN C22S
336 HEN C22T

| | | |
|---|---|---|
| Name | (PLEASE PRINT) | |
| Address | Apt.# | |
| City | State/Prov. | Zip/Postal Code |

* Terms and prices subject to change without notice. Sales tax applicable in N.Y.
** Canadian residents will be charged applicable provincial taxes and GST.
 All orders subject to approval. Offer limited to one per household.
® is a registered trademark of Harlequin Enterprises Limited.

SUP00                                    ©1998 Harlequin Enterprises Limited

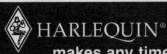

## #930 THAT SUMMER THING • Pamela Bauer
*Riverbend*

Charlie Callahan is the original good-time Charlie. At least, that's what everyone thinks, especially Beth Pennington. After all, she was once briefly—disastrously—married to him. And now she's sharing an inheritance with Charlie! Isn't it ironic?

*Riverbend, Indiana: Home of the River Rats—small-town sons and daughters who've been friends since high school. These are their stories.*

## #931 P.S. LOVE YOU MADLY • Bethany Campbell

Darcy's mother and Sloan's father are in love. But Darcy's sister is aghast and appalled. And Sloan's aunt is appalled. And that leaves the two of them trying to make everyone see sense. No problem, right? But then their parents break up just when *they're* falling in love.... Compared to what these two go through, Romeo and Juliet had it easy.

Guaranteed to be one of the funniest romances you'll read this year!

## #932 CATHRYN • Shannon Waverly
*Circle of Friends*

Cathryn McGrath of Harmony, Massachusetts, is the ideal wife and mother—her children are happy, her house is beautiful, her marriage is perfect. Except it's not.... Her husband is having an affair with another woman! Then Cathryn's marriage irrevocably ends, and she resumes her friendship with Tucker Lang—former bad boy of Harmony, who shows her that there's life after betrayal, love after divorce.

## #933 HITCHED! • Ruth Jean Dale
*The Taggarts of Texas*

Rand Taggart may have been swindled out of a fortune by his old college roommate, but he can inherit a *second* fortune—provided he's happily married by his thirtieth birthday. In order to save her sister's name, Maxi Rafferty is going to help him out—and complicate her life and Rand's with this seemingly straightforward marriage of convenience!

## #934 HIS DADDY'S EYES • Debra Salonen
*A Little Secret*

There's one thing in Judge Lawrence Bishop's past that could come back to haunt him. Two years ago he spent a weekend in the arms of a sexy stranger. Then Lawrence learns the woman is dead—but her fifteen-month-old son is living with her sister, Sara Carsten. Lawrence does the math and pays Sara a visit. What he tells her—and what he sees with his own eyes—rocks both their worlds.

## #935 DEEP IN THE HEART OF TEXAS • Linda Warren

Heiress Miranda Maddox has been kidnapped and held prisoner. Jacob Culver, a fugitive and the man known as "the hermit," rescues her, and against his own inclinations, agrees to guide her back to her home. In the process, Miranda discovers that someone in her family ordered her kidnapping—and she learns to trust Jake. She also learns that sometimes trust leads to love....